T4-AUC-510

Subversion

Science Fiction & Fantasy

Tales of Challenging the Norm

Crossed
Genres
Publications

SOMERVILLE, MA

The stories in this anthology are works of fiction. Names, characters, places, and incidents are products of the authors' imaginations or are used fictitiously and are not to be construed as real. Any resemblance to actual events, locales, organizations, or persons, living or dead, is entirely coincidental.

SUBVERSION: SCIENCE FICTION & FANTASY TALES OF CHALLENGING THE NORM

Copyright © 2011 Crossed Genres Publications. All rights reserved.
All stories are Copyright © 2011 their respective authors and are used with permission.

No part of this book may be used or reproduced in any manner whatsoever without written permission, except in the case of brief quotations embodied in critical articles and reviews. For information, contact Crossed Genres.

Queries: questions@crossedgenres.com

FIRST EDITION: December 2011

Edited by Bart R. Leib

Cover art: "New Generation of Leaders"
Cover art copyright © 2011 by Brittany Jackson
http://liol.deviantart.com

Cover design by Bart R. Leib

TABLE OF CONTENTS

FOREWORD
JENNIFER BROZEK

'Traitor' or 'revolutionary.' These labels are two sides of the same coin, just as 'hero' or 'villain' depends on the point of view of the person telling the story. These are obvious concepts when spelled out in clear cut settings. Because of this, how one goes about subverting the norm (as a traitor or revolutionary) is based on what the norm is. What is normal in one society can be, and often is, taboo in another society. This allows tales of subversion to be subtle, blatant, personal, communal, and endless in variation.

In this anthology, *Subversion: Science Fiction & Fantasy Tales of Challenging the Norm,* each story has its setting and its protagonist (or perhaps this should be 'antagonist') and that protagonist rebels against something. Or incites an uprising. It all depends on which way the reader chooses to ponder the story. Some of these traitorous actions bring calamity to all while other brave deeds bring personal, intimate triumph.

One of the best aspects of this anthology is the number of different types of subversion showcased. There is the obvious fight against a reigning government as well as the rejection of long held religious tradition – to both good and ill effect. But then there are the stories of personal subversion: of building or destroying what is a family; of how to stop violent plans as well as do the right thing, while working for the Man; of giving up oneself in order to save both yourself and a loved one. Each story of subversion is different from the rest while remaining cohesively within the whole of the anthology.

Designed to entertain, *Subversion* is also built to encourage discussion amongst its readers, even if that discussion is a private mental one. The stories are layered in what is being rebelled against and which norms – societal or personal – are being subverted. While the authors lay out the setting and have their own bias towards the story they tell, it is up to the reader to reflect on what they've read and decide for themselves if the rebellion succeeded and if it was just.

A Thousand Wings of Luck

Jessica Reisman

On the fourth of the Nine Days of Luck, the luck moths rose up out of the forest and descended on The House of Wren in a dry, rustling mist. They floated on eddies of river wind coursing down the house's stone corridors, massed in the air above terraces, obscured the gray and blue slate of the Wren School roof.

Rael, out in the garden between house and school digging carrots, looked up as the moths descended. The late sunlight steamed gold off the river, hazing the air as twilight seemed to seep up from the water's cold depths. There were clouds of wings: wings like thin tissues of gem and breaths of frost, like silk and dark water, wings colored silver, white, citrine, the fragile green of a new leaf, the rose-wash of blood in cheeks.

They lit on her, hands, nose, shoulders, and knees, clothed the ground and speckled the garden fences. Rael lifted her hand, made one with the trowel by a moving layer of moths. Tiny legs tickled her skin and clung to her clothes. Slowly, she stood and twirled, arms lifting out. Moths drifted up into the air.

***

Built in the grip of the forest at a bend in the River Shoon, the House of Wren and the Wren School had been much blessed by Luck. The school owned reputation up the river to the great cities of the north, and down to the rich houses of the south.

The Shoon's swift, deep waters connected house to town to village to city for a thousand miles. The forest sheltered in a craggy land that grew only steeper on its way to the mountains. Cliffs and towering trees cast the House of Wren in blue shadow for long hours into the morning.

When Rael and her cousin Garo were children, her uncle took them to explore the caves that riddled the ground under the cliffs, one of the moths' spawning grounds. Giant formations made up of thousands of individual cocoons hung in the crags and shelves of rock like strange, misshapen fruit. Stories were told, legends, of moths that cocooned for human lifetimes and only emerged once every hundred years, deep essence of the stuff of Luck.

As the moths descended, Rael thought of those caves, of the white globes of the cocoons, the air that smelled like spice and fern, and the way the place itself – something in the shadows, a turning in the slant of light – twitched at her skin

2

and itched inside her skull.

A phrase from the Grot she had lately been annotating as her third-year project brushed through her thoughts. *Chaos, their white-eyed fire came, the elder ones, to carve into the skin a map of chance – now skin touches the unseen currents of ever-rippling fate.* It was from the final volume of Grot's tetralogy, a work most scholars agreed had been written when Grot was quite insane.

***

Rael took Garo's place at the kitchen sink as he hefted a pot of water to the hearth. Prithen, a sixth year student with no family to go home to during the holiday, stood at the counter kneading dough. Rael watched his hands a moment, then caught herself and turned to the carrots. She'd only been sleeping with Prithen the last half a year; it was still new.

When she turned from the sink with her bowl full of clean carrots, she saw a silvery moth fluttering down toward the uncovered hearth bed.

"Garo, the mesh!"

The moth blundered closer to the open flames. Garo lunged, sweeping it clear. Prithen resecured the mesh while Garo, cradling the moth between two cupped palms, took it outside. When he came back in and returned to snapping beans, his hands trembled.

Prithen observed him, shook his head just slightly, and went back to rolling out dough. Dry and bony as an oak stick, his long brown hair worn in a topknot, Prithen was already a published scholar, his reputation beginning to be made, his work on Thantuvius well regarded. As a Thantist, Prithen didn't believe in the Luck, but he acted with respect for the beliefs of the House.

Garo rubbed his face. "I can't believe I left the mesh open."

"It's okay," Rael said, "No harm, Garo. All's well."

She caught Prithen's expression and gave him a severe look. Then Garo caught it, too.

"Shut it, Prithen."

"I didn't–"

"You didn't have to. I know what you think about the Luck. Being the scholarly light of Wren doesn't make you right."

Prithen's mouth twitched. "No, it doesn't."

Rael focused on the carrots under her knife.

"Schools downriver have banned Thantuvius," Garo said.

"I know."

Rael winced; Prithen was annoying to argue with because he seldom got the least bit ruffled. In Prithen's mind, every school of thought deserved consideration, and no inquiry was without merit.

Once, after Prithen had engaged a visiting lecturer in a dialogue more interesting than the lecture had been, Rael had followed him to the library. She'd been ten, and it had been Prithen's first year. Curious, because they'd never had a

Thantist at Wren, she asked him, "Do you really believe the Luck is nothing but superstition, Prithen?"

Already too tall, and at the time even more cadaverous, he'd looked down at her and nodded gravely. "I do. Of course the power of superstition should not be underestimated either."

Custom, faith, and law were on Garo's side, however. During the Nine Days of Luck, no moth should be killed. Though they would all die naturally within days of their arrival, to be swept up and burned in a ritual fire, until then every effort would be made to prevent the premature demise of any single moth.

If any member of the household killed, or, through negligence, allowed the death of a moth, it threatened the Luck of the House.

***

At supper, the few of them left at the school clustered near one end of the long, heavy wood table.

Only one moth had found its way in before the tall windows were all closed. The dark red of garnet, it floated in the heights among the unlit lamps. The hall was stuffy with the windows closed, and dim with only the evening light from outside and a few enclosed lanterns on the table, casting everyone's shadows in huge and shifting mantles on the walls.

Rael's aunt Teasel and the school warden, Sarduth, sat at the head of the table. Sarduth's appearance, as always, matched his acutely ordered mind. Teasel, in comparison, was wispy and unkempt. Her small hands were ink-stained and her thoughts forever tangled in the intricacies of her treatise on Luck doctrine, a work she'd been at for the last five years. It was Sarduth who kept the school and household running.

"Relays say Jummer's boat is due in tonight," Sarduth said.

"Oh?" Teasel looked up from some inner contemplation. Her fork had been hovering halfway between plate and mouth for a while.

"Yes," Sarduth said patiently. "Perhaps you could let me know if you need anything?"

Rael knew the warden had told Teasel this twice already in the last several days. Sarduth had already gotten a list of things needed and desired from everyone else. Rael kept the gardening and goat supply inventories and had asked for a new tiller. The librarian had ordered paper for Wren's new edition of first year texts. The cook had left a list detailing non-local foodstuffs to augment the larder, otherwise fed by their own gardens, an orchard, goats and chickens, river fish, and local inland farms.

"Oh. No, I can't think of a thing," Teasel said. She put the forkful of food back down onto the plate. "I suppose, since they're arriving during the Luck, I'll have to host Jummer to a sit-down welcome."

"That would be courtesy," Sarduth agreed, obviously relieved.

Garo, quiet and broody all through the meal, now looked up. "Teasel, the petition tokens, remember?"

She turned to her son. "Garo, we discussed this. Wren doesn't need to petition the Arcadia. Our Luck is not in question. And you know how I feel about petitions."

"But," Garo said, then sighed. "It's only–"

"Garo," Teasel said, suddenly quite focused, "what is the fourth doctrine of Luck?"

Garo pressed his lips together, but then he said, "Luck does not rule the intimacies of individuals, but only the balance of fortune and opportunity."

Since his father had left in the night on a tradeboat, Garo had believed that Wren Luck was turning. He took every mishap and setback, both personal and school-related, as evidence of such, begging his mother to petition the Arcadia with Luck tokens and House writs of promise.

Petitions, however, were a latter-day reform addition to Luck doctrine of which Teasel, wholly traditional and orthodox in her fashion, disapproved deeply.

A husband leaving, she had told Garo more than once, was not a turning of the Luck. Over the years, though, she grew ever more abstracted, and Rael knew that Garo felt the loss of her emotional presence as another signal of Luck's loss. No matter what the doctrines might say.

Rael attacked her food, frustrated and annoyed with both of them.

As she took her plate to the kitchen, another phrase from Grot went through her mind. *There is no luck but luck, a fish in shadowed waters, a fish with silver scales, flashing.* She thought on the words. By *no luck but luck* he meant that Luck was not good or ill in itself, but only in the way humans received it; the fish in shadowed water and the double meaning of its 'scales' addressed the endless turnings of luck on every breath and action of the world and the beings inhabiting it. Which went much against the way people wanted to think of Luck – as stable, dependable, with laws and structures that could be studied, quantified, understood. Grot had never been popular – and then he'd been insane, but she was drawn to his work.

***

Jummer's tradeboat arrived in the dark with a hail to the house. It moored at the dock, deck lights shining on the water.

While Teasel and Sarduth met with Jummer over tea and tobacco in the house's courtyard, Garo joined Rael in the kitchen, taking up the spices she'd set out. The scent of coriander rose into the air as he ground the pestle into the mortar with a frown.

Rael told herself just to let it go, but instead found herself saying, "Garo, the school prospers, we have food and shelter and warmth and light. You can't hold the actions of individuals against the Luck. People leave, people die, they disappoint you, surprise you – that's what they do."

"You see how Teasel is – how is that lucky? How is that good?"

"It's not good or bad, Garo, it's just the way she is. She's still here. My parents died when I was two – should I curse the Luck and sit on the steps of the Arcadia with petitions for the rest of my life? Have you ever wondered what it would really mean to lose the Luck?" She gestured around the kitchen, towards the rest of the house. "It's not as if the goats' milk runs curdled or we don't have money for trade. The river sickness passed us by last year, but even if it hadn't, or if our enrollment dropped for a turn of seasons – Garo, don't you see, we'd still–"

"Don't say things like that!" He slammed the pestle into the mortar and turned on her, furious, voice tight. "You sound like Prithen – cold as a fish."

That brought the blood up in her face with a wash of anger and she snapped, "You're the only ill luck in Wren, Garo."

Silence attended the remainder of their kitchen work, but, unwilling to let it go, he appeared at her door as she was getting ready for bed. They talked, argued about Teasel, about Luck, for several hours. They were both exhausted when he finally fell asleep at the end of her bed.

Rael slept eventually, a few hours wrestling through thick, prickly dreams. When she woke, Garo was blessedly absent from the end of her bed.

She leaned on the wide sill of her bedroom window, reading the second volume in Grot's tetralogy with fractured attention. Her thoughts echoed with the previous night's discussion, the whole question of Luck and the individual. Expectation, perspective. That fourth doctrine Teasel was so fond of: *Luck does not rule the intimacies of individuals, but only the balance of fortune and opportunity.* Could you, though, truly separate fortune and opportunity from the daily twists and turns of life, or from the relationships between people through which life was lived? Most people didn't see the Luck in that larger tapestry, but in the intimacies of life lived moment to moment, breath to breath. Didn't the loss of a parent affect the balance of fortune and opportunity? If the whole of the river reaches suffered some natural cataclysm, how could one say that had nothing to do with daily moments?

Was Prithen right?

Bah. Enough. She focused on the text.

A delicate moth with trailing amber wings and another of searing green landed on the page she was trying to read. She blew them off impatiently. A copper-winged moth took their place.

"Muck," Rael said. She slammed the book shut. The moth fluttered free at the last moment, dipped onto an upshaft of air from the courtyard several stories below and sailed away.

Everywhere moths clung to the architecture like many-colored lichens. Most were sluggish in the daylight hours, but here and there one turned lazily on the air.

Rael stared out through blue shadows to the Shoon, its smoke-dark surface deceptively still-looking. She opened the book again and found her place.

Another moth, the color of biscuits, fell out of an eddy of air onto the page.

Rael considered it for a moment, considered Garo and the question of Luck. Anger and an edge of challenge clicked over in her blood like a clockwork gear.

Very slowly and carefully she closed the book and mashed the moth.

She heard a noise and her heart jumped. Prithen leaned in the doorway. If he had seen what she did, though, he gave no indication.

"Sarduth needs you to choose which tiller you want; it seems they have an abundance. A good year for garden implements, apparently."

She left the book with the dead moth in it on the windowsill.

***

Jummer's wheelboat was wide and flat-bottomed, with an upper two half decks and ample hold below for trade goods. Including Jummer and his daughter there were nine crew, a Luck number. Jummer, small and deeply muscled with sun-toughened skin, consulted with Sarduth on the school's list, discussing payment in monies and trade goods – Wren's orchard fruit, jams, goat cheese, herbs. Teasel, having fulfilled her duty the night before, was not in evidence.

Rael chose between the two tillers Jummer had on offer, and then leaned beside Prithen on a barrel. The breeze off the Shoon blew chill and the boat knocked up against the dock with an arrhythmic thumping. On the far side of the river, the forest grew thick up into white and grey cliffs. Moths hung languorous on the wood of boat and dock.

Bargaining completed, Sarduth and Jummer shook hands.

"You three," Sarduth said with a gesture to include Prithen, Jael, and Garo, "go get what I noted here from the stores." He handed the list to Rael and she followed behind Garo and Prithen onto the slightly swaying railed plank to the dock.

As Garo went carefully ahead of her, a fish jumped high out of the water below, splashing a number of moths, which fluttered up into Garo's face. He waved a hand at them, missed his footing, tripped and fell over the rail before Rael could do more than reach a hand out. She heard a crack as one of his feet caught in the railing. Then a splash drenched her as he went in the Shoon.

She hurried to help him out, Prithen beside her. Garo was white-faced as he grabbed their arms and sagged to the deck.

"My leg," he gasped.

Sarduth knelt by him and felt up his calf lightly. He nodded. "There's a break."

No one said anything else for a moment, but several of the boat crew stepped back from them.

Rael watched them do it and cold shock pulled the blood from her face as she thought of the moth smashed in the book on her windowsill.

"Jolie," Jummer barked, "get the bottle of kava from my cabin." When his daughter came back with a dark bottle, the captain, instead of moving away from them, came in close and put a hand to Garo's shoulder. "Here, drink some of this, it will help." He ran a disapproving gaze over his crew. With a general ducking of heads, they withdrew to tasks elsewhere on the boat. "Don't mind them; the idea that Luck is catching, one way or another." He dismissed the notion with the fingers of one pudgy hand. "Pay them no mind," he said again.

They got Garo to the kitchen, where Sarduth, who doubled as school healer, straightened and set the bone.

The afternoon sun moved a slow fraction, light crossing the kitchen floor. Moths lifted and fell in the light and shadows outside the kitchen, clung to the walls inside.

***

That afternoon the fish and the bread for supper burned, when small emergencies elsewhere distracted those responsible at exactly the wrong moments. The school's printing press, acquired at great expense and recently fixed – at great expense – broke down for no reason that the librarian, who knew the machine inside out, could find. A hard, unripe quince fruit dropped from its tree into a small bee hive, causing the bees to swarm just as Jummer's daughter Jolie was taking a walk in the orchard; she was much stung and rather swollen. Both Wren's and the boat's nets came up entirely empty of fish.

Rael tried to work out whether all of this was her fault, while the rest of the household grew silent, their faces thoughtful, grim.

Over a meager dinner and the lingering smell of burnt food there was no conversation.

***

That night the moon stared through the forest's tall trees and the air smelled of rain coming.

Rael went by Garo's room to check on him and collect his dinner tray. She found him sitting up in bed, pen moving intently over the top sheet of a sheaf of paper on a lap desk. The one lantern on the bedside table cast a dim puddle that barely reached his work, and moths spotted the wall and empty dishes on the dinner tray beside it.

He barely looked up as Rael gathered the dinner tray, the pen moving furiously.

"I'm going to do the writ myself. I've saved from the copy work I did last session, so I can get the petition tokens." His face was set in its most stubborn expression as he paused and looked up at her. "But I have to have the Wren seal on the writ for promise and Teasel won't give it."

"Garo–"

"You can forge her writing and sneak the seal out, you always could."

Rael sat on the end of the bed, the tray in her lap, her thoughts circling like scavenger birds.

"You saw what happened today," Garo pressed, "the Luck is turning; if we petition before it's totally tainted we're more likely to heal it. Do you want to end up like Branth House?"

"Branth! Garo – Branth House is a child's tale."

"Tales have truth in them. Please, Rael, just help me do this?"

She took in his pinched face and set mouth. "Okay."

He smiled, face lightening, looking less like a pucker fish.

"I'll try tonight – no guarantees, though."

First she went to her room and sat at the window, staring at the book. After a while, she opened it to the dead moth and carefully shook it out. It left a splotchy, silvery stain.

Small sounds of night drifted through the window; music came faintly from the tradeboat. She picked up the dead moth and removed the globe from the lamp, set the moth on the flame and replaced the globe. The smell of burnt moth rose into the room.

Outside of Teasel's study she stood to listen at the heavy wooden door. She held her breath, one hand to the stone of the wall; this deep in the house no moths had penetrated, and the covered lamp hanging from the high ceiling was un-attended by fluttering wings. Memory echoed all the times she'd stood here, since childhood, listening to see if Teasel was there.

She heard the rustle of pages and was about to move on and leave the seal until later when she heard something else; the rough drag of sobs.

She eased the door open. Teasel, red-eyed and damp, sat drooped over some papers at her desk. Rael was trying to decide whether to go in or slip away when her aunt looked up, wiping tears back into her tangled hair.

"Rael."

"I'm sorry, Teasel, I – what's wrong?" This last as her aunt heaved another broken sob.

"Wrong? This day, Garo's leg, the press, poor Jolie, and then, then, this," she gestured at the papers she'd been crying over. "The Council of Schools says they never received our licensing fees – they were sent months ago, and a runner brought me this today, just today, saying our failure to attend to the oversight has accrued us a huge fine. I don't know what to do, we can't afford the fine, and the damage to our reputation if we're shut down while it's sorted out–" She stared into the space between them. "Has Garo been right all this time? I know I'm not an attentive parent…but, is all this because of me?"

"Teasel, no."

"Garo – what must he think now, what will he think," she gestured to the papers again. "He's begged me to petition the Arcadia so many times."

Rael said softly, "Maybe you should."

"What? But it goes against everything–"

"Aunt Teasel, isn't one of the reasons for petitions for the sake of attitude, of hope? Garo needs that."

Teasel's next words were bleak and quiet, "You think Wren is losing its

Luck?"

"No, but–"

"I do," Teasel interrupted. "I do. But petitions – no. No."

"For Garo – surely to do it out of love, that's not a violation of doctrine, not really?"

Teasel shook her head, deep in thought. Rael watched her. After a few moments with no answer, she slipped back out of the room, her stomach muscles tightening into knots.

Outside, the moon rode high; the tradeboat rocked on the river in a cradle of dark broken only by one lantern. Moths brushed by her in the chill. She smelled thyme on the shifting wind, then goat.

In the residence wing of the school she found Prithen's door ajar, a golden line of light cut into the hall, the scritch of his pen audible. She pushed the door open without knocking. He looked up, welcomed her with a slight nod, and went back to writing. He sat on one end of an old couch at his desk, his hair down. Rael curled up on the other end and waited for him to finish his page. It smelled of Prithen in the room, a dry musky smell she'd come to love, and of the citrus oil he burned in his lamp. It was expensive oil, one of his only extravagances. Its sweet, clean scent always made Rael a little drowsy.

As he set the pen down and blotted the page, Rael said, "Isn't there a saying somewhere, the first sign of Luck's turn will always come by water?"

"Yes, it's from Faren, I think."

"And a fish made Garo break his leg."

"I wouldn't say that was precisely correct."

"It's my fault," Rael said, brushing his objection aside.

He sat back, brows raised. She told him about the moth, and he was still quiet.

"I know," Rael said to his silence. "It's just…you've read Grot."

He nodded.

Rael shifted restlessly. "Do you accept the assertion that he was insane when he wrote the tetralogy?"

"You don't?"

"I'm not sure. I guess I don't. Something happened to him, no question. The style of the tetralogy is cryptic and murky, full of ambiguities, but…I just feel like he understood something." She shook her head and looked up into his eyes. "Prithen, what have I done?"

"Rael, if it's a proof you're looking for, you'll have to give it more than one day."

She thought of Teasel and the council letter. "Wait for Teasel to fail in some duty and Wren's reputation to wane? For sickness to strike or the roof to fall in?" She wrapped her arms around herself.

Prithen shifted closer. "Would those events be proof? Can we foresee the consequence of every broken moment, lost opportunity, or wrong action? No. *That* is the fallacy of Luck law."

She hid her face in his hair, just breathing in the scent of him, but her thoughts kept straying to fish and Grot's "elder ones" and a particular reference in Grot about propitiation.

***

When she left Prithen, all of Wren was silent. Instead of going back to her room she went to the library.

The familiar dim cavern of the great room was comforting, even in the deep of night. Taking a lamp from the librarian's desk, she threaded among the shelves of books, scrolls, manuscripts, and maps, under carved stone arches and high windows. Far back in the stacks she found the volume she wanted and took it to a carrel.

The book was a copy of an ancient text which Grot had argued to be a primary source behind the origins of Luck Law. Most scholars and all the orthodoxy disagreed with him and dismissed the work as a collection of dark and rambling tales in vaguely poetic mode.

An hour later, beyond tired, her eyes burning, she finally located the passage she was looking for. She only had a reference to it from Grot's cryptic writings.

It was even more cryptic and strange than Grot's work.

The passage spoke of a ritual of propitiation undertaken when the *connected limbs fall under angry shadow*. The ritual seemed to be a simple one in which the seeker journeyed to the *fruited groves of night's children* and offered the *body's humors* to an elder multi-deity which the text referred to only as the *white-eyed ones*.

Fruited groves of night's children: a breeding ground of the moths. That she thought she understood.

***

Retrieving a jacket, a lantern, and a small knife used to trim lamp wicks, Rael went into the forest and was quickly deep among vine-hung trees. Going slowly on trails that rose and fell raggedly, Rael moved from familiar paths to less-known ones, searching out the route her uncle had taken them on so long ago, finding her way with the shielded lantern and the moon's light.

Eventually she came among a set of tall standing stones. Moss grew damp and thick on them. Ferns, grey in the moon's light, overhung the walls of a small cliff. A cave breathed cold and dark from behind the ferns.

"Well," she said aloud, and felt the word eaten by the dark. Setting the lantern down, she knelt in front of the tallest stone. Several feet behind it was the cave in which Rael remembered seeing the clustered cocoons of the moths as a child.

The body's humors. She pricked one finger with the knife until blood welled, then smeared it on the moss at the base of the stone.

"I'm sorry I killed that moth," she whispered. "Please… please restore Wren's Luck."

She sat there feeling stupid for a few breaths, and a few more.

Then a chip of deep darkness detached itself from the cave's depth. It floated out into the glen. She wasn't sure she really saw it until another followed. And another – and then many others.

Moths.

Thousands of soot-black wings cloaked the air. One drifted close to Rael. Small, burning white spots on its wings winked in the dark.

Grot's white-eyed ones?

She lifted a hand and a moth landed on her bloodied fingertip, wings slowly moving. Another landed in her palm, another on her arm. One by one they settled all over her.

A small sting of pain in her palm startled her. She watched a drop of blood well beneath the moth and stared, not comprehending.

She began to feel pin-pricks of pain all over.

In a rush, she thought she did understand. She brushed at the moths, but found herself falling. She hit the wet ground and, in helpless horror, realized she couldn't move.

More and more moths brushed their wings across her skin, settled into her clothes, pricking her. They landed over her eyes, covered her nose and mouth, found their way into her ears, crawled down her shirt, over her thighs and groin, pricking through cloth as easily as into bare flesh.

Just under her skin, all over her body: a shiver. It pulsed down into her blood, tiny needles stitching fine thread through her, stitching her to the air, to soil and stone, to the pulse of life behind her own breath.

Her blood burned white fire, the fire that smoldered in the moths' eye-spots, the fire at the heart of the world.

A rush of wings turned the wind, and a single brush of one wing turned a footstep. Cause or reaction, was there a difference? The thousand facets of the air, of all breath, into the throat of time and out.

***

She woke to wet cold. Rain sounded softly in the trees, down to the bracken; the ferns dipped and showered continual beadings of silver water. Rain-light pooled down from a grey morning sky.

Rael clutched fingers in the bracken, found she could move, climbed slowly to her feet and stood there swaying. She pulled off her jacket and looked at her arms, turned her palm to the dim morning light. No blood, no wounds – but patterns traced over her skin, the silvery, opalescent tracings on a moth's wing, faint, but visible.

She made her way back to the house through the rain and was able to slip past Teasel as she drifted distractedly onto the porch with a cup of tea in her hands.

Once in her room, shivering, Rael tore off her wet clothes and dried off, wrapped her hair in a towel. Then she examined her body.

The moth patterns covered her all over, light and dark by turns, a moiré that shifted as she moved. She looked at herself bleakly in the tarnished mirror.

...to carve into the skin a map of chance.

Bloody Grot.

With angry jerks she pulled on a long-sleeved shirt and pants, leaving her hair loose to cover her neck. But the patterns were on her face, too.

When Prithen came to see why she hadn't appeared for breakfast, she hid under the covers and said she felt ill.

Despite the turmoil of her thoughts, she fell asleep, exhausted. When she woke in the late afternoon, she watched the day's light die slowly away at the window. Wings brushed through her mind, things shifting, Grot's words and the shiver of something – knowledge? – that now owned her blood gaining clarity. The turmoil in her mind was gone, though its remnants were jagged.

Prithen came up with her supper. As he set down the tray and leaned over the lamp, he said, "Teasel signed Garo's writ, then gave her seal – can you believe it? And the council sent a runner to tell Teasel something had been a mistake, I don't know what, but she seemed very relieved."

He finished with the lamp and turned, coming to join her on the bed. "So you see, your concerns were unfounded."

It wasn't until she shifted, moved somewhat, that he saw. He fell absolutely still, staring.

"What – what did you do?"

"What Grot did, I think. I think now I can see why he became somewhat lunatic, though I don't feel inclined to do so. He must have been unstable to begin with."

"That," Prithen said, "does not answer the question." He took her hand and pushed the shirt sleeve up, turning her forearm slightly in the light. The moiré patterns glimmered and faded from view, glimmered back. "That's... remarkable."

"It was something in Penorin, that Grot references: a ritual to propitiate the elder gods of Luck when you've trespassed on Luck Law. There were black moths, a kind I've never seen before. They...well, they did this. And..."

Prithen waited.

Rael looked down, turning her hands and watching the patterns move. "I don't know if killing that moth really affected the Luck at all. But this," she shook her head. "It's like I tore at the fabric of Luck and...and made myself part of it in a different way than before. We're all part of it, obviously, but now...I think I'm like some kind of Luck rod, or catalyst, or something." She pulled the sleeve back down over her hand. "It's just a feeling. Connections, I don't know, movements, or currents, I can sense somehow now."

"A Luck rod? Like a lightning rod?"

Rael nodded. "Which means I should leave Wren. My being here could cause the Luck to turn again."

"If it ever really turned at all," Prithen said mildly, but with a firm expression on his face. "No, Rael, you can't leave. At least, not yet – or how will you, or any of us, know if what you say is true?"

"I don't want to be a–" *a freak.* All right, she was, but, "I don't want to become some kind of scholarly exhibit to study."

"Rael," he spread his hands helplessly, "You have to talk to Teasel, and just – give it some time. What would you be if you leave? A traveling exhibit? At least here you're home. And, who knows – you might end up making Wren's reputation beyond the river reaches."

"Is that supposed to make me feel better?"

"You could change all we know about Luck – maybe you'll even convert me." His twitch of a dry smile made her shake her head, almost ready to meet his challenge and laugh, but not yet.

***

For the next few days Rael kept to her room, hiding in shadows when others came to check on her.

One night the moths began to die, falling to the ground in drifts of color. In the blue shadows of the following morning, Rael watched Teasel come out into the courtyard with a broom and begin to sweep the moths into piles. Feeling the shift in currents she couldn't yet read, Rael went out to help her.

Jessica Reisman's stories have appeared in numerous magazines, as well as in anthologies such as *Cross Plains Universe*, *Passing for Human*, and *Otherworldly Maine*. Five Star Speculative Fiction published her first novel, *The Z Radiant*, in 2004. She lives in Austin, Texas and likes a Mexican martini with extra olives. For more exciting information, visit www.storyrain.com.

And All Its Truths

Camille Alexa

She's not a number. She's a creature of flesh and desires and the thousand burning stars of her wounds. Constellations of agony, those wounds. Galaxies of pain.

"Prisoner 7537 will come forward for nutrient dosing."

The mechanized voice is the only one Prisoner 7537 knows anymore. Her own voice is as lost to her as the name she doesn't remember, though she senses the lingering of its previous existence. Her name has left behind ghost pain, like an amputated limb.

"Prisoner 7537 will show efficient compliance in five seconds. Four. Three. Two ... 7537 is cited for non-efficiency. Forced dosing sequence activated."

Doors roll back on invisible steel tendons, the bone and sinew of Machines. Built of oiled tubes and metal cables, they sound like Death when they move. Death comes rolling in on wheels – no, not Death; just Death Deferred. The Machine sprouts wings: tiny, articulated wings of whirling metal, which quickly blossom into the many-segmented limbs of a torturer. She who once had a name and a voice is caught, pinned against the hard cold floor like an insect on a slab. Though she doesn't cry out loud, she screams inside.

The Machine doesn't gloat, doesn't require her submission or revel in her pain. It's a social efficiency Machine designed to keep Earth Colony IV in perfect running order, and exists solely to do the bidding of its Program. Unruly citizens are not efficient, and at this instant, this particular Machine exists to ensure the thousand tiny healing wounds of inefficient prisoner number 7537 are wounds, renewed.

***

Sister Beatrix of the Order of the Third Supreme Deity pushes the gurney and sloshing bucket down the long narrow hall. Trails of warmish soapy water follow her like charmed snakes across the dank metal floor of the automated prison. Water sploshes, soaking the heavy fabric of her leggings.

She wipes oil-smeared palms on her woolen smock and with impatience shoves a stray black curl back under her linen wimple. She squints at the tiny digits on the data card she took from the slot by the prison entry.

Prison light is not good for inefficient human eyes.

"Seven, five, three, seven," she reads aloud. "Interesting."

She doesn't consult the dull glow-map on the wall representing the tight angling corridors of the Compliance prison. She's been here eight times before, and the design is very efficient if one has a good head for recalling numbers.

At the stained steel door of cell 7537, Beatrix drags her cart to a halt, sticks the data card into its slot. A mechanical voice programmed to ring with maximum authority echoes in the empty hall: "*Data card received. Entry permitted.*"

"So let me in already," says Beatrix, hand on hip, one foot tapping to invisible drummers. "Ali Baba and Open Sesame."

The corroded door rolls away. Beatrix heaves her bucket with both hands and lugs it into the dark room, water sloshing. Her eyes sting at the scents of old blood, stale urine, rancid machine oil. "Where are you, poor primie?" she calls, as if expecting an answer. *Primie* is what she calls all these last survivors, these prisoners left only with prime numbers instead of names or flesh or life. "It's just me, Sister Beatrix, come to offer Final Solace."

She plunks down her bucket and peers into the gloom. Thin pale light filters from a narrow horizontal slit high in the wall, too high for Beatrix to touch even if she stood on her own shoulders and lifted both arms over her head. But she sees well enough the steel bench, the filthy toilet basin in the corner, the metal platform of the only bed, without pillow or blanket but with the bony ankle protruding from beneath.

Beatrix's heart crimps into what she imagines as tight, mathematically perfect spirals. She controls her breathing and kneels. Gently – as if mottled bruises on skin across tissue-covered bone are still capable of feeling pain – she tugs the ankle. Cold leaches into her kneecaps through wool. Fluids glint on the dead primie's vacant face: blood and spittle, and oozings from a thousand tortured places. Beatrix winces as the body scrapes across cold gritty floor.

Sister Beatrix of the Order of the Third Supreme Deity is small, but the inert form on the floor is little more than scab and bone. She rolls the body onto the metal sleeping platform. "Poor primie," she says. "Not much left of you, is there?" She straightens the body's broomstick legs and folds the scarecrow arms across the sunken chest, humming a wordless tune. Lullabies for the dead. Or perhaps to comfort herself, the living.

Beatrix straightens the corners of her wimple and reaches for the soapy rag to bathe the chilled surfaces of the skin-covered bones. She begins at the cold flesh of the bare feet. She moves across the bent ankles mottled with bruises from the manacles of the automated nutrient enforcers. Beatrix washes away machine grease and the rust of dried blood from the thousand pinpricks of dosing needles: fluids from the veins of human and Machine mingling on the cold flesh of prisoner 7537, who is, according to her data card, the last human occupant of the Machines' Compliance prison.

"It's part of their original programming that people be allowed to confirm the prison's dead," she tells the dead woman. "More efficient for settlement population records and whatnot. Not that there's a settlement anymore. Or a population to speak of. Or a Colony, really, unless you count this place."

But the dead woman doesn't answer, leaving Beatrix to wipe the pale mottled flesh in silence and cold and stillness. The only sounds are sloshing water and Beatrix's own voice.

She always talks to them. For four years, three months, and two days it has been her duty to regularly check the slot by the prison gate for data cards, to come offer Final Solace, to prepare the bodies for immolation. So much went wrong in those mechanical minds, with their evolving efficiency programs designed to help the small colony survive so far from Earth. Is it irony that Machines have maintained one of the least efficient human methodologies, the opportunity for Final Solace? Or is it something else: fate? Or perhaps a joke played by the Third Supreme Deity — if you believe in her, which Beatrix does not. She is *not* a very efficient member of her Order.

"I've seen the same thing, performed the same Solace for eight others, all with prime numbers encoded on your data cards," Beatrix tells the dead woman as she dabs her with the damp cloth. "You're my ninth. Nine's not prime, but it's lucky. A lucky number, like in the sequence: one, three, seven, nine, thirteen, fifteen, twenty-one..." The spirals blossom again in her chest and her breath catches. She waits, hand midair, for the feeling to subside. When she resumes, she whispers in awkward apology, "Not lucky for you. I'm sorry."

She bathes the shoulders, the arms, the pitifully gnarled claw-hands dangling from wrists with identical bruises to the ankles like a matched set of vulgar jewelry. As Beatrix runs the cloth along the bony lengths of the woman's fingers she murmurs, "That's an old, old hand you've got, primie, for a woman probably much younger. How old are you? Thirty-five? Forty? You've spent at least twenty years here. The Machines stopped incarcerations then; nobody left to take, practically. Everybody in the Colony settlement had been incarcerated or eliminated for non-compliance, for physical imperfection, for personality irregularities, for resistance to social efficiency..."

Gently she scrubs the neck, wipes the brow and the cheeks and the needle-pricks across their surfaces. She smooths her hand over the shorn head. The woman's skull looks delicate in the faint light, her hair prickling from her scalp like the tender, stubbled feathers of a newborn chick. Even the lids of the closed eyes have the round red welts of the dosing Machine littering their papery surfaces.

"You're the last Colony inmate by three months, four days, and nine hours according to your data card. That's three, four, nine; and three hundred and forty-nine is another lucky number. A lucky *prime* number." Beatrix reaches for the satchel beneath the folded canvas on her gurney. "But it's always like this when they post a card outside, when I come down the mountain to perform Solace. I always feel the person might still be alive, like the chest still rises and falls. But wishing and hoping doesn't make it so."

Beatrix watches the dead woman's chest rise and fall, knowing it for an illusion. The Sisters say it's the Order's continuing sacred duty to the Third Deity and to the Colony to check prison postings, to confirm and record the deaths and offer Final Solace. Beatrix wept countless impotent tears of rage for the prisoners when she was old enough to understand, taking no comfort when the Sisters cited the unknowable will of the Third Supreme Deity. For a time she left the abbey each afternoon to hide in the cliffs above the prison, to spy on its stark metal angles. But by then nobody ever went in or out anymore. Not even Machines.

After all these years the prison has become part of the landscape, unmovable as the mountains. The Sisters say she's too young to recall the scent of charred flesh as the Machines rampaged and burned, efficiency programs run amok. And here in the sunless cells of the automated Compliance prison, Beatrix's skin grows clammy and cold, until the waxy quietude of the dosed and the dead are of a oneness with her own flesh. All she has to do is wrap up this primie, load her onto the gurney, and wheel her to the immolation chamber. This final witnessing of the dead is her duty, and this is the last time she will perform it.

Without knowing exactly why, she bends to kiss the dead woman's lips before covering her face with the cloth. Beatrix is startled to find herself looking directly into a pair of very green eyes, which are very not dead.

***

The woman doesn't recall being folded nearly double and smuggled from the prison on the undershelf of a rolling cart along with buckets and sponges and the items of ritual for Final Solace. She doesn't remember being strapped to the back of a huffing donkey, or immersed in warm water at the abbey and scrubbed clean and placed in a real bed with real sheets and blankets. All she knows is, she's not a number.

She's a creature, and when the soothing murmur of a fellow creature finds its way through the canals of her ears, across the tautness of drums and the softness of minuscule hairs and into the lonely corridors of brain; when that murmur finds its way, she wakes, and listens.

"...And so I said to myself: Beatrix, you're not a very good Sister of the Order of the Third Supreme Deity, may your Sisters forgive you, but *numbers*, numbers you do get, and they get you. And if seven plus five plus three plus seven equals twenty-two, well, that's a master number."

Warm water from a warm sponge, wielded by a warm hand, crosses her temple.

"And I tell myself: Beatrix, if this primie – whose prime number is seven thousand, five hundred, thirty-seven – if she's your ninth, and that's a lucky number, and she's a master number too, well then that's someone very special, in truth."

She's reluctant to open her eyes; every time she does is perhaps the time she wakes. And then there'll be only hard metal and the interior echoes of her own silent screams and the embrace of cold limbs of segmented steel. And so she does not, *does not* open her eyes, but sobs instead. Sobbing she has done a hundred times, a thousand times, a million. But never once in these past two decades has it been answered with an embrace from human arms.

***

"...So I'm certainly not going to mind if you aren't talkative." Beatrix ducks her head beneath the ribs of the cow, milking with renewed vigor. "I go days here at the abbey without hearing a single other human voice. Vows of silence are a tradition with the Sisters, and there aren't so many Sisters left anymore. If I'm the only one for myself to talk to, might as well keep myself company. It's all I've got, other than the dozen Earth books hidden in the abbey belfry by some long-gone Sister before I was born, when Social Efficiency programs first started getting out of hand." She smiles askance at the other woman. "Books promote deviance from social norms, you know. Very inefficient!"

With an affectionate slap to the cow's side, Beatrix stands, stretches. "Besides," she says, reaching to adjust the blanket across the other woman's bony shoulders, "maybe you don't understand a lot of what I say. The Sisters say the original settlers came from several Earth origins. You could've been practically anybody, done practically anything for the Machines to put you away. Or done nothing: turns out the most efficient human settlement has no humans in it at all."

Beatrix looks into the other's green, green eyes. "Sure you don't remember anything? From before?" The silent woman shakes her head, her movements slow, painful to watch. Beatrix squeezes her shoulder before turning to put away the milking stool. "That's okay. Those Machines nearly wiped out every human on the planet, but they weren't built to last. Just a generation or two, until the settlement got on its feet. Problem now is, they're smart, see? They learn, their efficiency programs evolving, teaching them new stuff. All these years of nothing, and now they're making a new wing at the back of the prison. For all we know, they're building machines to build Machines. If they do, well..."

She studies her tiny, work-roughened fingers. "Well maybe I'll just have to learn to pray to the Third Deity after all. Come on, then," she says, straightening. "Let's get you inside. Hey, we'll go to the belfry! I'll read you one of Scheherazade's stories to the King, about how Sinbad escapes the rocs in the valley of diamonds. His method isn't very efficient, but it's *very* effective."

***

Beatrix leads through cobbled-together whitewashed halls. Older portions are built of stone or wattle and daub; newer are built of salvaged settlement detritus, cinderblock and chunks of cement and hammered metal or crumbling plastic. The silent woman stops to run her crooked hand along a plaster section embedded with empty glass bottles. The bottlenecks open to daylight, the

19

bottoms glowing circles of brown, gold, blue, green: a multi-hued constellation of beveled suns.

Running both hands along the uneven surface of dimpled glass, Beatrix says, "I call this the Augustine Wall, after an ancient Earth philosopher from my hidden belfry books. See that brown bottle? Only two of those. Seventeen gold, fifty-nine green, one hundred and three blues." Her finger brushes each color as she names it. "Two, seventeen, fifty-nine, one hundred and three: all prime numbers, together equaling one hundred and eighty one – also prime. Subtract back out the first two browns, and that's one-hundred and seventy nine, which is twin prime to one-eighty-one. And *that*," her hands drop to her sides, "is how I figured my path to Truth wasn't through prayer and silence, but through *numbers*. Earth Augustine wrote, 'Numbers are the Universal language offered by the deity to humans as confirmation of the truth.' If nothing else, I do believe in Truth."

Sister Beatrix leans to kiss the closest blue circle before continuing down the hall. With only brief hesitation, the silent woman trails after, leaving behind the bottles and the wall of multicolored light and all its Truths.

***

Beatrix drops her hoe, careful to aim its fall away from the tended row of little cabbages. She rubs both hands along her spine and grimaces. "If hoeing vegetables didn't eventually lead to eating them, weeds would lead a happy life."

The other woman unfolds slowly from her hunched position. She places her hoe carefully alongside the other on the ground and massages the stiffly bent twigs of her fingers.

Stepping to her, Beatrix closes her strong little hands with their tidy calluses over the scarred ones with the twisted lumpy joints. She smiles. "Stronger, Lucky. Much stronger this week. 'Heal Thou all my bones'..." Smiling, she smooths a wispy lock off the woman's forehead. "And your hair, almost as long as most of the Sisters' at the abbey now, though twice as fine." She curls one tendril about her finger, but that's the extent of its length, and it slides away. "Like the silky ends of the embroidery thread the Sisters are forever despairing me to stitch. And brown; brown as the bottles in the Augustine Wall."

She stoops to retrieve her hoe. "Goodman Cropper has requested Final Solace for his mother," she says, returning to her labors. "They're an old family, worshippers of the Third Supreme Deity from before the Machines, like the Sisters. Not many Sisters left, Lucky. They found me at the abbey's postern gate when I was a baby, but their order was modest even then, and the youngest not so young. I'm the only one left can easily make the trip over the mountain." She pauses, tilting her head to meet the green gaze of the other woman. "Thought you might like to come."

The other woman, as always, says nothing. Beatrix shrugs, the movement lending momentum to her hoeing. "Final Solace is really for those left behind. Earth Augustine writes: 'Human friendship also is endeared with a sweet tie, by

20

reason of the unity formed of many souls.'" She pauses again to study the other woman. After a moment she nods, deciding. "Good. We leave tonight before dark."

***

She sits, cleaving close to the small, solid, wool-covered back of the one before her. Her legs stretch astride the barreled ribs of the fat donkey, and it's torture, yet also pleasure, a wonder that limbs once so turned upon themselves can bend now to suit other geometries: the geometry and cylindrical dimensions of the fat and swaying beast beneath her, her arms forming the circumference of embrace about the woman in front, her torso a perpendicular line with her spine an imperfect rod between ground and sky.

"There, there, Panza; gently over the gully. Good donkey..." The other croons on, singing gentle praises to the fat animal and its labors on behalf of the two women, in the service of the dead and their living. "Good donkey, good little friend..."

Sometimes she feels she's the other's shadow, always following behind. *Shadow* implies mere proximity to a solid thing, but being a shadow is vastly better than being nothing at all. Nothingness is what she would've been but for her. Nothing except torture and pain; those things first, forever, and only after that the nothingness.

She listens to the other's words – confident, comforting, nonsensical words. She remains the shadow, indicating only the presence of a caster nearby. She's just the hollow number. Nil and zero.

No. Not a number any longer. A name, not quite right but close. *Lucky*, the other calls her, and though she knows it for an artificial construct, it's no more a construct than the possessing of a name has ever been. A name: designation of identity for the convenience of an external classification system. Efficient.

But that's not right either. A name, a human name, holds also joy, and inclusion, and lends the simple comfort of self-identity, however tenuous. While *Lucky* isn't the name she had once, it feels close. It might be just as descriptive of *what* she is as any other, similar device, though her mind still shies from the thousand burning needles of the question *who?*

The fat donkey, puffing, crests the rise of the final hill. Twilight has grown just dark enough so woodsmoke rising from the Cropper cottage chimney isn't plainly visible, though it's easily detectable via other senses, the sharp tang of smoke, bitter to the nose, tasted at the back of the throat. A low line of gold sky lies crushed beneath a heavy twilit quilt of purple, while spiky pine branch fingers loom to frame the gentle curve of the valley below.

After the small woman slides from the donkey's back, her tall shadow follows to land on the awkward stilts of her legs. She towers above the small one and her fat donkey, feeling less human for it. She pictures the abbey's salvaged metal spire and thinks it must get lonely so far above the tended rows of

21

vegetables residing close together in the garden below.

The door to the cottage falls open, light like nugget gold spilling out into the crepuscule. Silhouettes framed against the hearthlit doorway remind her of her own shape, the lank and lean of it, the shadow nature. But coming inside from the dark, she sees these figures, unlike herself, are fully-realized.

How long since she experienced the unhindered society of humans? The silent figures of the Sisters aren't like true society; they too are withdrawn from the human world. They strive for immolation in a different Universe, that of their Supreme Deity. The fire of their faith burns them if they're fortunate, and the bodies left behind are only mute echoes of their souls. Staying at the abbey is like living with a host of silent ghosts.

Only their Beatrix can draw smiles or frowns from even the most insubstantial of them. She's their tether, the anchor to the humanness of them, keeping them earthbound. But perhaps it's no favor: is it kindness to ground a kite which yearns for fiery oneness with the sun?

***

The cropper and his family crowd close to Beatrix. The grubby hands of an alarming number of offspring tug and clutch at her tunic. Children always like her, enjoying the compact smallness of her person, an adult close to their size.

"Thank you for coming, Sister," says Goody Cropper, whom people will soon call the more formal *Goodwife Cropper* now her mother-in-law lies dead in the next room with her arms folded across her still chest. Beatrix kisses Goody Cropper on each cheek. She moves about the cottage, kneeling to listen to the whispered secret of a child here, pausing to shake the hand of Goodman Cropper's brother there. Throughout the whole, her shadow hangs back, balanced on the threshold: life and death inside the cropper's cottage before her, the nothingness of night spilling behind.

At last Sister Beatrix steps through another doorway to the chamber beyond. Her shadow follows. In the small room is a narrow bed and on the bed a woman. The late Goodwife Cropper's daughter and granddaughters have already bathed her body and redressed it in their best linens. Her eyes are closed, her hair braided, her empty face serene.

Beatrix shuts the door, pulls objects from the satchel slung low across her back: a shallow wooden plate; a slender vial of thick, clear liquid; two small wax candles; two little linen sacks with corded drawstrings.

She begins humming her customary lullaby – breathy, almost inaudible – as she digs for a slender tin of matchsticks. To the low music of her humming she lights a candle and uses its flame to affix its fellow to the bedpost. She repeats the process, softening wax with the heat of the other candle and pressing it, molding it, to the wood of the opposite post. The wooden plate she places on the dead woman's chest. There she drops a pinch from both small sacks: one of earth, one of salt. From the vial she drips lavender oil on the dead woman's forehead,

22

murmuring words of comfort, strings of sequential calculations which sound like prayer.

A few moments of silence, then everything but the candles are returned to the satchel. Beatrix smiles down at the woman on the bed and gives her inert shoulder a tiny pat – of recognition, of kinship, of sorrow – before blowing out the candles, leaving only the dim light of an oil lamp and the sliver of yellow glow beneath the door. "We die, Lucky. It's the one thing we can all count on, right? And if death is the sole universal human experience – next to birth, that is – it makes us all more akin to each other than we would be without it. Our commonality is our most human part, right? And without humanity, we may just as well be Machines."

She tucks a stray dark curl under the edge of her wimple, then reaches to grasp the other woman's hand. She turns, and opens the door to the living.

***

Invitations to share the evening meal are readily accepted. Shadow-she moves about the room, touching things on shelves and mantels and in the other hundred nooks an active family finds to stash the accumulated objects of their daily lives. Touching their things, she briefly feels closer to them.

The small one also moves about, but under her hands wiggle more obvious signs of life, the children. They cluster and flock to her, moths to flame, geese to crust. The laughter in the room complements the silence and quietude of the room beyond, two facets of a human whole. Not disrespectful, but joyous, uncontained, *alive*.

Around herself, the shadow, exists a circle of hush. People in the room don't shy from her, but neither do they gather close; she's not a part of them and they can tell. She doesn't mind. Is in fact relieved. She finds herself looking away from their laughter as from the brightness of midday sun. Already she feels burnt.

And then she moves though a patch of coolness in the room. It's like wading through a deep cold current in a warm and shallow lake. She looks up, sees him seeing her.

He sits at a table. Not the main table covered with crockery and dishes and the crisp linen squares of napkins, laden with baskets of bread and bowls of glazed potatoes and the tiny green pearls of peas. No; his table against the far wall is covered with what look like maps, and blue-tinted diagrams of buildings, and what she vaguely understands are the technical drawings of a Machine. She can't help recognizing sketches of cables and sprouting arms – she understands too well the purpose of those segmented limbs with their hundred sharps. She can almost hear the rolling of those rounded gripping wheels against the necrotic metal of the Compliance prison floor.

He looks a little like the small one, she thinks. He too has dark, loosely curly hair. He too has pale grey eyes, though not laughing like the other's do. His lips and the planes of his face aren't cruel, but they are hard, unhappy. It's that, the lack of happy, which connects them like a thread across the ocean of laughter.

She walks to him. Darting children and bustling adults carrying milk and wine and vegetables part before her. He stands, and when she reaches his side she finds they're of almost equal height, though he's slightly taller, standing straighter. She's so used to being the steeple above the cabbages, she finds herself surprised.

***

"This is my brother, who fancies himself a scholar and a settlement scavenger," Goodman Cropper says to the silent scarred woman who inexplicably slouches after the delightful Sister Beatrix everywhere she goes. "My brother," he repeats louder when the woman fails to acknowledge his presence, "Samuel Smith."

She glances at him briefly, the unnatural greenness of her eyes making him shudder. Goodman Cropper moves hastily away as his brother takes the woman's hand. It's bent, that hand. Against the expanse of Samuel's calloused blacksmith's fingers it looks crumpled, like tin too near a forge.

"Join me," says Samuel, making room on the bench. She sits. The warmth of his thigh along hers seeps through the coarse wool of her leggings and her tunic, into the outer layers of her skin. He resumes studying the lines of diagrams spread on the table, making no attempt to speak. But neither does he remove his hand from hers. And when Samuel is called to take his place at supper he draws her to her feet and leads her, settles her next to himself among his relatives.

There's no prayer to the Third Supreme Deity, no marking of the meal's start other than a "Go on, then," from Goody Cropper to her eldest daughter. Conversation around the table barely lessens, children relating to Sister Beatrix tales of their cow's new calf, and how the eldest Cropper girl fell into the mud by the edge of the pond, and how Grandmother Cropper always liked glazed potatoes best and so everyone should enjoy them extra-special in her honor.

"Will you stay the night, and join us for the burial tomorrow, Sister Beatrix?" asks Goody Cropper, passing her more bread.

Beatrix nods, her linen headdress bobbing, and swallows her mouthful of glazed potato. "We would love to join your family for their last farewells. Right, Lucky?" She looks at her companion and all faces at the table follow suit, no sound in the room but muffled chewing and the crackling fire at the hearth and the expectant non-sound of curious eyes.

And then the silence breaks, Beatrix laughing, nodding, filling the blank space until everyone surges on and flows forward, an unstoppable brook of human living. The silent woman was only a branch caught in the mud of the bank, to be flowed around and over and past.

After dinner, Beatrix joins Samuel at his curling papers. She frowns, leaning over the blue lines and tiny numbers, the unrolled diagrams, the maps of Machine physiology. "Settlement scavenged?" she asks. He nods. With her finger she traces mathematical formulae in columns along the edges. "Keeping these old documents is just begging death to come find you," she says. "Even in the mountains, though no Machine has come up these slopes for ten years or more. They could. They still could."

But behind her words, her interest flares bright and involuntarily eager. He says, "There's new building going on at the back of the prison. I used to think we could wait them out, but if they evolve, learn to build a new generation of themselves, what would that generation learn to do? And the next?"

Grey eyes stare into grey, unblinking. "Studying the mechanics of a thing won't give it meaning," says Beatrix at last. "Meaning lies with us, not them. Even their meaning began with humans, back on Earth."

"Then let it end with humans here," he says. "We can't wait for another colony ship to show up from the other side of space – though who knows what's happening back on Earth? And if another ship arrives, what will these evolved Machines make of new settlers come to build a home on Colony IV like our great-grandparents?"

Frowning again, Beatrix pulls a diagram from beneath others, shifts a blueprint to the top. She doesn't look at the woman behind her.

But the green-eyed woman is content merely to be in the presence of both of them: the light spark and the dark, each connected to her center. She senses these connections, imagines them as cords of wool – no, rope; no, smith-forged chains – fastened somewhere in her middle close to where her heart would be if she could feel one.

Later, sweet, chubby Panza is bedded for the night with other livestock. Children are kissed and sent to pile together into bed like kittens in a box. Sister Beatrix of the Order of the Third Supreme Deity is thanked and thanked and thanked for the great service she has done the Cropper family. Goody Cropper gives her human guests soft blankets and a cozy corner near the fire.

The two women lie side by side in the warm, human-scented darkness, each pretending to sleep, but both seeing in their minds' eyes the dark blue lines of diagrams, the sketched skeletons of Machines and the numerically-described pathways of their metal fortress and their mechanical intestines.

***

The burial takes place the following morning at first light. It's an informal, quiet affair, the adults holding hands and singing, the children telling remembered stories about their grandmother. As they talk and congregate, sweet contented feelings of family flow around the hollow woman, almost fill her. But no: the human fullness washes through her, past her, leaving her empty again but for the bindings around her core, those tethers looping outward to both Samuel and Beatrix. The tethers are tentative and fragile, but she takes comfort knowing they are there.

From this side of the Croppers' mountain, dozens of thin, straggling fingers of smoke can be seen where homesteads dot nearby mountainsides: proof of other Colony survivors.

Beatrix notices the path of her gaze. "I wonder what the world looked like last time you saw it, Lucky. You lived in the settlement? Well now it's just a scraped place in the ground with no trees, everything portable scavenged and carted off years ago by survivors brave enough to rummage so close to the Compliance prison. Everyone out in the woods, the desert, up in the mountains – we lie low. Lower than low. Like ghosts, invisible even to each other for the most part, though nobody's seen a Machine in the countryside for years." She laughs, hard and short. "Too inefficient to round up those living scattered and without technology. To a Machine designed to regulate Colony IV's social efficiency, a biological creature without organized society is no different from Panza, eh? A donkey. Or a squirrel or a bird. No need to enforce social efficiency on a lizard."

The burial closes simply, everyone working together to pitch shovelfuls of dark earth. Afterward the family walks arm in arm and hand in hand back into the house to eat, to offer each other small courtesies and affections. Only Samuel remains behind, dusting his large palms on the front of his smithy's smock. He meets the grey gaze of Sister Beatrix. "I spent all yesterday at the base of the mountain, laying lines, placing charges, doing what needs to be done," he says. "You should come."

The tall silent woman steps from the short Sister's side to take Samuel's hand. He smiles, curls his thick fingers about her thin crooked ones. But he watches only Beatrix.

"I've studied those plans for years, trying to get up courage, to find strength," he says. His fingers tighten around the hand he holds. The tall woman leans closer. "Or maybe I've been waiting for strength to find me."

Tilting her head, Beatrix squints up at the dark height of him.

Samuel smiles, a tightening of lips across teeth. "All our lives we've been taught to lie low, to do nothing, told that if we act and fail, the Machines will come and we'll all lose – instantly, horribly, in fire and blood like the original settlement."

"And if we don't try," Beatrix says, "then we lose slowly and in increasingly smaller numbers, like a collapsing spiral. Our children lose, and their children, until all is lost for good. It's true. And as Earth Augustine says, 'Entrust Truth, whatsoever thou hast from the Truth, and thou shalt lose nothing.'"

Samuel nods once. He turns to stride toward a small stone hut some distance from the Croppers' cottage, pulling the silent woman after him by the hand. Her grip on his tightens convulsively, her knuckles white points of bone thrusting from the melding of their fingers, her feet each tripping over the other as she follows him.

"Truth it is, then," Samuel calls to Beatrix over his shoulder. The small Sister clamps her wimple to her head with her fist and runs to catch up.

***

It's late. It's after dark, and she's sleepy. Samuel has spent hours showing Sister Beatrix diagrams and plans; explaining how he located *these* ingredients or *those* by hoarding, by trading, by raiding the outskirts of the ruined settlement below; how he discovered the forgotten mining shed in its shallow mountainside grave with its explosives and texts, and mixed *this* reagent with *that* according to the instructions of diagrams and illegal books.

It's their united love for illicit books which cements the bond between the grey-eyed two.

Though she doesn't share the color of their eyes or the excitement of their convictions, she's content to simply watch their dark heads press close together; to listen to their voices and hear the meeting thoughts of two beings so different from each other and yet both so compelling to her. If only she could join them, become more than a hollow thing without title, without name, without meaning other than that gleaned from those around her.

She falls asleep to the murmur of their muted voices, the heat of their bodies warming the small stone hut. She doesn't wake when someone tucks her into the folds of woolen blankets and kisses her goodnight.

***

She is not a number.

When she wakes, it's to the thin light of early morning and the coldness of an empty room. The other two aren't in the yard, or the larger cottage. The donkey Panza stands alone by the gate, ignoring Croppers scurrying through morning tasks: milking, chopping, sewing, herding stubby grey sheep or fetching water from the silty stream over the rise.

She doesn't know where the two have gone, but her feet carry her to the tethered donkey. Without conscious thought she unties him, pulls herself up onto Panza's wide back. With no urging he begins plodding away down the hill. His hard donkey hooves scatter small pebbles, his heated breaths puff warmth into the air.

It's not toward the abbey that they head. She understands this even from the first step. It's as though she and the donkey both seek to be reunited with *her*; as though he too feels only empty hollowness when they are apart.

The hour it takes to descend the mountain passes quickly. They come upon the others camped on the crest of the last ridge, the one overlooking the automated prison. From this vantage it's no more than a squat, perfectly square box of black corrugated metal stretching across an acre of brittle winter grass.

She looks down at the place where her name was taken, filed off and obliterated. Nobody speaks as she slides from the donkey's back, though both the tall man and the tiny woman reach to catch her. They stand, caught in an awkward three-way embrace. She breathes deeply, inhaling their human warmth. For the first time in more than twenty years, something stirs inside where her heart used to be.

As the sun crests the rim of the mountain, the lit fuse finds the explosives nestled in the rock. Though the flare and flash of the explosion renders her momentarily blind and the boom leaves her ears ringing, she doesn't flinch or look away.

When the dust clears, there's little left. Carefully-placed charges on the cliff have triggered an avalanche of dark rock. A single crumpled metal corner of the automated prison is barely visible, but nothing more: just grass, and sunshine filtering through clouds of dust, and the sharply irregular outline of the new, unweathered cliff-face of raw rock.

She becomes aware of pressure on both her hands. Her vision clears enough to see Samuel, though the questions in his eyes are nothing she can immediately decipher.

Beatrix grips tight her other hand.

"Lucky," she hears Beatrix shout past the ringing in her ears, "Lucky, it's done..."

And she who's not a number, has never been a number, returns the pressure of their hands. "My name," she says, "is Lucy."

Camille Alexa lives mostly in the Pacific Northwest, usually in a century-old house, sometimes writing fiction. Her first book, *PUSH OF THE SKY*, earned a starred review in *Publishers Weekly* and was a finalist for the Endeavour Award. She loves cool sunny mornings and hot running water, and hates the thought nuclear winter could deprive her of both.

More at http://camillealexa.com.

PUSHAWAY
MELISSA S. GREEN

Esti Gusev wasn't the name she was given at birth. It was the name she'd taken. She'd damn well earned it.

And wasn't that how they worked things in the Consensus? You earned your place. You Examined for it. You got what you got by merit and heart.

Now she had name and place and a ticket printed with both. "I'll sure miss you," she said, "but I won't miss here."

"Yeah," Michel said. "Let me see."

It was just a small, square card, but it was proof: in three days, she'd board a mag capsule and push away from the planet. She might never see Mars again. She might never see them again, either.

Michel passed the ticket to Jaime and looked up with a sad little smile. "You're really going to do it, then."

"She won't go *that* far," Frieda said. "She'll get to Earth, she'll never want to leave it." Her voice was well-controlled, but Esti heard her envy. Frieda had wanted to go to Earth herself. She just hadn't wanted it enough.

Anyway, Earth wasn't Esti's final destination. She felt it in her blood, the same sure conviction that had fueled her since reading Meikäläinen eight years ago, and then learning about Consensus and its project to the stars. She'd do what she was going to Earth to do, and then she'd be stuffing that data into suitcases for the trip across the Long Dark her very own self.

"Esti Gusev," Jaime read off the ticket. "Leaving your real name behind, too, eh?"

"*That's* my real name," she said. She shrugged. "And now it's official."

He shrugged back.

"When did that happen?" asked Michel. "Weren't there court fees–?"

"Not my problem. Change of citizenship, change of name, same difference – that's what Mordecai said. Consensus doesn't care if Mars Government stamps the papers in advance. Especially since I'm launching from Biblis instead of climbing the rope."

Which was to say that she'd be squished back into her seat under a couple or three Earth-g's and shot up from a Consensus-operated mag launcher, instead of taking the much slower but far less physically stressful ride into orbit from Pavonis summit. Biblis Launch was cheaper, too, and Mordecai appreciated that.

In fact, he'd told her Consensus Library wanted her on in the data acquisitions project in Vancouver so badly that Consensus would pay her court fees *and* first class fare up the space elevator if she wanted to take that choice. She hadn't expected that, hadn't planned for it either. She'd always reckoned she'd have to be strong to stand on Earth – strong, for that matter, to live on a Consensus ship or one of the settlements in or beyond the Belt, almost universally kept centrifugal at Earth g. But for damn sure she'd have to be strong to withstand the crushing force of a mag capsule catapulting up from Biblis Tholus. She'd worked for that strength – vibe plates, 'fuges, weights, the works.

She kept her mouth shut now about Mordecai's offer. Frieda in particular would moan the next three days straight if she knew Esti was passing up a free chance at a luxury class ride up the rope. But Esti had earned her strength as much as she'd earned her name. She meant to use it.

***

She didn't like when Mama spanked her. It was mean, especially in front of everybody. The hug afterwards only made it worse. So she tried to push away.

But Mama wouldn't let go. She pulled her in closer, shushing in her ear. "It's all right, honey, I still love you…"

No, Mama didn't really love her. Mama only said so because she was supposed to. Brother Easton was watching. So was Papa and Uncle Philip and everybody else. She could see their faces through the blur of her tears, watching her from their sleeping bags or the benches along the wall. The bigelow was the only building in New Nazareth that could keep the dust out, so everybody stayed there while the dust storm kept going on forever and forever, and now all of them were watching her. She hated it. She tried to squirm away.

Mama held her tight. "Shhh, shhhhh, you just have to do better next time… but don't worry, Mama still loves you…" But she wasn't crying because she was afraid Mama didn't love her. She was crying because she was *mad*. It made her even madder that Mama wouldn't let her go. The harder she pushed away, the tighter Mama hugged her close.

Yesterday Mama had spanked Elijah when he fussed and wouldn't eat his food. He cried and cried, but when Mama hugged him afterwards she wasn't all stiff and hard like she was now. That's how she knew Mama didn't love her. Mama said she was "oppositional," but Elijah was just "boys will be boys." She'd spank Elijah just hard enough to make him cry, and then hug him all warm and soft and cuddly and Elijah would go limp in her arms and stop crying and even smile and laugh at what she whispered in his ear. Then he even ate his food, even though it was horrible and it was mean for Mama to spank him for not liking it.

"Shhh," Mama said, "shhhhh." Then she knew she was supposed to do just like Elijah. She was supposed to do like Amelia did with Aunt Sarai. She was supposed to stop crying or squirming to get away. She was supposed to let Mama hug her and comfort her like it was someone *else* who had put her over her knees to slap her bottom and make her hurt so bad, not Mama at all.

But it was Mama who did it! It just made her *mad!* But she couldn't think how else to get free. So she held herself still and gritted her teeth and forced herself to stop crying. But she couldn't make herself go limp like Elijah did. Just the thought made her feel dirty inside. She just held herself still, made herself as stiff as Mama. Finally Mama gave her a last squeeze and let her go.

***

The dirt was so dry and loose she hardly had to dig, just sift her fingers through it to capture the little potatoes hiding in it. They came out tiny, hardly big enough to eat. They were really hard too, like little pieces of hard candy from Dao Vallis. Uncle Philip said there wasn't enough water. There used to be water here, a long long time ago, but it disappeared long before Earth people even invented telescopes or sent Spirit Rover to look.

New Nazareth was cold, too, too cold for the most important crops. That was why the farm was inside a greenhouse. It was like the bigelow, except bigger and transparent. There were compressors and generators to make the air thicker than outside and warm enough for the plants. It was even warm enough they didn't have to suit up. And there were sunlights because the real sunlight wasn't strong enough to make the plants to grow right, even with the orbital mirrors. Aunt Sarai said the lights also gave them vitamin D, so *they* would grow right. But the sunlights didn't make up for not enough water, and Uncle Philip said the dirt wasn't very good soil either.

The grownups argued about it at meeting. Brother Mikkelson said the greenhouse didn't have a good seal and let too much water escape no matter how many times they tried to fix it. Sister Caritas said how much it cost to rover supplies in from the nearest maglev at Apollinaris. Brother Esteves visiting from Axius said the South Hellas churches were worried because New Nazareth was costing more instead of less like it was supposed to by now. Uncle Philip said they should move closer to Apollinaris where there was more water and they were closer to shipping and help from the churches there.

But Brother Easton looked angry and said no, God wanted New Nazareth to be where Spirit led. He said it wasn't accident that Spirit Rover landed in Gusev Crater – he said it was God's plan to show them two hundred years later where He wanted His people to live, and God was in charge, not Man.

She sat back on her heels. Her bucket was less than a quarter full and the potatoes were tiny and dry. "Brother Easton always says God is in charge," she said. "But God is never at meeting. At meeting, Brother Easton is in charge."

Amelia looked around from her own work, eyes wide. "Don't say that!"

"It's so," she said. "Look, the dirt is bad, your Papa says so and everyone knows he knows more about growing food than anybody. But Brother Easton says we have to stay here even though the plants don't grow good and we don't have hardly any water."

"But Spirit is here!" Amelia protested.

31

"Spirit is an old machine that died a long time ago," she said. She had thought that ever since they went to see it, the old robot rover in the little museum building Mars Government had built long ago on Husband Hill. It made a big scary hole in her tummy to say it aloud, even to Amelia. But she knew she was right. "Spirit Rover isn't the same as Holy Spirit."

Amelia's face got even whiter under the orange dirt smudged all over it. "Don't say that!" The boys were so near they might hear, but that wasn't all making her scared. She was hearing blasphemy. That had to be what she was thinking. "Unbelievers sent Spirit," Amelia said, "but God used them to leave a sign for us!"

"Brother Easton says so, but how does he know?"

Amelia looked troubled for a moment, but then her face cleared. "Mama says he's a prophet, like Elijah and Isaiah and John. God is in his heart."

Now it was her turn to frown. She scooted herself along the ground to the next section and drew her bucket after her. If God was in his heart, and God was in charge, then that explained how Brother Easton was in charge. But then she remembered that Brother Easton also said God is in *your* heart. *Everybody's* heart. He even quoted Lord Jesus. *The Kingdom of God is in your heart.* She put one dirty hand to her chest and felt it there. God was in her heart. It felt right to think so. Yes, she was sure it was right.

She pulled her other hand up out of the dirt and sat up again. "But remember when he said, God is in everybody's heart? So if God being in your heart means you're a prophet and you're in charge, then doesn't that mean *I'm* in charge too?" She thought for a moment. "Or at least part of me? And so is your papa. So when your papa said we should move because we don't have enough water and we can't make the dirt into real soil here, we should listen to him."

***

"Who told you that?" Papa asked. He stood over her where she sat on a chair in the middle of the room. Papa wasn't very tall for a grownup man, but he was lots taller than she was, and he was angry. "Who told you Philip should be in charge?"

They had sent the boys away, but Brother Easton was here, sitting right next to Uncle Philip at the table. His face was all red-splotchy like it got when he preached Moses coming down the mountain with the tablets and finding the people worshiping the golden calf. She thought if he had a stone tablet he'd come break it over her head. He was even scarier than Papa.

Papa bent down and shouted in her ear. "Who told you that?"

"No one told me!" she said again. "I never said Uncle Philip should be in charge, I just said he knew best about farming and everybody should listen to him!"

"She has the devil in her," Uncle Philip said. He was scared too. She could tell. He was scared and it made him hate her.

Brother Easton looked at him. "Maybe she does. Or maybe she overheard something. Maybe she overheard Brother Bienbenidos say something to *you*."

"No!" Uncle Philip said. His face was all pale and sweaty.

She remembered Brother Bienbenidos. He was in the rover that came with Brother Esteves and some other Promised Land people and they stayed for a month. Except she never heard him say anything except at meeting or common meal where everybody else could hear him too. And he never sat next to Uncle Philip.

"That's telling a lie!" she said, "I never –"

"That's enough!" Papa yelled.

"– heard anyone – God is in charge, and God's in everyone's hearts, and God is in Uncle Philip's heart, and he knows –"

"That's *enough*!" Papa yelled, and he slapped her ear.

"– about farming, and we should listen –"

"Silence!" Brother Easton stood and walked right up to her and looked down, and she looked back up. He was taller than Papa, and he was scary, but she looked right back at him even though the sting of Papa's slap had brought tears to her eyes. "Your uncle is right about one thing, little girl." He leaned down and she could smell his breath all hot on her face. "It's not God in *your* heart, but the devil." He gave Papa a look and walked back to Uncle Philip.

Then Papa grabbed her up with his fingers digging into her shoulder and armpit and he dragged her home. He spanked harder than Mama did. A lot harder.

***

One day three rovers came up the Ma'adim Vallis. But rovers only ever came from the north, sometimes Promised Land rovers with visitors, but mostly their own freighting supplies bought in Apollinaris with donations from the churches. She always knew when they were coming because Papa kept them in repair. That was his job. He went on some of the trips, too. He was on one now and wasn't due back for three days yet, which was good because Papa was mean. But it was bad too. Uncle Philip was even meaner because it was her fault Brother Easton didn't trust him. But he didn't live in the same habitat with them, and Papa did.

The new rovers were coming from the south, up the Ma'adim, and they had just one day warning about them. "They're coming to spy on us for Mars Government, and they want to catch us at something," Elijah said, which probably was what Brother Easton had said. Elijah always repeated what Brother Easton said. She couldn't think what Mars Government would catch them at, and she thought it would be stupid for them to send three rovers through the chaos lands south of Gusev Crater where nobody lived for thousands of kilometers just in order to spy on New Nazareth. But she kept her mouth shut because Elijah always repeated what *she* said too, except in her case what she said got her punished. She still had big bruises on her back and behind from the last time he told on her.

Anyway, even if they were spies for Mars Government there was nothing Brother Easton could do to keep them away. Mars Hospitality Law said travelers had to be welcomed. It was a law so old it predated Mars Government, because Mars was dangerous and it could mean life or death to say go away to a traveler.

That was how she met Sioloa. She was her same age so they sat together at common meal, along with Amelia and Elijah and Conlee and Sioloa's little brother Etano, who was a year younger than Elijah. They were the first people she ever knew who weren't New Nazareth or Promised Land. They wore blue coveralls with the orange big-ball-of-Mars patches of Mangala University that she had only ever seen before in pictures on the computer. Their rovers were big expedition-class rovers that they had already lived in for eight months.

"We're on a science survey," Sioloa bragged, but of course it was her parents and the other Mangala grownups who were the scientists, not her and Etano. She talked like they helped with some of the science work though. Their survey team was just one out of four, she said, and they were doing a big study for Mars Government. Elijah nodded and gave her a big look like, "See?"

She thought he was wrong, they weren't spies, but she didn't care. She could feel her heart beating and she put her hand up to her chest. She'd never been so excited in her life, not ever. Sioloa was so different. She was smart and funny and she bragged like a boy. She wasn't afraid to say what she thought.

Like after common meal when they went outside to play, and Conlee asked, "Why are you so strong?" and it was true, Sioloa was stronger than any of the New Nazareth boys, and Etano was too even though he was younger than Elijah and Conlee both.

"Why are you so weak?" she shot back. "Don't you have vibe machines? Don't you have a 'fuge?" The Mangala rovers, it turned out, all had vibe machines, and everyone in the expedition including Sioloa and Etano used them every day. New Nazareth had only two machines that the boys used every other day, and the girls only once a week. "That's stupid," Sioloa said.

"No, it's not," Elijah said. "Girls aren't supposed to be as strong as boys."

"Girls and boys doesn't have anything to do with it," Sioloa said. "If you don't use them enough your muscles and bones get weak and you get sick easier and die younger. Once a week isn't enough."

"Who says?" Conlee challenged.

"My aunt says. She's a gravitational physiologist."

"Well, Brother Easton says girls go only once a week," Elijah said, "and besides, girls are supposed to keep their mouths shut. He knows best because he's a prophet."

Sioloa made a face and rolled her eyes. "No, he's a despot."

She didn't know what that word meant, except Sioloa didn't like Brother Easton. Elijah didn't know what it meant either, but before he could ask Brother Easton and Brother Mikkelson came out with the Mangala people, and Mama

34

and Aunt Sarai were talking with Sioloa's mama.

Then she got really lucky, because Sioloa asked her parents if she and Elijah and Amelia could stay that night in their rover. They asked Mama and Aunt Sarai and Uncle Philip, who came out late. Mama was caught by surprise and said she and Elijah could, before Uncle Philip had a chance to forbid it. But he wouldn't let Amelia go. If Papa had been home, she wouldn't have gotten to either. So it was lucky he wasn't home.

Sioloa's rover was wasn't really that much different from the rovers Papa kept running except it was bigger and newer and had lots of strange instruments. Elijah asked all kinds of questions, but he kept interrupting when Sioloa tried to explain, and Etano wasn't as good at explaining. She wanted to ask her own questions. What was it like to live in a rover? How did they go to school? What was a despot? How could Sioloa speak her mind so freely, without fear? But Elijah was there, and her own fear held her back.

Then Elijah interrupted Sioloa again and she made a face again and rolled her eyes and said, "Let's go to my quarters" – that's what she called them – and they left the boys behind.

Sioloa's quarters were small, but they weren't cramped like she thought they would be. "Good design," Sioloa said, "look at this!" She just reached up and pulled, and suddenly a second bed sprang down from the wall so that they both had one. They sat down on them and looked at each other. "You don't talk very much, do you?" Sioloa asked.

She didn't know what to say.

Sioloa frowned and tried again. "Your brother isn't very nice."

She looked to the door – what if he heard?

"Etano's quarters are the other side," Sioloa said. "He won't bring your brother down here, I already asked him because I wanted to talk with you."

She didn't know what to say to that, either. Nobody ever wanted to know what she had to think except Amelia.

"Elijah said mean things and I could tell you didn't like them, but you didn't say anything, and neither did your cousin."

"Amelia," she said.

"Amelia. How come you didn't say anything?"

She'd only known Sioloa a few hours, but already she was the best friend she'd ever had. That was the feeling she had. Her heart beat fast and hard, and then became calm as she felt this feeling, this strange feeling. Could she trust it? But it felt right. God is in my heart, she thought. God is in charge. She looked up into Sioloa's eyes and she knew it was right.

So she told her.

***

When she was in hospital at Apollinaris, Sioloa sent a book she downloaded to her new pod about a place where people came out of hard times, all kinds of hard times, and healed from all their hurts the best they could, and found the way that was theirs. When they arrived at this place, they were all given names different from what they were called in the Real World, and in finding their own way some of them renamed themselves.

There was no forest on Mars quite like the forest in the story. But sometimes after a session with the Carmen, her physical therapist, she'd go sit in the most dense bamboo thicket in the hospital garden and pretend she was in that forest with those people sitting around that fire, telling stories and, like them, happening by accident into other stories that told them who they were and how to go on living.

If she were to arrive in that forest by that fire, and go to the red oak and put her hand in its hollow, what name would she draw out of it?

She thought it would be Gusev. Not New Nazareth, but Gusev, which was the real name of the place when Spirit Rover came to it, and the official name that Mars Government gave it. It was what the Mangala scientists had on their maps when they came up the Ma'adim, and it was because they followed those maps that she met her first real friend. And out of that, eventually, New Nazareth came to an end, and Brother Easton and Papa and Elijah couldn't hurt her anymore.

Gusev was, on top of it, a name every Martian knew. Maybe everyone in the Solar System knew it by now, it was on the vid all the time. It was *notorious*, that's what Carmen said. There had been bloodshed, and Brother Easton and Brother Mikkelson had actually been killed. But even more important was how unhealthy and sick most of the people were, even the men, because of not enough food, not enough water, and weakness of bones and muscles just like Sioloa had said, and even worse how the women and children got punished all the time and all the meanness and craziness of the place.

Because of all that, Gusev would be a name that turned the screws in people. And they all deserved it. She knew now what she hadn't known then, that Mars Government had known all along what things were like years before the Mangala rovers came. They said things like "religious dictatorship" and "violations of the Mars Charter of Human Rights," but what it had really been was being beaten and made to feel wrong just for having God in her heart and being in charge of her own thoughts and Brother Easton and Papa and Uncle Philip and even Mama wanting to beat it out of her. And teaching Elijah to do it too. And Amelia... well, Amelia's heart had been beaten out of her before she was even old enough to talk. Mars Government left them all there for that long, and so Martians deserved to be reminded of it every time they said her name.

In her imagination she wouldn't need to explain the meaning of her name to any of the other people in that forest, around that fire, even though the author who wrote the story had been born and died long before Mars was even terraformed. They'd all know. But they'd also all know that if her name when she came into the woods fit her life as it was, then she was in search of a new name. And that she would find it.

Just like Rachel Meikäläinen had, who claimed that even though the story was completely made up, it was also a true story. So why shouldn't it be true for Gusev too?

After hospital, she was sent to the Children's School in Dao Vallis because Papa was still in prison and she refused to go back to Mama and Elijah. Dao Vallis was pleasant, even beautiful. It wasn't dry like New Nazareth, but was set on the shore of the first sea on Mars, the Hellas Sea, and she made friends and had good teachers, and she was able to stay in touch with Sioloa and Etano, even being allowed to visit them once at Mangala.

But she felt that something was still wrong inside of her, so she downloaded Rachel Meikäläinen's book to her pod to read it again. One day she sat reading it in Sungari Park among the trees, imagining the fire, the forest, the red oak, how she had drawn her name Gusev from the hollow in that oak, and what kind of story she would go into to find her new name – when a boy came along and, seeing her, stopped. "What you reading?" he asked.

He was another "orphan," as Children's School residents styled themselves, though most had living parents – kids who, like her, had fallen victim to "violations of the Mars Charter of Human Rights." Michel, his name was. She'd never talked with him much, and didn't much want to then either.

But later she was glad she did, because when she named her book, "Meikäläinen!" he exclaimed immediately. "Yeah, she wrote this other thing, it's behind all those anticorporate socialist sociopaths who think they can run Outer System on their own." Suddenly Rachel Meikäläinen became more than just the name of the person who'd written her favorite book, but someone who'd had an important effect in the universe.

Meikäläinen's other book, according to Michel, had provided a philosophical foundation for the Ceres Rebellion some forty years ago, by means of which the deep space mining and energy workers in the Main Belt and beyond had seized the assets of the megacorporations that had controlled their lives. They formed their own government, the Consensus of the Outer System, which was increasingly in the news nowadays ever since the Treaty of Ceres that had been signed just three years before, normalizing relations between insystem and outsystem for the first time since the rebellion.

As Michel had to explain to her, since she'd never paid much attention to Consensus before. Her own fascination was with Earth, its wealth of stories and legends and beliefs, for good and ill. Somehow she knew it was necessary work if she wanted to unravel her own story, but it hadn't previously occurred to her that others of the human diaspora in the solar system owed just as much to the heritage of Earth.

The book *Whole Numbers* wasn't anything like Meikäläinen's story about the forest and the fire, except that it was just like it. It was unlike it because it didn't have a forest or a fire or people going into stories by accident, it didn't contain fantasy, it wasn't imaginary. But it had imagination. It had names: the names of words, and what they meant, and how that carried out into the world.

For example, "The root of the word *integrity*," Rachel Meikäläinen wrote, "is the Latin *integer*, which means, literally, *untouched*. And so an integer is a number that hasn't been broken or fractionated. It is complete, a whole number. Something which is *integral* is something which is essential to completeness, something which is *integrated*, which is to say, something which has been incorporated into a functioning and unified whole. And so to have *integrity* is to have wholeness, completion, undividedness.

"But if *integrity* is undivided, unbroken, untouched – then what, in this context, is it to be *touched?*"

Touched. Reading the word sent an unexpected wave of horror through her, as if Brother Easton stood over her again, breathing his hot breath into her face, signaling to her Papa what he should do. *Touched.* It was a nondescript enough word, really, but "in this context," as Meikäläinen wrote, was it really? If *integrity* was *undivided, unbroken, untouched* – its opposite was *touched, broken, divided.* And it came to her that if *Gusev* was a screw turning in people who must call her by that name of ugly repute, it was a screw that turned in her, too. *Touched.* She had been. Touched and broken.

"Touch is not a bad thing, usually – but in this context," Meikäläinen answered herself, "to be touched is to be breached, broken, violated. That's at its worst, anyway. But the worst happens, over and over. Even when no harm is intended, harm often comes; and often, of course, harm *is* intended. The harms may be physical; the harms may be emotional or spiritual. Abuse. Coercion. The most common harm of all to human beings – the one that most harmed me – was the simple and common harm of those who convince themselves that they are well-intended when they attempt to coerce an individual into behaving according to *their* arbitrary standards, rather than according to the individual's *integrity* – to what should properly be understood as that individual's true selfhood."

She recognized that. *The Kingdom of God is in your heart. God is in charge.* The one true lesson Brother Easton had ever taught, and then had tried violently to unteach, all the days of her childhood. Mama did, too. She remembered as if it had just happened moments ago being bent over Mama's lap and spanked for a reason she didn't remember, if in fact she'd ever known, and everyone watching. And her tears. And Mama's embrace, that she had tried to push away from because it was a lie even meaner and deeper than the spanking itself.

"*Integrity* is whole," Meikäläinen wrote. "The root of the word *whole* is the Old English word *hal*, which is also the root or closely related to the roots of the words *heal, hale, holy.* To be truly whole, to be fully and completely healed, would be as though one had never been touched by the harm that had in fact touched one. But if you *have* been touched, how can you become *untouched* again? It's a paradox: you must *incorporate* the experience of that touch, that harm, into yourself. Meaning literally – because *incorporate* comes in part from the Latin root *corpus* meaning *body* – that you make that touch, that hurt, part of your body: but in a hale, healing way. How? When you eat an apple, does it stay an apple inside your stomach and gut? No: your body transforms it with its acids and enzymes and all that other stuff that goes on inside the body. Call it *incorporation*, call it *integration*: transformation comes with the territory of it. You have no choice about the harms that others inflict upon you, but if they haven't actually killed you, you may still have much more choice than you realize to transform them within yourself and integrate them into a new whole, a new integrity. You are not exactly the same self you began with; but you are still your own self. The Self itself is change."

The Self itself is change.

She thrust the pod aside. It was too much, to ask her to incorporate *that*. To make what Mama and Papa and Brother Easton did to her part of her body and mind? Her spirit? No. That's what Amelia was, a girl so lacking in self that she wouldn't let herself be rescued from Uncle Philip, who should be in prison too. The hurt, the harm, all memory of New Nazareth was something meant to be pushed away, rejected, and forgotten. How could she integrate *that* into who she was?

She picked up the pod again because she had to: it had everything on it by which she lived her life now, schedule and coursework and Earth studies. But it was a long time before she opened Meikäläinen's book again, and that too only because she had to, for a course on the history of the Consensus that was now part of the standard curriculum. How in hell could Meikäläinen's philosophy-through-etymology have any possible relevance to the political and economic and social issues that had pitted the workers at Ceres against the corporate bosses and owners of He-Three and Deep Space Energy and Mining? That was the question she had now. Meikäläinen had shaken her before, but she was older now; she reckoned she had a distance now from her past, and the histories and commentaries would take her through Meikäläinen's stuff without hitting her in the gut.

Older? A whole half-year older. Not much, really, especially when you were only 8 – or a year older at age 16 by Earth count – that's what she reflected after Meikäläinen punched the bravado out of her. Shit, Meikäläinen was as violent as Elijah, she thought, even if all she used were words. Those passages of *Whole Numbers* brought back every physical memory – the spanks, the slaps, pinches, beatings, hunger. The fear. The weakness from being kept off the vibe machines except once a week, and never having access to a 'fuge to begin with, such that she was severely handicapped by the time Mars Government swooped in and saved them all. Well, some of them. Saved her at least. But it took a lot of doctoring to make her healthy again. And then the daily agony and sweat since then to accomplish the strength gained, first with Carmen at Apollinaris and now at the gym in Dao Vallis.

Maybe it was like just like that for Talvi and Cheng and Dabrukas and the others at Ceres and Vesta and the moons of Jupiter and Saturn when they threw off the corporations. The histories said the corporations used intimidation and torture, even murder, to keep the workers in control. So those workers would have been just as squashed, just as broken, just as violated. And it all started with just with one person forcing – not just asking – another person to do his or her bidding. But the cure started in the same place, with the refusal of the self, of the Kingdom of God, to be snuffed out.

The Self itself is change.

When she read those words this time, something like a voice at her right shoulder whispered in her ear: *Gusev.* It was the name she'd pulled from the hollow of the red oak in Meikäläinen's story. It was the name fitted to her by the tale of her own life to that point – the name she herself had written into Meikäläinen's story, because it was fitting. All that stuff was already inside her, part of her... her name said so, and it was a true name. It was the reason for her night terrors. It smothered her just like that forever and forever storm of red Mars dust that had kept them holed up in the bigelow for two months of her childhood. Maybe she couldn't cast it away. Maybe Meikäläinen was right. Instead of rejecting it, maybe she had to take it in on purpose and transform it. Since she couldn't get rid of it in any case.

A few nights later she and Michel watched a docco about *Celeritas*, one of the ships Consensus was building out in the Belt that they intended to send across interstellar space to a terrestrial planet in a nearby system. It would take years to complete *Celeritas* and the other ships. Once launched they'd be decades reaching their destination. Decades more again before the planet on the other end would be as habitable as Mars. And they'd be carrying with them, like Noah's Ark, animals and plants and knowledge. Human knowledge.

Just like that it all came clear. She found herself saying to Michel, "I'm going to be on one of those ships," and holding her hand up to her breast, feeling the beat of her heart in her chest, she knew it was true. Even Meikäläinen and her etymologies made sense. To carry the life of Earth to another star, one must carry the lives and genetics and seeds of Earth. And words, the meanings of them, what Meikäläinen called *the wisdom of the first coiners of language...* they would need those seeds too, and all the knowledge packed into them. That was her job, her purpose, the meaning of her heartbeat that Brother Easton had tried to pound into submission so that she couldn't fulfill it. If he'd been the CEO of Deep Space Energy, it would be just the same: he'd want to stop her, and she wouldn't be stopped. She belonged with the other people who wouldn't be stopped.

"I know what my name is," she said slowly, turning to Michel who was sitting there on the couch beside her, his mouth already wide open from her first realization. "Doesn't *Esti* mean *star*? My name is Esti Gusev."

It might take as long as getting to the other star for her to find the healing Meikäläinen insisted she could find. But somehow that made sense too. Some stories went long.

***

The pressure wasn't just on her chest. It was against her face, her eyelids, her legs, arms – hell, her lungs, she had to labor to breathe – she was squished back so hard she swore she'd go right through the back of her seat before this capsule was aloft. But just like in the centrifuge, just like standing in a wind being blown like a tree – she found it was something she could bear. And then the pressure eased off, and she didn't have push away any more.

※

Melissa S. Green works by day as a publication specialist at the Justice Center, University of Alaska Anchorage; by night (and lunchtimes) as a writer, poet, and blogger. She's an editor and writes on Bent Alaska, Alaska's LGBT blog; her own blog can be found at Henkimaa.com. "Pushaway" is set in the same story universe as the short story "Cold" which appeared in the November 2009 issue of *Crossed Genres*.

Phantom Overload
Daniel José Older

I'm late to a meeting with The New York Council of the Dead so I swing by my favorite Dominican spot for a ferocious coffee. It's kind of on the way, but mostly I do it to bother my icy, irritating superiors. I'll roll up twenty minutes in, smugly caffeinated and palpably disinterested. I linger even longer than I have to, partially because I'm in a good mood but mostly because the counter honey's strapless shirt keeps slipping up like a curtain from her paunchy little tummy. Every time it happens my meeting with the Council becomes less and less important.

The spot's called EL MAR. It's one of those over-decorated 24-hour joints that always has dim lights and a disco ball. Corny papier-mâché coral reefs dangle off all the walls and there's usually a lively crowd of stubby little middle age couples and taxi drivers.

"My friend Gordo's playing here Friday," I say, aiming for casual chitchat but achieving only uninvited randomness. The counter honey raises two well-threaded eyebrows and pouts her lips – which I roughly translate to mean *"Whoopdeedoo, jackass."* But it's spring outside, a warm and breezy afternoon, and my good mood has granted me temporary invincibility. Besides, I like a girl that can say a lot without even opening her mouth. "The big Cuban guy?" I offer. "I've never seen him play before but I hear it's amazing."

She softens some, leans back against the liquor cabinet and exhales. "Gordo's a friend of my tío. He alright." The shadow of a smile is fluttering around her face, threatening to show up at any moment. I try not to stare. "Brings a weirdo crowd though," she adds.

Here's the part where I'm supposed to hand her the dollar, letting the touch linger just a fleeting moment longer than it has to so my fingers can tell her fingers about all the rambunctious lovemaking I have planned for us. But my skin is inhumanly cold; my pulse a mere whisper. I am barely alive at all, a botched resurrection, trapped in perpetual ambiguity with not even so much as a flicker of what life was like before my violent death. Surely, whatever flutterings of passion trickle through my veins wouldn't make the jump from one body to the next. Plus I'd probably ick her out. I put the money on the counter and walk out the door.

***

42

The New York Council of the Dead holds court in a warehouse in the industrial wastelands of Sunset Park, Brooklyn. The outside is nondescript: another towering, dull monstrosity clustered between the highway and the harbor. Inside, a whole restless bureaucracy of afterlife turns eternal circles like a cursed carnival ride. Mostly dead though I may be, it's here that I always remember how alive I really am. Everyone else in the place is a shroud, a shimmering, translucent version of the person they once were. The glowing shadows spin and buzz about their business in the misty air around me. After five years of showing up here every couple weeks for a new assignment, the presence of this walking anomaly doesn't even warrant a sidewise glance.

I stroll through chilly little crowds of ghosts and into the back offices. I'm a good half-hour late and still murkily ecstatic from the nascent spring and my non-conversation with Bonita Applebum. Unfortunately, they seem to have been waiting up for me.

Chairman Botus' hulking form rises like a burst of steam from behind his magnificent desk. He's the only one of the seven Council Chairmen that anyone's ever seen- the rest lurk in some secret lair, supposedly for security purposes. "Ah, Carlos, wonderful you're here!" Something is definitely very wrong – the Chairman is never happy to see anybody. Botus smiling means someone, somewhere is suffering. I grunt unintelligibly and sip at my lukewarm coffee. There's two other ghosts in the room: a tall, impish character that I figure for some kind of personal assistant or secretary and a very sullen looking Mexican.

"Carlos," Botus grins, "this is Silvan García, spokesman for our friends out in the Remote District 17." The Mexican squints suspiciously at me, nodding a slight acknowledgment. His carefully trimmed goatee accentuates a severe frown. "Silvan, Agent Delacruz here is our leading soulcatcher prime. An investigator of the highest spiritual order. He's done terrific work in the Hispanic communities."

I don't believe in animal spirit guides, but if I had one it just curled up and died. Nothing marginalizes marginalized people like a dead white guy talking sympathetically.

Plus he's managed to deflate my rare bout of perkiness. The secretary, apparently unworthy of any introduction, just stares at me.

"It seems Mr. García's community is experiencing some, er, turmoil," Botus grins hideously down at Silvan. "Is that the word you would use, Sil? Turmoil? Anyway, in short, they're in Phantom Overload and need our," another smirking pause, false searching for the right word, "assistance."

It's a tense moment. The Remote Districts are a few scattered neighbor-hoods around New York that unanimously reject any interference from the all powerful Council. Instead, they deal with their own dead however they see fit. I believe 17 is the strip of East New York surrounding the above ground train tracks on Fulton Street, but either way, for them to ask help from the NYCOD means something's really messed up over there. Unfortunately, I haven't peeked at my terminology manual, well, ever, so I just nod my head with concern and mutter, "Phantom Overload, mmm."

The meeting wraps up quickly after that: many nods and smiles from Botus and grimaces from Silvan García.

"The fuck is Phantom Overload?" I say once the curt spokesman has floated briskly away. Shockingly, Botus' smile hasn't evaporated along with his guest. He appears to be genuinely happy. It's a terrifying thought.

"Oh, Carlos Carlos Carlos," he mutters, letting his long cloudy form recline luxuriously behind his desk. "You're weird and of questionable allegiance, but you're the best we got and I like you."

"You're sinister and untrustworthy," I say, "and I can't stand to be around you. What's Phantom Overload?"

"It means our good friends at RA 17 can't handle their business. No surprise there of course. Seems they have a bus that makes a routine drive through the area picking up souls, collecting the dead, you know – it's all very quaint."

"Until?"

"Until the motherfucker disappears!" Botus lets out a belly laugh.

"The ghost bus disappeared?"

"Can you imagine the irony? Is there anywhere Mexicans *don't* go stuffed into buses? Man!"

I have this blade that I carry concealed inside my walking stick. It's specially designed and spiritually charged to obliterate even the toughest afterlifer. In moments like these that I have to work very hard not to use it.

"Anyway," Botus continues once he's collected himself, "yeah, the ghost bus gone and disappeared, or ain't showing up for whatever reason and so yeah, of course," he rolls his eyes and makes an exaggerated shoulder shrug, "they're gonna go into Overload. Phoebus, tell him what Overload is."

The slender secretary ghost, who had become so inconsequential that I'd actually forgotten he was there, suddenly leaps into action. "It means, sirs, that the souls are all hanging around and can't be carted off to the Underworld and instead congeal and cause havoc and generally make nuisances of themselves. The situation can be exacerbated by high murder or infant mortality rates and can reach a critical point in as few as 72 hours."

"Critical point?"

"Would be classified as an utterly overwhelming level of chaos derived from the overcrowding and massive spiritual collisions."

"A fucking disaster, Carlos," Botus puts in. "A Mexican clusterfuck of the highest order. Trust me. You don't wanna see it. It'd be like 9/11 for the dead, but worse. Or like that other thing that happened, the one with the levees and whatever."

"So they sent an emissary?"

"To beg for help. Cocksuckers refuse and refuse and refuse assistance from the Council for decades. No, it'll compromise our autonomy, it'll create dependency on the COD. Blah blah blah. You know the whine. What can you do? Wait around till some shit pops off they can't handle. Fine. Here we are.

Took a little longer than expected, but no matter. We'll move ahead as planned."

"As planned?"

"Like I said, we all knew this was gonna happen. It was only a matter of when. So did we have a plan in place for when the inevitable occurred? Of course we did, Carlos, that's what the NYCOD does: it prepares. That's how these things work. Stay ahead of the game and you rule the planet. Come unprepared and the world will fuck your face and shit in your soul."

"Is that what it says on your gravestone?" Botus chuckles mildly and I start getting antsy. "So you want me to…"

"Set up in RD 17 and lay some preliminary groundwork for an incoming squadron of soulcatchers. It's gonna be a hazy mess in there, kid, and I'd like things to be a little ready for our boys when they show up. Minimize damages, if you know what I mean. You start tomorrow. Phoebus here will be your partner."

My what? I gape at Botus for a full three seconds before recovering. "My what?"

But the matter's closed. The Chairman has already immersed himself in some other paperwork and Phoebus is hovering eagerly beside me.

***

I'm heading back towards Bushwick, running through all the reasons why the Phoebus thing is a whack disaster. Number one on the list is Jimmy. Jimmy's a high school kid, my friend Victor's cousin, and a freakish incident with a granny and some soul-eating porcelain dolls a couple months back left him able to see afterlifers. He's not half-dead like me but he's definitely another uneasy interloper between two worlds and I've taken him under my wing to thank him for making my unusual status that much less lonely.

But with winky little Phoebus tagging along, I'll have to explain why I'm bringing a live teenager around in flagrant disregard for the most basic NYCOD protocol: stay the fuck away from the living. Whatever, I'll figure it out.

I find Jimmy playing checkers on a little sidestreet off Myrtle Ave. Even sitting down, the kid towers over the table and has to squint through his librarian/Nation of Islam glasses to see the board. He's playing against Gordo, a great big Cubano cat who's down with the living, the dead and probably a whole slew of saints and demons that no one's even heard of yet. Says it has something to do with the music he writes. He plays a mean game of checkers too, and from the look of it he's hammering Jimmy something fierce.

"If this were a real game, like chess," Jimmy is saying when I walk up, "you'd be on the floor beggin' me for mercy."

Gordo just grins and smokes and triple jumps across the board.

"How is it," I say, pulling up a chair, "that you can be such a freaking wizard at a game as complex as chess and get your ass handed to you in a glorified Connect-4?"

"Who asked you?"

I gank one of Gordo's malagueñas and light it up. "I need you both tomorrow." Gordo raises an eyebrow but keeps his concentration on the board.

"What you got?" Jimmy asks.

I explain more-or-less the situation, eliminating the part where I had to ask what Phantom Overload was.

Gordo's looking interested when I finish. "This ghost bus – she just disappeared? She estopped coming completely?"

"Apparently. Maybe it's on strike. The little irate Mexican Silvan said he'd try to arrange a meeting for us tomorrow with the ghost bus driver but it wasn't a guarantee."

"Silvan García?" Gordo says. "He's Ecuadorian."

Figures my oversized living friend would know more about my assignment than me. "Either way," I say, "he's already given me the dirty eye cuz Botus did his poor Hispanic communities routine and now I look like Malinche again."

Gordo lets out a long exasperated sigh. "One day, Carlos, I am going to kill your boss." It's not an idle threat but he'll probably have to wait in line.

"Who's Malinche?" Jimmy asks.

"The chick that helped a couple white guys on horses take down the whole Aztec empire," I say. Jimmy looks crestfallen. "Or got kidnapped and forced into being a historical scapegoat, more than likely."

Gordo looks very sad all the sudden. "It is always easier to blame one of our own."

"Oh and there's more," I say. "They stuck me with a partner. Some doufy little guy named Phoebe or something."

"Phoebe's a girl's name," Jimmy informs me.

"Either way, I want you to tag along. Should be an interesting mess. We'll work it out with the partner. Gordo, can you mingle around Fulton while we meet with Silvan, see what you can find out?"

Gordo nods and then jumps Jimmy's last two checkers.

"Fuckassshit."

Gordo just chuckles: "Should've stuck with basketball."

***

"Who's that?" Phoebus wants to know when I show up to meet him with Jimmy in tow. It's the beginning of a beautiful breezy spring night. The whole world seems to be milling pleasantly about under the Fulton Street train tracks. It's gametime and gossip hour outside the bakeries, dollar stores and beauty salons of East New York. I'm in another weirdly chipper mood but I don't let it show; instead I get up in Phoebus' face.

"Listen, partner," I say real slow and menacing, "I'm glad you have the protocol book memorized and got good grades in the academy, but now you're in the streets and it's a different game." Okay, I got the speech from a cop flick I was watching the night before, but it translates pretty well. "Now we gonna play

46

by my rules. Got it?"

"Got it," Phoebus mumbles. "But who's that?"

"That's Jimmy," I say. "He's my trainee. And he's coming with us."

"Nice to meet you," Jimmy says, smiling down at Phoebus.

"He can see me?" The new guy is scandalized.

I'm about to spit out some other slick line I had memorized when I notice it: with the coming dusk, the ghosts have floated gradually out into the streets and there's hundreds and hundreds of them. More ghosts than people. Phantom Overload. What's more, they're bustling about and interacting with the living like it's just the way things are supposed to be. I'm rendered speechless for a few seconds. It's disturbing but strangely beautiful too. My first instinct is just to leave Phoebus and Jimmy behind and go for a jaunty stroll down a street where for once, the two disparate halves of me are happily cohabitating.

"This is all highly irregular," Phoebus sputters. I can tell from Jimmy's awed face he's as entranced as I am. But there's business to be taken care of. Several battalions of soulcatchers are gearing themselves up and will soon be on the way to wreak havoc on this quiet intermingling. And we still have no idea what's going on.

"Phoebe," I say.

"Phoebus."

"Phoebus, keep an eye on things over here. I'm going to meet Silvan and the bus driver at the abandoned lot."

"We're not – uh – we're not supposed to split up."

"And yet: off I go."

"Oh."

I almost feel bad, but then I remember that Phoebus is just a feeble extension of Botus. Sympathy dissolves into disdain. Much better. Jimmy and I walk off towards the lot.

***

"Turns out you're not Mexican," I tell Silvan when we reach the top of the dusty trash-strewn hill where he's waiting for us. "You're Ecuadorian."

"I know," says Silvan. "But you fucking Dominicans can't tell the difference."

"I'm fucking Puerto Rican."

"I know that too."

So a little Latin to Latin humor is not the way to start things out. Live and learn. The busdriver and Jimmy are looking uncomfortably back and forth between me and Silvan.

"Um – con permiso," The busdriver ventures timidly. He's a tall, round ghost with big bulgy eyes and three days of stubble. His beat up old van idles a few feet away. "You think we could get down to business? I can't stay long."

"I'll be brief," I say. "I don't know what the problem is, sir–"

"Esteban Morales, from Michoacán." The bus driver's wide eyes dance across the abandoned lot like shivering searchlights.

"Señor Morales, The New York Council of the Dead has been anxious for any excuse to kick some Remote District ass. Now, I for one, don't want that to happen, and I don't think Mr. Silvan here does either, ornery bastard though he might be, but believe me when I tell you they are on their way and it won't be pretty. So, Esteban, please, tell us what it will take to get you to start collecting the dead again."

"No," Esteban says. "No se puede."

"What do you mean no se puede?"

"It means it can't be done," Silvan says.

"I know that," I growl. "I mean why not?"

"It's that the dead won't let me take them because they aren't from my jurisdiction. They're not from here. They're our people but they're from faraway."

Immigrant dead? That in its own right isn't so unusual – when you die and get carted off you can turn up any damn place or nowhere at all. Thing is, it's really not up to you and you certainly can't go moving from place to place in packs. You're basically stuck in whatever city or township you pop up in. At least, in the States that how it works...

"It seems," Silvan says, "that several communities around Latin America have figured out how to travel in the afterlife."

"And they've come to be with their families?" Jimmy blurts out. "That's sweet!"

"It is sweet," Silvan nods, "but unfortunately it is also an untenable situation. Resources are running dry. Overcrowding has become the constant state. We are quickly approaching critical point."

All this terminology is getting on my nerves. I'm about to say something slick about it when I notice a rustling motion at the foot of our trashy hill. A crowd of ghosts is waiting down there, glaring icily towards us. Their wraith clouds wave gently like drying laundry in the evening breeze. They look pissed.

"We're not leaving," a tall gangly ghost calls out from the crowd. "Never leaving. Not by force and not by choice. And not in the damn bus."

Esteban takes his cue and makes himself scarce. The ghost bus leaves a puff of exhaust behind as it sputters off into the night. Jimmy is suddenly very anxious. I can feel his jitters sparkling around him like eager fireflies. The crowd of ghosts is hovering slowly up the hill.

I take a step towards them. "Look, I'm from the Council but I hear where you're coming from. I don't want this to get messy."

"Then get out of here, güey, and take your Council goons. We've come this far to be with our families. We're not going nowhere." A general hoorah goes up. As the ghost mob starts to clutter closer around us I notice most of them are carrying chains and clubs.

"The Council goons are coming regardless of what I tell them to do," I say. As if to prove my point, the mournful battle howl of the approaching soulcatchers rings out in the night air. It's not a comforting sound. "They wanted an excuse to get in this place and you've all given them one. I know you want to be with your people, but all you're doing is putting the ones you love in danger."

"You really believe that mierda, compadre?" the tall gangly one demands. He steps a few feet out of the crowd. He has a scraggily black beard and eyes that keep rolling in different directions. An epic adventure is scrawled in tats over his translucent skin. Jimmy takes a step behind me, but surely his skinny-ass moose head is poking out well above mine.

"We are happy here!" gangly says, to more uproarious applause.

"Tell 'em, Moco! ¡Dile la verdad!" someone yells. "¡Sí se puede!"

"No," I say. "No se puede. Something must not've been working out because..." I have to stop mid-sentence because my mind is suddenly too busy working things out to bother making my mouth move. "Silvan!" I say quietly. "Jimmy, where's Silvan?"

"Dunno, Carlos."

I whirl around but the slippery instigator has vanished. And here I was thinking I was the Malinche.

"Your representative is the one you need to talk to, people," I announce. "García went to the Council begging for help. Probably received a pretty payoff from it too. The wheels are in motion now though, there's no stopping it. You have to clear out."

"We'll crush The Council!" Moco yells, his eyes boggling wildly. Another hoorah goes up.

It's getting to be time for me to leave. I back up a few steps to position myself behind a rusted out refrigerator. At the edge of the field I see my new partner Phoebus at the head of a group of armored soulcatchers. He looks different, Phoebus. His whole demeanor has changed – he's floating upright instead of in the usual cowering posture he'd been using. Also, he's yelling out orders. But I don't even get a chance to think it all through because then Moco spots the soldiers.

"¡Compadres!" he hollers. "Let's kill the insolent pigfuckers!" Doesn't take much poetry to rile up a bloodthirsty crowd. The angry ghosts rush towards the edge of the lot, chains and clubs swinging wildly above their heads. At a command from the newly non-doufy Phoebus, the soulcatchers jump into a defensive position: a solid wall of impenetrable supernatural armor. It looks fierce, but some of those boys are pissing themselves with fear. The mob moves as one – they surge suddenly up into the air above the lot and come crashing down on the heads of the waiting soulcatchers like a damn tsunami wave. How many times have I tried to tell the Academy instructors that frontward wall posture is only worthwhile against the living? The dead float – it's a whole other dimension of combat. I guess there hasn't been much experience with large crowds, mostly one on one shit.

You can see right off the bat it's not going well for the COD boys. Armed with the superior numbers, the fury of the righteous and those nasty clubs and chains, the mob is laying a solid beating on the dozen or so soulcatchers. Three fellows in straw hats have cornered a soldier and are laying into him with their clubs – I hear him screaming in agony as the blows pierce through his armor and shred his translucent cloud. Moco storms furiously through the melee, his chain whipping in a vicious circle above his head. The thrill of victory is in his stride, a casual overconfidence that I know well.

"What you wanna do?" Jimmy says behind me.

"This whole damn situation is starting to feel like one big setup, kid."

"Silvan?"

"Definitely in on it, somehow. I don't like it. Feel like a damn pawn and I'm not even sure whose."

"Can we go?"

I realize Jimmy's trembling. It wasn't so long ago he was having his living soul torn out by those American Girl dolls, so I can see where he'd be a little hesitant about the vicious battle raging a few feet away. "You go head, kid. I have to see this one through."

"'salright," he says, fixing his mouth into a determined frown. "You stay I stay." Not bad. "You got a plan?"

"Nope. Gotta see what happens next."

***

The fighting has scattered out into the streets now and it sends a vicious whirlwind of combat swirling around beneath the tracks. The few living folks walking by recognize something wrong and take cover in shops and behind cars. Seems the soulcatchers have rallied some: they've slashed a few mob members into tattered ghost shards that lie motionless on the pavement. Suddenly Phoebus rears up above the fighting. I'm still stunned by his transformation from dweeb to superghost. "If you won't heed the Council," he calls out over the din of battle, "perhaps you haven't fully understood what is at risk to you and your loved ones." Jeering and shouts from the crowd as a few objects fly up towards him. Undeterred, my deceptive partner nods at four of his men and they immediately detach from their adversaries and bee line it into one of the storefront churches on Fulton.

"Stop them!" Moco hollers, but the soulcatchers have already returned out onto the street, each wrapped around a living, breathing, screaming person. The fighting, the yelling, the sound of weapons tearing into dead flesh: everything stops. The angry mob is suddenly very quiet as they turn and stare at the hostages – two middle aged women, a guy in his twenties and a fourteen year old girl..

"That's my granddaughter!" an aging guajiro ghost yells, throwing down his club and stepping forward.

"And my nephew, Juan José!" calls out another.

"¡Mi hija!" screams a middle aged ghost as she rushes forward.

"I thought the NYCOD wasn't supposed to fuck with the living!" Jimmy

50

whispers.

"They're – we're not." I realize now I'm trembling. For all the chaos, everything's still feeling like it's playing out according to some heinous plan. "Someone high up must've given them the authority to..." Nothing is what it seems. I already knew that but it seems I have to learn again and again. I'm getting ready to hole up for an extended hostage negotiation when the four soulcatchers wrap their arms around their hostages' faces like cellophane. I think the crowd is just too stunned to react in time: after about five seconds of squirming each living human goes limp and then sprawls out lifelessly on the pavement.

The crowd surges forward en masse, toppling the four soulcatchers and instantly tearing two of them to shreds right then and there. I hear Jimmy throwing up behind me. In the chaos of it all though, I notice the remaining COD soldiers jump into motion and sprint away from the fray. "Now that you see what we will do to your beloved families," Phoebus yells at the crowd, "maybe you'll rethink sticking around. We're pulling back, but not for long. Regroup yourselves and come to your senses, rebels!" The soulcatchers pour out of the shops and salons, each wrapped around a struggling human, and fall back towards the abandoned lot that Jimmy and I are hiding in.

"Get out of here, now!" I whispershout at Jimmy, who's trying to spit the last bits of vomit out of his mouth. He stands but just stares past me, eyes wide. "Go!" I say. "Not the time to be all heroic, kid, just get out!" He's still not moving, just staring. Finally, I turn around to see what he's looking at.

"They've got Gordo," he says. And it's true.

***

The Council soulcatchers are all in a tizzy as they retreat up the hill towards us. They're young, barely older than Jimmy, and by the look of their crisp, unstained uniforms and shiny helmets, brand new recruits. A few of them are injured, limbs hanging useless at their sides. Whatever plan is in place, these kids were clearly kept far out of the loop. Gordo walks calmly along with his fatigued captor. He's trying to appear unimpressed but is probably terrified. Or maybe I'm projecting.

I grab Jimmy roughly around the neck and throw him on the ground as they walk up. A couple of the boys I've seen before come running up to me first. "Where you been, Carlos?" a kid named Dennis asks.

"Yes, Agent Delacruz," Phoebus says, eyeing Jimmy. "Where have you been?"

"Infiltrated the rebel mob," I say. "And I took a hostage of my own while I was at it."

"We're not really gonna kill these ones too, are we?" Dennis says. You can hear a quiver of fear in his voice. A few of the hostages are sobbing.

"We can't!" another one yells. "The mob'll tear us to pieces! This is crazy!"

51

"Everyone shut up," Phoebus snaps. "You're soldiers, soulcatchers. You will not show fear. You will not retreat or give up, ever. Understand?"

"But you knew they would rush in on our guys when you had them kill those hostages, didn't you?" Dennis demands. "You did that on purpose."

"It's not for you to question my decisions," Phoebus says. He's seething with restrained rage. "Now, everyone fall into line and shut up." There's a few murmurs of frustration and the soldiers fall into a tense kind of quiet. Shouldn't take much to rile 'em back up though.

"I heard the mob is planning an ambush," I say. "There was a few lurking around here I had to deal with before you guys showed up, but a couple got away. They're probably crawling all over this place by now."

"Oh shit oh shit oh shit," one of the soulcatchers starts chanting.

"What's the matter, Tyler?"

"I thought I saw something move over there by that old car!"

"Where?"

"By the car, asshole, by the fucking car!"

"Wait!" I yell pointing at some random spot in the dark lot. "What's that over there?" Everyone turns and gapes into the emptiness.

"This is fucked up," someone says.

"Calm down!" Phoebus yells. "Everyone calm the fuck down!" I suppress a chuckle.

"Listen," I say. "I have orders from Botus. Everyone is to remain here with the prisoners. Phoebus and I are gonna go politick with the rebels and see what we can work out to end this mess peacefully." A general murmur of approval rises from the frantic soldiers.

"Now now," Phoebus stutters, "let's not be rash. Let the fools have a moment to discuss…"

"Every moment more we give them is a moment they have to plan another attack," I say. "Rebels love ambushes."

"He's right!" Tyler declares. "Go now!"

"It's true," says Dennis. "Wrap this shit up quick."

I start walking down the hill. "You coming?" I can feel Phoebus' furious glare on the back of my head as I hobble awkwardly down the hill on my cane. He growls and then floats after me, frowning.

"How quickly your young friend went from student to hostage," Phoebus muses when we round a corner onto a quiet residential block. By way of an answer I pull the blade out of my cane and swipe at him. He hurls himself away just a split second too late and I hack a sliver of cold cloud off his form. Before I can swing again, he's on me, icy hands wrapped around my neck, cool breath on my face. I push forward against him, throwing us into a brick wall. Phoebus loosens his grip just long enough for me to shove him off and stumble backwards a few steps. I raise my blade. "Alright, Phoebus – or should I say Chairman Phoebus?"

He pulls his own blade out and grunts with irritation.

"You can act, I'll give you that," I say. "Definitely had me convinced you were just a sniveling little new guy. But why bother? You could've just waltzed in as is and torn shit up."

"But you see, we don't trust you, Carlos." His voice seethes with hatred. "We wanted to see what you'd do. Keep an eye on you. For the plan to proceed, it had to be kept completely secret."

"Even from the youngens you got doing the dirty work."

He lunges forward, blade first, and I parry off the attack and sidestep out of the way. The Chairman is panting heavily now.

"What I want to know," he says, "is are you just a renegade dickhead or are you working for someone?"

"Too many questions," I say, making like I'm going to swipe at him again. When he goes to block I stab forward instead, catching him right in the core of his long silvery body. Chairman Phoebus lets out a howl and stumbles forward, forcing the blade deeper into himself and pinning us both back against the brick wall. Higher ups are usually crap at one-on-one combat.

"You can't...kill me," he gasps and for a second I'm afraid he might mean that literally. Did the bastard figure out some slick supernatural way not to die again? But then he finishes his thought: "...I'm a Chairman..."

"Guess now there's only six," I say, pulling out my blade. He's oozing out all over, his flickering corpse now a dead weight draped over me. Don't know if I'll ever be able to shower enough to get that feeling away. I heave him off me as his whole body sheds itself into an icky mess of tattered shiny ghost flesh. I don't feel bad, just grossed out.

***

The angry mob has transformed itself into a confused support group when I find them huddled in a storefront church. A few of the ghosts are sobbing inconsolably while others pat them on their heaving backs. Moco is walking in anxious circles, trying to rile folks up again.

"Listen up," I say, walking into the dusty church, "we can end this now. It's only gonna get worse if we don't." I send Moco a piercing stare, which isn't easy the way his damn eyes keep boggling, but he seems to take my point and stays quiet. "I can tell you that any battle that comes after this won't go well for you, and it'll go even worse for your loved ones. It's not a threat – I didn't know it was going to go down like that tonight, and I'm sorry it did." Ghosts are looking up at me with sorrow and fear in their eyes. "I know you just came here to be with your families, to carry on in an afterlife that's harmonious with the living. And believe me," I had been in let's-clean-this-mess-up mode but I'm suddenly choking over my words, "I want as much as any of you to see that happen, here in New York." They believe me. Even I believe me. I guess it's cause it's true, but still – I'm startled. "But it's not time yet. There's more work to be done. Foundations to be laid. I dealt with the dickhead that ordered your living relatives to be murdered." A cautious hurrah rises from the mourning ghosts, startling me again. "But I'm going to have to say that you did it so I can keep working things from the inside." That seems to be alright with everyone.

"You can't stay here in RA 17 though, you have to scatter." More nods and whispers. "Moco and I are going to go back to the Council soulcatchers and work out the arrangements."

***

"What do you mean they killed Phoebus?" Botus is livid, which means somewhere an angel is getting head. "I don't understand. Which one of them? We have to exact revenge!"

"Well, that won't actually be so easy. He was kind of torn up in the mob, it wasn't like one or the other. And they're all gone now anyway. Scattered."

"What do you mean they're all gone?"

"Isn't that what we wanted?" I'm trying so hard not to smile that it actually hurts. "Phantom Overload no more. Situation remedied. Voilà. A few them lit out for Mexico I think. Shame about Phoebe though."

"I don't understand," Botus says again.

I light a Malagueña and exhale thick plumes of smoke into his office. "My full report's on your desk, sir. Just had one more question."

Botus barely looks up. "Eh?"

"Where might I find Silvan García?"

***

It's another beautiful afternoon. My mark is hovering in a quiet reverie on the walking path that winds alongside the Belt Parkway, not far from the Verazzano Bridge to Staten Island. Perhaps he's contemplating the sun sparkling on the water or the way the lapping of waves contrasts with the rushing traffic. Either way, he's about to get sliced.

I come up quietly, trying but failing, always failing, not to look too sketchy. Standing by a tree on this twinkly spring day with my long trench coat and walking stick. There's something definitely off about that guy, the joggers are thinking, where's his spandex and toothy grin? Why no headband or fanny pack?

I'm just biding my time, waiting for a break in the constant stream of exercise dorks so I can make my move. When it comes I take one step forward before a thick, warm hand wraps around my arm. It's Gordo, looking cheery as always but a little worse the wear after his harrowing hostage experience. I already apologized too many times to him for that and he's already swatted away each one jauntily, so I just nod at him. "What are you doing here, papa?"

"I am estopping you."

"What you mean?"

"Not this one. This one is not for you."

"Gordo, if it wasn't for this asshole…"

"Yo sé lo que hizo. And it doesn't matter." His hand is extremely strong and me tussling with a fat old guy would not be a good look right now. "It's not right and you know it's not right."

I'm about to argue with him when I realize he has a point. Ending García gets us nowhere and risks blowing my cover. It was Botus, after all, that told me where to find him. The trail would lead right back to me. All I'm left with is 'but I want to' and that's obviously not going to get me anywhere. "It is always easier," Gordo says, "to blame one of our own."

I shrug my acceptance and Gordo cautiously releases his hold on my arm. We turn together, away from the water, away from Silvan and my useless vengeance schemes, and begin walking back into Brooklyn. "You are coming tonight?" Gordo wants to know.

"Wouldn't miss it."

***

Six mojitos deep, I stumble towards the counter honey. Around me, the living and the dead are bopping up and down together to the sacred and sexy rhythms coming from Gordo's motley crew of musicians. Even a few of the soulcatchers showed up, including Dennis and Tyler, which I found kinda touching once I was drunk enough not to be eeked out by it. Moco is dancing up a storm towards the front, apparently in a world all to himself. The music is pounding and relentlessly beautiful. It strips us, if only for this night, of all inhibitions and traumas.

The counter honey's making eyes at me. I think. She's smiling even. Maybe at me. I'm not so sloppy yet, just have a little extra swing to me. I've been watching her and she's not fazed by the ghosts. The bar must be its own little Remote District – outside the Council's grasp, free of the fears and taboos of the living.

"What's your name?" I say, careful not to slur.

"Melissa." It's a little plain for how pretty she is, but I don't mind.

"It's a little plain for how pretty you are." Oops. She looks me dead in the eye and then laughs.

"You don't like to touch people?" she says, still burrowing her gaze right through me. "We're Latin, man. We touch. Get with it."

"I know, I know," I say, putting a hand to my face. "It's that, I'm…I'm like them." I nod at the ceiling, where a few adolescent ghosts are grinding their crotches into each other in anxious imitation of adulthood.

"What, a horny teenager?"

"No!" Ah, she's laughing again. She also touches her hair, which my best friend Riley once told me means she wants me to eat her ass. I manage to keep that insight to myself though. "No, I'm partially slightly dead. I died. But I came back."

"Ah." She nods knowledgably, like customers tell her that all the time. "That's cool."

It is? I mean, I knew it was, to me anyway, and to my dead friends, and to Jimmy, who's gawking at me rudely from a few barstools away, but I never thought it was alright to someone like Melissa. Someone pretty. "I don't know how I died though. Or how old I am." I put my hand on the bar and squint up at nothing in particular, trying to look thoughtful.

Melissa reaches over, in this room full of stunning music and the pulsating, celebrating bodies of the living and the dead, and puts her hand on mine.

Daniel José Older's spiritually driven, urban storytelling takes root at the crossroads of myth and history. His work has appeared in Strange Horizons, Flash Fiction, Crossed Genres, The Innsmouth Free Press, and the anthology Sunshine/Noir, and was featured in Sheree Renée Thomas' Black Pot Mojo Reading Series and The New York Review of Science Fiction Reading Series. When he's not writing, teaching or riding around in an ambulance, Daniel can be found performing with his Brooklyn-based soul quartet Ghost Star (http://ghoststar.net). He is represented by Linn Prentis of Linn Prentis Literary. You can read about his paramedic adventures at www.raval911.blogspot.com.

Cold Against the Bone

Kelly Jennings

From the moment he took her hands, cold as the stone of the tank, Jeno knew Kip would not send him away. This had been the one thing he feared, because Kippen Hawes had no time for sentiment. She meant to be a real hero, like those in the files she had linked when they were young: William Morris. Harriet Tubman. Ichiro Rayne. Rabbi Hillel. A skinny red-haired holder boy, shivering with terror over what might be done to her, what place did he have here?

"The road leads where the road leads, Jeno," Kip said, crouched on the filthy mat in the cell, the tightness of her grip belying the ease of her words.

He was not able to find any of his famous skill with speech. "I wish..."

She grinned. Bruised and scabby from the beatings the Labor Security had given her, she was still Kip. He still loved her like his own bones. "Wish in one hand," she told him, "spit in the other. See which fills up first."

***

He had been the younger son of Harper Estate. She had been contract labor, raised with her brother across the yard by a boss's wife, rather than in an orphanage where she belonged. When he was little, Jeno hadn't seen why this mattered. He just knew Kip and her brother were the only children his age on the estate. He was always luring Kip into running off with him to hide from his tutor in the greenhouses, to climb trees in the orchards, to thieve horses from the paddocks and ride off to the hills. Kip got whipped for these crimes; Jeno got lectures from his father about responsibility toward contracts.

"Kip's not my contract," he had argued. "She's my friend."

His father told him not to talk back, which always put Jeno's neck up.

"Anyway, she can't be contract labor." Even at nine he could slash straight for the flaw in any argument. "Contracts can't be sold until they're twelve. Kip's eight, Grant's not even six. And they've lived here – they've always lived here." He stared across the study into his father's eyes, the same yellow-amber as his own.

"Stop acting like a child," his father ordered. "We hold their contracts. You have a responsibility to put her welfare before your whims."

He remembered frowning at his father, trying to see what premise he had

57

missed.

Later, his older brother Istvan, the heir of Harper Estate, had laughed at him. "You can't be that soft. Are you telling me you really believe Mother went to live in the West Country because she preferred the climate?"

In truth, Jeno barely remembered his mother. A smell, fierce words, long dark lashes. The sense, growing to conviction, that something was gone forever. He stood at his window above the contract dorms, three long wooden shacks with the bosses' tall houses at their north end, watching the cots messing about on their sints and handhelds, playing tup on boards drawn in the dust, working their gardens. Kip and Grant were among them, barelegged in the summer evening heat. He watched Kip helping Desi strip mani, Grant running the ball field with the men. His fists clenched the iron bars of the nursery guard that covered his window. The metal had burned cold under his fingers, cold against his bone, cold as her hands now.

***

Everyone in the Rift Valley told the story, how those Harper boys ran wild after their mother left, while their father spent his days smoking and his nights across the yard.

Once Istvan went off to the University in Kadir, he just got worse. It wasn't six weeks before Security had him in the tank for off-market drugs; three times Kadir's disciplinary council brought him up. Everyone said he would have been the first Lord Holder in Kadir's history to be expelled for cause, if he hadn't killed himself driving too fast on the icy mountain roads that winter.

Jeno happened to be in the house when the provost arrived. Ever since his father had sold Kip and Grant, he had made it his habit not to be around. But that morning when the sedan from the University came crunching up the gravel drive, by chance he was on the veranda. He had seen the provost emerge, dressed in dark clothing. He had gone down through the house to stand outside his father's study while the provost spoke; he had watched his father's face through the cracked door. He had thought – well, what had he thought? That his father's nature would somehow change under this seismic shift in the world? Why would it, when nothing else, not the loss of his wife, not the sale of his children, not his oldest son's hatred and contempt, had ever done anything to him?

"Come in," his father said, when the provost was gone.

Fear Jeno had not known he possessed surged up inside him. He stood frozen in the dusky corridor, wanting to run. Run where, though? In all the world lived no one at all who would believe he needed help; not Jeno Lord Harper, heir to Harper Estate. Forcing his spine straight, he moved into his father's reach. He was thirteen years old.

***

Contract labor rebellions were common. Kip had taught him this. She had hundreds of examples banked. Ditching his tutors and her work, they had hidden in the hills, wandering streams, talking endlessly, watching animates, reading her files. So many, Jeno remembered thinking. He had three tutors then: one for math, one for science, and his general tutor. This tutor covered the history of The Republic of Sovereign Planets, including how the system of contract labor had come into being, without ever mentioning contract rebellions.

"Almost none of these succeeded," Jeno pointed out to her.

She grinned, showing her missing front canine. Like most holders, Jeno's father provided only basic medical for cots. If a tooth went bad, the dentist yanked it. "I noticed that too," she said. "A bit discouraging, is it?"

They were lying by the Rift River, the spring sun warm on their backs, the river's current rushing past. Come summer it would dry to a sullen creep. His chin propped on his arms, Jeno mulled. "We should create a database. Analyze for points of failure. And…"

He became aware of her gaze. "What?" he asked.

She didn't answer, just flicked her finger against his silk and linen shirt, very different from her rough Nartec. He caught her hand and put it against his chest, where his heart banged hard. "My blood is yours," he said fiercely. "It is."

She laughed, tears bright on her lashes, in her amber-gold eyes.

It wasn't a month later that his father posted her contract, and Grant's.

Jeno had thought it his fault, because he kept taking her off from her work. He had gone to speak to his father. What happened then should not have been a surprise, though it was. His father had no idea that he had been spending time with Kip, no idea she had been missing work. "Just as well," Lord Harper said, "if she's that sort. But it's no matter. We're short of funds, and overstocked on contracts. I'm selling off thirty of our most useless."

Jeno stared. "What?" His father waved a hand in dismissal. "You – Useless? Kip and Grant?"

Lord Harper looked impatient. "Contracts the Estate can do without. The unskilled, the redundant. Those who cost more than they produce. It's a simple cost-benefit analysis."

Jeno shook his head. "You can't sell your children because they're not profitable."

His father raised his voice to call for Jeno's tutor. Jeno raised his own voice: "Cut expenses somewhere else! Spend less money on clothing. Sell the horses! Sell some land! Don't sell your own–"

His father shouted: "*Be quiet!*"

Jeno stared at him.

"Sell the *land*?" His father leaned his fists on the worktable, his yellow eyes narrow. "I would sell *you* before I would sell a fistful of land. This land is all we are. Without this land, we are nothing but cots ourselves."

Jeno could not move.

"Get out of my sight," his father ordered.

***

He bent to his studies with a fury that astounded his tutors – he had been a haphazard student previously, excellent if interested, appalling otherwise. Now he surpassed every expectation, doing particularly well in math and science, and won a scholarship to the University at Al-Tayib at fourteen, the earliest possible age for admittance.

He had already learned enough about writing code to infiltrate his father's bank, so he knew where they had been sold. Though he had been saving for years, he didn't have enough to buy them out. He knew his father would up his allowance once he was at university; he posted his estimates of what he could save to Kip, now a kitchen girl on a Naoko Estate holding in the high North Country.

Grant had been sold to Alhamini mines. Jeno had not been able to get through their shieldwall to track him further than this. Alhamini mined both coal and silver. It depended on which they put Grant to, how long he might live.

When Jeno was in his third term at Al-Tayib, something happened. He didn't know what, only that Kip stopped answering his posts, and, weeks later, posted to say she was in the fields now. She didn't say why. She did ask if he had learned anything more about Grant, which he had not.

He was learning everything he could at the University at Al-Tayib, where he was doing history, math, and science for his trium: everything they would teach him, everything he could learn on his own. He was terrified he could not learn fast enough. He joined clubs determinedly, and made friends the same way. From his analysis of successful revolutions, he knew influential friends would be essential. Though he was careful to befriend men, since men held most of the obvious positions of power on Julian, he also courted women. It was Kip who had pointed out to him all the research showing that young women were the true agents of change in most cultures. "Men hold things," she said. "Women change things. You need them if you want to control the agents of change."

He never went home, not for Ends or holidays; not even for Winter holiday.

At the end of his third term, he traveled to the estate that held Kip; but the estate manager first could not understand why a Lord Holder would visit a field cot; and, once he learned which cot Jeno had come to visit, ordered him off the estate. Jeno considered sneaking into the dorms after dark. He knew who would suffer if he got caught, though. He remembered the whippings he had cost Kip when they were children. In the end, he just went back to Al-Tayib and doubled down into his studies.

It was a month or so later that he finally got good enough at packing code to slip a tunnel through Alhamini's shieldwall.

***

The Security Officer unlocked the cell. "Time to go, sir."

Jeno sat back on his heels. "Suppose you just log me as having gone, Wilder."

During the week since he had arrived, Jeno had taken care with the JFS assigned to the tank, asking after their families, discussing their prospects. He knew who had a cat and who a sweetie, who liked rum at the End and who preferred smoke. Each one of the squad believed he was Lord Harper's blue-eyed favorite, Officer Wilder along with the rest.

Wilder smiled. "I can give you another hour, sir. Then Sergeant Karif comes on. He's like to run a RT check, we'll all be in it then."

Once he was gone, Jeno settled close to Kip, trying not to think how short an hour was, how brief the time she had left. His mind kept circling, trying to find some path he had not tried. He knew no path existed. He had begged his father; he had gone himself to the Prime Minister, pleading for a pardon; he had spent his savings on lawyers; tried to engineer an escape. All useless. Useless. "I wish I hadn't told you," he muttered now. "I almost didn't."

Kip straightened from his embrace. "Jeno." He turned his face away. "You couldn't have done that. Lie to me about that? You know you couldn't."

He shook his head, letting her think this was agreement. But fiercely within himself he knew it was not. He would give anything to go back to the day he had learned that Grant had died in the Alhamini silver mines. Jeno had read Grant's scanty contract file: the captures taken when the boy had been sold (with numb bitterness, Jeno had seen his father's claim that Grant was twelve, though Grant had been barely ten): a full-frontal shot of the child's face, looking like a slightly darker Istvan; another full shot of him standing naked, his eyes wide and scared, his ribs and shoulder bones knobby. The brief description written by the boss who had raised him, claiming he was mild and biddable. Under that had been entries from the bosses at the mines. Grant had done what he was told. He had worked hard. He had never required discipline. He had been injured, twice, once when a cart struck him in a narrow adit, and once during a "fight" in the barracks. This second injury had required a week in the mine infirmary. The boss had also recommended Grant's transfer to a different barracks. Once he had understood what wasn't being said in those paragraphs, Jeno had to shut his handheld off.

It was likely because he was still so unsettled that he had posted Kip about Grant's death. If he had been thinking at all, he would have – he should have – what use, to tell her? What did he think would happen next?

"You had to tell me," Kip said, as if she could read his thoughts, which maybe she could. No one had ever been closer to him than she was. No one ever would be again. She put her scabbed hand on his face. "Jeno. You know you had to. You have no right to try to control the world I can know about. What are you if you do that?"

Hot tears stung his eyes. You would be alive, he thought. I would not care what I was then, because that would be the world where you would be alive.

"Jeno," she reproached, and slipping her arms around him, pulled him close.

***

Perrin Lord Kadir had brought the post to his attention. He'd been in session with his tutor, and arrived late to hall. Since she was the only one still dining, he sat with her. She turned her handheld to show him the screen: *Uprising on Naoko Estate: Blood-Soaked Fields!*

"Isn't that where you visited last break?" she asked, her grey eyes glinting.

***

He wanted to be angry. It had been a stupid attack, making nearly every mistake they had ever noted, in all their analyses of failed revolts. She had moved too fast, not keeping her planning team small or organized into cells; she had chosen weak allies; she had not bothered to build in back-up options; she didn't wait until she had sufficient numbers or weapons before she attacked. Worse, she had no clear goal. Slaughtering bosses and burning property, Jeno wanted to shout at her, how was that a goal?

Resting his head on her shoulder in the icy cell, he whispered, "I can't save you, Kip."

She hugged harder. "I know."

He slid his hand into his jacket, bringing out the medical kit: chased silver, very pretty. It had been Istvan's. Opening it, he took out the sheet of patches, round light green circles. Extremely off-market. "It won't hurt," he said. "The dealer promised. You fall asleep. Your breathing stops, and then your heart. It takes about twenty minutes."

She was silent. He looked up, into her dark golden eyes. He wet his lips. "It looks like death by natural causes, afterwards. A cardiac event."

Her bruised mouth curved up. "In a fifteen year old, Jeno? Really?"

"Stress," he said. "Or some genetic defect. They'll believe it."

She reached to shut the kit. Then she kissed the side of his face. "It's fine," she promised. "I'm not afraid."

Which was the worst moment of all, hearing in her voice how scared she was, and having to pretend, because of how much she wanted it, to believe her. It ripped at his heart like hot steel; but he did it for her.

***

He was not in Al-Tayib when Labor Security took Kippen Hawes back to her Estate, put her on her knees before all the contract labor from the barracks, and put a bullet through her head. He did not see her body doused with coal oil, did not watch them run it up the flagpole, did not watch it burn. The captures were linked off Parliament's main page, as was standard practice, so that everyone could see that justice had been done. Jeno Lord Harper did not link to these. He never would, not ever, not then, and not through all the long years of his life.

He returned eventually to the University at Al-Tayib, where he shifted the focus of his trium to geology, literature, and art. This mystified his tutor, who had him in for an interview. Jeno presented the tutor a bland face he would get better and better at adopting over the next fifty years, saying mildly that he'd grown bored with math and history.

"But you can't do anything serious in these areas!" his tutor cried.

"Oh, surely you exaggerate," Jeno said. "Poetry is the unacknowledged legislator of the world and all that?"

His tutor gaped.

His new tutor was an idiot – no shock, since Jeno had chosen his new concentrations with an eye for the tutor he might get assigned. He spent the rest of his university years unchecked, learning the bare minimum necessary, while using most of his energy on his true agenda: planning the Revolution. Educating himself toward the Revolution. Equipping himself with allies for the Revolution. Putting in place the structures that would become the Contract Labor Revolution on Julian and, eventually, fifty years down the road, the war that would, at length, destroy the Republic of Sovereign Worlds.

It would take years, he knew, before the shadows in his head became the world. This did not disturb him. He had years. He had his entire life, which he would use for this one end. His sister and his brother were bones and ash, but they were not dead for nothing. He would slaughter the system that had slaughtered them.

Toward the end of Spring Term, five weeks after Kippen Hawes had been murdered, he considered whether it was time he began spending his holidays with his father again. Spring holiday. Fall holiday. Summer. He would take his time. He would wait. Next Winter holiday would be time enough. His father was still smoking and drinking himself to a stupor every night. Easy enough to slip in, once all the house contracts were asleep. A cardiac event: sad, but hardly unexpected, not in a man of his age and habits.

Jeno Lord Harper, seventeen years old, got up to pour another cup of tea, his long face calm with easy humor. When his friend Luke stopped by to ask if he was coming along to dinner with the Hegelian Club, he smiled and said of course he was. Later everyone would remark on it, how well he was recovering from that late unpleasantness.

Raised in New Orleans, **Kelly Jennings** is currently teaching hungry young writers in northwest Arkansas, where she is also a member and co-founder of the Boston Mountain Writers Group. She has published fiction in *Crossed Genres*, *The Future Fire*, and *Strange Horizons*. Her first novel, *Broken Slate*, was recently released by Crossed Genres. You can find out more at her personal blog, http://delagar.blogspot.com,or at the SF/F blog FanSci, http://www.fansci.org, which she runs with Marilou Goodwin and Barbara Ann Wright.

*Hesch —
Great knowing you!
Barbara Kras[noff]*

THE RED DYBBUK

BARBARA KRASNOFF

Marilyn wanders among the tombstones. The Long Island cemetery, a place for the Jewish dead for generations, is crowded with graves; appropriate, she thinks, for those who lived their lives crowded in the cities.

The grounds are so vast that guests come with maps in hand. Most drive to a specific section, park halfway on the grass (trying not to violate one of the graves), and make their obligatory visit, leaving small stones as markers of their presence. But Marilyn doesn't need a map – after losing both grandparents and a father, she usually parks at the cemetery's main gates and strolls to the section where her family lies.

It's not hard to miss. Marilyn knows she's come to the right place when she spots, high against the early afternoon clouds, a statue of a woman in coveralls, fist thrust to the sky. She continues slowly, unhurried, careful to avoid a small funeral some yards away, where about 15 people stand and chant Kaddish. Otherwise, on this weekday afternoon, she is alone.

She walks through the small, rusty gate that marks the beginning of the section. Other areas were sponsored by synagogues or organizations based around whatever Eastern European town the family escaped from (one of the first tasks on any immigrant Jew's list was to make sure they had somewhere respectable to bury their dead). But this piece of land was bought by a union of fur workers. The union was eventually purged of its radicalism during the 1950s when union officials began to court respectability – and avoid the taint of left-wing radicalism. But the graves, and the memories they evoke, remain.

She runs her hands along slowly fading carvings of Jewish stars, upraised hands, and hammers and sickles, and haltingly reads Yiddish poems by long-dead writers foretelling the triumph of the working class. Finally, she stops by a modest black stone that has no verse or statue, but just two names, two dates, and two small, oval black-and-white photos. A round-faced young woman and a thin man with a mustache stare solemnly out at a long-dead photographer.

"Grandma," she says to the woman, and then, in halting Yiddish, "Bubbe, what have you done to our baby?"

***

"I know you're not going to like this, but I'm leaving college."

Marilyn stopped chopping celery and stared at her daughter. Keep calm, she told herself. You knew that something was coming. She's 18, she's the age at which she's going to make you insane.

"May I ask why?" Marilyn said, trying to keep her tone even.

Annie, her baby, her only child from a marriage that faded long ago, was still not fully grown in Marilyn's eyes, but all long legs and thin arms and short flyaway hair. The girl reached out and took a piece of celery in an obvious attempt to be casual, but Marilyn could see her hand was trembling slightly. "Well, last weekend I went to great-grandma's grave – you remember, you told me that I should go there to see some family history? And I saw all the graves of the people who spent their lives fighting for what they believed in, and I became ashamed of how I was wasting my life. I'm going to live here for a while, take some courses in Somali and French, maybe in farming or first aid. Refugees are starving while we play student and teacher; I can't sit by while that happens."

"I see." Marilyn put down the knife, not only so she could give her daughter her full attention, but because she suspected that it was not the best time to have a knife in her hand. "What brought this on?"

Annie shrugged. "I just realized that I was wasting my life sitting around in classrooms listening to a bunch of overpaid bourgeois tutors tell me how to spend my life as a willing victim of American consumerism."

Since Annie had, until recently, been a very willing consumer of media players, computer games, expensive shoes and the occasional tattoo, Marilyn was a bit worried. Also, since when was her daughter using words like "bourgeois"?

She placed a solicitous hand against the girl's forehead. "Are you feeling well?" she asked. "Are you running a temperature?"

Annie pulled away irritably. "I'm fine," she said. "Really, mom!" and she flounced off, taking a loud bite out of the celery stalk.

***

"She's going through a phase," said Marilyn's best friend Sandy when they met at the Ginger Cafe the next Sunday. "It could be worse. She could have found religion and ended up sleeping with some middle-aged guru out in Oklahoma like Sarah's daughter."

"Bite your tongue," Marilyn said, shocked and appalled. "My baby wouldn't do something like that."

"Your baby is a human American girl, and so is going to do at least one or two crazy things before she settles down and becomes a boring adult," said Sandy. "If what she does is get a political conscience and perform a few good deeds, all to the better."

Marilyn, whose mother had lost her teaching job during the McCarthy era and who, as a result, could never rid herself of a sneaking fear of doing anything that might place her name in a file somewhere, just nodded and mentally crossed her fingers. Hopefully, the phase was indeed a phase, and would be over before

Annie could get herself in trouble. Or actually leave college.

***

Marilyn sits cross-legged in the narrow grassy lane in front of the grave, shrugs off her backpack, reaches in, and pulls out an old, perilously yellowing album. She places it on her lap and opens it to the first photo. Three children stand stiffly in uncomfortable poses, carefully groomed for what must have been a special occasion for turn-of-the-20th-century youngsters.

"You want a prayer?"

She looks up. An elderly man in a worn, faded suit, a small yarmulke askew on his balding head, stares at her disapprovingly. "You want a Kaddish?"

Of course, she thinks. As a woman, she can't say Kaddish; for a small fee, this man will say it for her. She is tempted for a moment – what could it hurt? – but thinks then of what her grandmother would say. "No, thank you," she replies, putting a slight edge in her voice to warn him not to press his case. He shrugs eloquently and moves on.

Marilyn looks back at the photo. A 10-year-old boy in short pants and cap carefully holds the hand of his sister, 8 years old and already showing the stubborn press of lips that, Marilyn remembers, lasted into old age. The girl, in turn, clutches the hand of her younger brother, a toddler with long curls and a sweet smile.

All gone now. They, and most of their children.

Marilyn puts out a finger and lightly touches the head of the little girl, who glares back defiantly.

***

The police station was a lot less frightening than Marilyn had imagined it to be, although it was just as seedy. The lawyer hired by the organization for which Annie had been demonstrating seemed to be a nice young man; Marilyn took his card and made a mental note to call her own lawyer when she got home.

It only took about 15 or 20 minutes for Annie, pale but determined, to emerge from a far door and walk over to her mother. A bored sergeant gave Marilyn a receipt for her bail. "Make sure she shows up for the hearing," he said, staring with tired disapproval at his pen, which seemed to be misbehaving, "And don't worry about it – the judge will most likely just throw a fine at them and lecture them for a few minutes, depending on how busy he is. Here's your receipt. Next."

It wasn't until they were in the car and at least a mile from the police station that Marilyn felt secure enough to say, "For God's sake, whatever possessed you to confront those protesters?"

Annie stared ahead stubbornly, with a new set to her shoulders that Marilyn found weirdly familiar. "Prejudice against any group is prejudice against us all.

Those small-minded bigots claim to be against terrorism, but they are using a tragedy as an excuse to terrorize those in our society who don't conform to their narrow definition of what is American."

"Why didn't you just start a Facebook group, or send some emails to your representatives, or do something digital?" asked Marilyn, wearily. "Why did you have to start tearing up their signs? Didn't you think that somebody might try to stop you? Like, say, the police?"

Her daughter shrugged and continued to look out at the road in front of them. There was a haunted look in her eyes that make Marilyn's stomach clench.

"Honey," she said, trying to keep her voice even. "Are you all right? Did anything happen in jail that you need to tell me about?"

"I'm fine," Annie said. "Just fine. Everybody was very polite. Except for one miserable son of a bitch who felt it necessary to push one of our group – Sophia – so she fell and skinned her knee. Of course, he chose the black woman to pick on, the goddamn racist schmuck, *a feier zol im trefen*."

Marilyn swerved the car into the other lane and almost clipped an SUV, whose driver cursed her silently behind his windows. She took a breath, kept her eyes on the road, and said steadily, "Honey, where did you learn that phrase?"

"What phrase?"

"The one you just used. '*A feier zol im trefen*.' It means 'A fire should burn him.' Where did you learn that?"

Annie closed her eyes. "I don't know what you're talking about. I'm tired, Mom. I'm going to take a nap, if you don't mind. We can do the whole mother-daughter you're-in-trouble-thing later, okay?"

That evening, Marilyn sat on her front porch and stared out into the yard, where a few of the first fireflies of the season were trying out their neon. The sound of her very American daughter cursing out the police in Yiddish kept running through her brain.

Then something occurred to her. "I suppose it's possible," she told the insects. She pulled out her mobile phone. "Hey, mom," she said when it was picked up on the other end. "Can I ask you something?"

There was a pause. "What's wrong?"

"Nothing's wrong, mom. I just wanted to ask you. When you were babysitting Annie, when she was small, how much Yiddish did you use with her?"

"What's wrong with Annie? Is she all right?"

"She's fine. I'm fine. We're all fine. But she used a Yiddish expression today that I'd never heard her use, and I was wondering – did you ever use the expression "*a feier zol im trefen*" in front of her?"

There was a short, obviously offended silence. "Of course not! You know I'd never curse in front of a child. Your grandmother, may she rest in peace, used that expression a lot, especially when she was talking about her enemies. And she had a lot of enemies. But she died before Annie was born, didn't she?" A pause – her mother's memory wasn't what it used to be these days. "Of course, she did.

Annie was named after her – how could I forget something like that? And she has your grandmother's eyes."

***

The next album has photos of Marilyn's mother, in calf-length dresses and high heels, dark lips that would have been bright red if the photos had been in color, grinning at long-dead young men in jaunty WW II uniforms. Marilyn turns to the last page: her mother's mother, now middle-aged, hands thrust into the pockets of a long fur coat as if to keep them still. There is a look of grim satisfaction on her face – she is obviously determined to enjoy the moment if it kills her.

"You loved that fur coat, didn't you, bubbe?" Marilyn says out loud. "You always said that Grandpa had ruined his hands curing furs for rich women to wear, and you were determined that at least one of those coats would end up on the back of somebody who actually deserved one. And then you gave it to me, your beloved granddaughter, and I refused to wear it because it was seal, and they were clubbing seals in the Antarctic. Cause versus cause, and who wins in the end?"

Living and dead smile at one another.

***

Marilyn had finally gotten around to reading this week's NY Times Magazine section, one eye on the umpteenth rerun of Casablanca on cable, when the front door opened. "Annie, is that you?" she called out. "Did you remember to pick up the milk I asked you to get?" There was no answer, just some footsteps in the direction of the bathroom. Marilyn stood. "You forgot, didn't you? Was it that hard to just write down..." and she stopped short at the bathroom door.

Annie was sitting on the closed toilet seat, a bloody washcloth pressed to her temple. There was dried blood under her nose and around her mouth, a cut on the bridge of her nose, and scrapes all along the side of her face and left arm. She was a mess.

"Oh, my god." Marilyn ran over and pulled the washcloth from her daughter's head. The cut was long and ugly looking, but didn't look very deep. Marilyn opened the bathroom closet, grabbed a roll of gauze, dampened a piece and began to carefully clean off her daughter's face. "Honey, what happened? Are you dizzy? Are you feeling sick? I think we'd better get you to the hospital–"

"I'm fine, mom," said Annie wearily. "Really. I just… We were just trying to keep some squatters from being evicted from an abandoned building, and we thought the man who owned it would at most call the cops, but instead these three thugs, these *shtarkers*, came and threw us out, and I fell down the stairs...." She started to cry quietly.

Marilyn didn't bother with any more details. She got her pocketbook and

68

her coat, guided her daughter to the car (there was no resistance) and took her to the emergency room. She told the receptionist and the doctors that Annie had been in the city, and tripped at the top of some steps, and was brought home by friends (all of which was true, in a sense). Annie needed a couple of stitches in her head, and there was a chance her nose might be broken. ("Let the swelling go down," the doctor said, obviously not all that interested in what to him was a minor case, "and then go see your regular doctor.") But that was all.

They got back around 1 a.m. The entire time – sitting in the waiting room, in the examination room, in x-ray – Marilyn just talked about everyday things: Calling Annie's friends to tell them she'd be staying home for the next couple of days, whether Annie could still go on a march that she had planned to attend in D.C. that weekend, Marilyn's plans to visit a cousin the following month...

Only once, when they were driving back from the hospital, did Marilyn venture a question. "Baby," she asked, "why did you go there? Didn't you realize what kind of people you were dealing with?"

Annie took a deep breath, and for the first time that evening, there was a tremor in her voice. "I don't know, mom," she said. "I just.... I don't know. It's just that... well, it's just that I have to help, I have to do these things. I just..."

Then suddenly she lifted her head and looked directly at her mother. "Somebody has to relieve the miseries that are inflicted on them by the ruling classes," she said, clearly and steadily. "If your generation chooses to ignore these ills, then it is up to mine. If your values don't include working for change and for the betterment of humanity, then mine do."

Marilyn stared back at her daughter. The girl's voice had acquired the Russian Jewish lilt that Marilyn remembered from her childhood, the same intonations that her grandmother had used all her life.

***

The last album is Marilyn's, from her childhood and young adulthood. She pages through well-remembered photos. A tiny version of her brother (now a pudgy executive with three kids and a third wife) grins at the camera. Her father sits in their living room playing Woody Guthrie tunes on an acoustic guitar to a crowd of fascinated children. Long-haired college kids dance enthusiastically in Washington Square Park. And a stocky woman in her 60s with white hair stands in a queue of older folks and students and grins sardonically at the camera.

"That was the afternoon I took you to see that Yiddish film," Marilyn tells her grandmother. "*The Dybbuk*. From the Ansky play? I'm sure you must remember it. About the poor yeshiva *bochur*, the scholar, who is not permitted to marry the girl he is promised to because of the greed of her parents, and who dies and then inhabits the body of his beloved. It is a fable, you said, of how money corrupts the older generation, and how only the dedication and passion of the younger generation can overcome their greed."

She drops the folder, kneels, and puts her hand against the stone. "But, bubbe, when the scholar Channon inhabits the body of Leah, it is with her consent, and it is two young people coming together after they have been told they can't marry. You are of another generation, another world, and you can't know what it's like for the children of Annie's generation. And even if your kind of work is still needed, how can you talk to children who have grown up in such a different world?"

Leaves crunch behind her and Marilyn looks up, embarrassed to be caught by some stranger. But it's Annie, standing tall and angry amid the tombstones and the dead.

Marilyn quickly stands. "Honey, I told you to pick me up around 5 p.m. It can't be that late yet."

"Is the fight all that different, even today?" Annie asks in quick, unaccented Yiddish. "Or has it simply been twisted by men in power who have used their money and influence to make socialism a curse word, to make cooperation and consensus a thing of the past, to make each worker a pawn in every government's fight to stay in power? Look around you. Are people not losing their jobs? Not being driven from their homes? How many people around the world have become simply statistics, irrelevant except as weapons in the wars of those who consider themselves better?"

Marilyn answers in English, in the language she knows best. She needs to be fluent. She is fighting for her daughter. "No, of course not," she says. "Things are as bad as they were – if not worse. But do you really know what is important in this world? In your day it was the bosses and the unions. In my mother's, it was civil rights and red-baiting. In mine, it was Vietnam. And what is it in Annie's? Global warming? The Middle East? The economy? Or are you going to drag her into causes that she wouldn't have followed herself, simply because they are your causes?"

Marilyn finds herself starting to cry, and bangs her fist on her thigh, trying to keep her composure. "Bubbe, you had your life. You fought the good fight, you joined with your comrades to keep the bosses and the police and the politicians at bay. You kept the unions going, you pulled your family through the Depression, you helped women get birth control. But your fight isn't her fight."

"It is all the same fight!"

"Is it? How do you know? Before you appeared, my daughter was in college studying, preparing herself for whatever her life will be. Who knows what she may be able to do years from now? Maybe she'll become a doctor or a lawyer or an activist. Maybe she'll create Web sites or work with technologies that we can't even imagine. Or maybe she'll choose to work quietly and raise children and have a happy, safe life. Why would you deny her that? Is she worth less than any of the people you fought for?"

Silence.

"Leave her. Now."

"I can't." Annie – both and one – cries out in pain and sorrow. "I need to work! I can't just rest and let the world go on the way it does. It is a sort of hell, and when my great-granddaughter, the darling, the jewel, came one day to visit me and talk to me, what else could I do? She welcomed me, and I came. What else could I do?"

Marilyn takes another step, until she is close enough to reach out and touch her daughter's – her grandmother's – cheek. "Leave her, bubbe. Let her make her own life. '

She pauses for a moment. "Take mine."

Annie steps back. "Mirele, what are you saying? Are you sure?"

"Yes. I am." Marilyn turns and looked out over the cemetery. "When I grew up, I knew what had happened to you, to my mother. I wanted to live a safe life – I got a safe job, married a safe man, divorced him in a safe manner, lived in a safe neighborhood and brought up a lovely, safe child. Now she's ready to go off on her own, and what do I have? My daughter is leaving, my husband is gone, life is starting to run short and I haven't done anything significant on my own, something so people will say, 'Look at what she did, how she helped.' I want that. I want to make a difference. And if I can't do it on my own, I'll do it with you."

She stretches out her arms. "Take me, bubbe. Live with me in my skin. We'll go out and together we'll challenge the evil that still stalks our world. You'll teach me how to fight, and I'll teach you how to live." Marilyn suddenly wants to laugh, as though she's found something she didn't know she'd lost. "The bastards won't know what hit them."

There is a moment in which everything is still. And then her daughter/ grandmother smiles, a lovely, joyous smile. "Come, my sweet child," she sings. "Come, my angel, my little bird, my Mirele. Let us change the world together."

Barbara Krasnoff's short fiction has appeared in *Crossed Genres, Space & Time Magazine, Electric Velocipede, Apex Magazine, Doorways, Sybil's Garage, Behind the Wainscot, Escape Velocity, Weird Tales, Descant, Lady Churchill's Rosebud Wristlet, Amazing Stories*, and the anthologies *Broken Time Blues: Fantastic Tales in the Roaring '20s, Clockwork Phoenix 2, Such A Pretty Face: Tales of Power & Abundance*, and *Memories and Visions: Women's Fantasy and Science Fiction*. Barbara is currently Features & Reviews Editor for Computerworld and a member of the NYC writers group Tabula Rasa. She lives in Brooklyn, NY with her partner Jim Freund and can be found at BrooklynWriter.com.

Pushing Paper in Hartleigh
Natania Barron

The lantern on Sir Gawen's desk was nearly out of fuel by the time they brought in Sally Din. She wasn't kicking and screaming, but she embodied a kind of dormant rage that Gawen could appreciate in a person. That six Roseguard had accompanied her was no miscalculation. Her face was a mess of bruises, and blood seeped down her hand from an undisclosed location further up. Her ankle was twisted, but she tried not to show it.

"I'm Sir Gawen of Fenlie. Captain of the Order of the Rose," he said, gesturing to the seat across his desk. "Please, sit."

"I know who you are," Sally said, with no sign of pain.

Prickly. Just like a cactus.

Behind the bruises, Sally had a wild look to her, not at all like the few women Gawen was used to dealing with. Her hair was unkempt beyond measure, plaited and beaded here and there like some savage. And she was dressed in chaps and trousers with a loose-fitting white shirt and unlaced vest. It was hardly the attire expected of one rumored to be the next Captain of the Order of the Asp – at least, it was so rumored before she found herself charged with a series of scandalous crimes.

Sir Gawen leaned forward and dismissed the knights who brought her in. Then he waited until they shut the door before speaking.

This was an interrogation, certainly, but Gawen was a man of etiquette.

"Nice of you to invite me to your ivory tower," Sally said.

He gave her a tight-lipped smile and nodded. With any of the other knights, he'd have taught them a lesson for a reply so glib. But she was a woman. The only woman in the five knighting Orders. It didn't feel right.

Though she was no ordinary woman, Sally Din, in no ordinary Order. The Order of the Asp was downright unpredictable.

"So, sit," Gawen said. "They tell me if you're compliant, I can give you some vialc for the pain. Personally, I'd suggest whisky."

Sally sat, folding her hands across her chest. She was suppressing a wince. "Whisky it is."

Just looking at Sally made Gawen remember what it was like, fighting in the field: the thrill of pursuing enemies, the feeling of the wind in his hair, the smell of dry earth and hot sun all around. Gawen had spent the best years of his life out there, knocking skulls and pulling steel, until the Queen had promoted him to his post as Captain. At the time, he had wanted it; it was an honor, after all. But he had not spilled blood in years, now, and he was beginning to forget the man he once was.

Gawen rose, and he watched her as he did so. He was a living legend, according to the storytellers and bards who still sang his praises. And in person, he was typically the tallest man in the room. People had a way of staring.

Sally didn't.

Gawen went to his liquor cabinet and poured the whisky into two matching glasses. He handed one to her, his hand dwarfing the delicate glass.

She tipped the whole three finger's worth down in a single swig.

Gawen retrieved some oil for the lantern, replacing the well with a new one, while he watched Sally out of the corner of his eye.

More light was better, but it brought out just how incongruous Sally was in his lavish office. Nestled high in one of Hartleigh Castle's towers, far from Queen Maelys's own quarters as could be, Gawen's office was impressive. High-ceilings, stained glass, carpeted floors. The fireplace roared, a welcome comfort in the dank spring season. Banners hung behind him, as well as ornamental swords and guns.

Though it was not to say all was for decoration. The guns on the wall once hung at his hips, and he was proud to wear them.

Just not any more.

"I gather you're not a woman prone to long discussion and deliberation, so I'll cut to the chase, aye?"

"Sure."

"We want Lee Renmen," Gawen said, taking one more sip of whisky. He needed it. Her presence alone was making him feel inadequate.

Sally made no expression. "You can't have him."

"You're aware that failing to comply is akin to treason, which is punishable by death?" Gawen asked.

"I'm aware," Sally said.

Gawen hadn't expected her to be compliant. He wouldn't have been, in her position.

He continued, "Aye, and when we find Lee Renmen – and we will, I assure you – he'll be hanged. The knights he's accused of attacking were high-ranking, trusted individuals, with not just my confidence but the confidence of the Queen and the High Counselor."

Sally gritted her teeth and looked away. She winced, just barely, and Gawen knew he'd hit a tender point. Emotion was cutting through the pain.

He pressed it again. "If you won't let me know where Renmen is, perhaps you'll enlighten me as to why you'd be willing to sacrifice your well-earned career and life for his sake. Seems a heavy price to pay, aye?"

"Career?" she said with a laugh. "What I've got ain't a career. That's what you've got. I'd kill myself in your position." She gestured to the papers.

"We're not talking about me," Gawen said, feeling the barb just the same.

"Surely you are a woman with ambition, otherwise you wouldn't have enlisted. But you are willing to throw that away. For what?"

Gawen could tell she was thinking. She had to be tired, too. They'd kept her awake in her cell since they brought her in the day before. No food, only drink. It was enough to render some men to tears by the time they got to Gawen's office. But not Sally Din.

"I trust him," Sally said at last.

"Trust?"

Sally shrugged. "He didn't mean to assault those men. He was asking some questions. But it didn't go so well."

"Questions about what?"

She paused, then shrugged and said slowly. "A conspiracy."

Conspiracy. Great. That meant even more paperwork. Gawen felt a sickly surge in his stomach. What was he doing, thinking of paperwork at a time like this? He had a crown to defend, after all.

Frustrated, Gawen went to the window. It was raining again, the panes were flecked with raindrops. In the distance he could see the *Queen's Mercy* rising above the east tower, the airship a perfectly oblong shadow against the stars. Why they were running that thing in the middle of the rain in the dark, he didn't know. As usual, life went on in Hartleigh while Gawen of Fenlie pushed paper.

He took a deep breath, measuring his words. "I find it more likely that he was simply taking out his aggression on the Roseguard."

"That ain't how it is," Sally snapped.

"Then what, did he just have a *hunch*?" Gawen asked with a laugh.

"Something like that."

Well. A fortuitous turn of phrase, perhaps. Not that it made much more sense. If Renmen acted on a hunch, chances were the man was insane. Which would mean another set of reports and a closed trial which would be exhausting to keep out of the papers.

Godsdamnit.

"A dream? A portend?" Gawen suggested.

"A *vision*," Sally said.

"Well, if he's mad–"

"He *ain't* mad," Sally said. "He's gifted. Listen, you wouldn't understand–"

"My dear woman–" Gawen stopped when she bristled, giving him a narrow-eyed glare like to wilt a desert rosette. He tried again. "My dear *Sir*. I'm Morish. Just because I work for the Queen does not mean I share Her views on religion."

"So? Don't change anything."

Gawen was feeling weary. And he ought to have just thrown her back in the cell. But he was tired of inaction. "While I'm hesitant to believe such a thing, my-self, I can still see your sincerity. That you would be willing to sacrifice every-thing you have earned for his life is remarkably telling, aye?"

Sally frowned at him, frowned at him good and long. Gawen held her gaze as long as he could.

Then she said: "Renmen is a good man. Standing up for him is easy. Everything else... that's where it gets complicated."

Gawen nodded. Most of what he was considering was far from protocol. But with all the paperwork incurred these days, Gawen wasn't feeling particularly overwhelmed with love for his monarch. In fact, he figured that with the mountain of paperwork he'd inherited as Captain, he didn't owe Her a godsdamned thing. She was not his keeper.

"Well, I'll give you a choice," he said. "I can put you in custody, but if I do, my knights will eventually find Renmen. They'll put him in irons and hang him for treason."

"Figures," Sally said.

"Or, as an alternative, you can take me to him and we can have a discussion. I can give you a draught of vialc, too. It will dull the pain considerably. Simple as that," Gawen said.

Sally Din stood up, leather creaking up and down the length of her. Gawen knew the feeling of bruised ribs, and watched as she held back a gasp.

Leaning forward, Sally placed both of her hands flat on Gawen's desk – grimy hands streaking blood on his paperwork – and stared him down.

Gawen did not move. He had seen much more terrifying things in his life, looked down their foul, sharp-toothed maws. It wasn't that Sally Din was not a terror, only that she was judging him. Yes, Gawen knew he was softer than he'd been in the past. He was buried in bureaucracy, half sick with it. But his heart still beat with the desire of adventure, his blood rushed at the thought of risk.

"Well?" he asked.

"I can't promise your safety," she said. "My men are unpredictable."

"I think I can handle myself," Gawen said, taking down his pistols from the wall.

"Oh, but it's been years since you've seen action, Sir," she said. "You still up for it?"

"Aye." Gawen felt rage flicker in the center of him. He placed his hand on his heart and nodded.

Sally smiled at his gesture. "Pour me another whisky and we have a deal," she said, spitting on her hand and offering it to him, streaked in blood and promises.

***

Sally walked with purpose, snaking through alleyways, her boot heels clicking over the cobblestones and her spurs trembling like punctuation, even with her limp. For someone who was born and raised far away in the Territories, she certainly acted as if she knew the place. Gawen followed after her, trying not to breathe so hard. He'd not been out for such a brisk walk in ages.

Then she stopped dead. "We're almost there," she said, thrusting her thumb behind her to a nondescript warehouse. A few lights were on at the base, golden lantern light flickering.

Gawen nodded. "Very well," he said. "Shall we?"

In the dark her expressions were even more difficult to decipher, but Gawen thought she had the air of someone considering her next moves very carefully.

"I'd ask you to try and keep a low profile," Sally said after a few more moments passed, "but everyone knows who you are already. Ain't no other redheaded giants in the service."

"Aye, I'm afraid the art of stealth is not my forte," Gawen said, taking a stab at humor. He shouldn't have even tried.

"You sure you up to this? There might be gunfire."

"Have you heard the stories about me?" he asked.

"Yeah."

"Most of them are true."

She sniffed. "Right."

No, she didn't believe him, either. But he had to believe it of himself. Otherwise it was crazy to descend into danger like this, alone and without backup.

When they reached the decrepit warehouse, they skirted the side and Sally picked up speed.

"This way," Sally said, pointing to an outcrop in the building.

A single wooden door presented itself, and when Sally opened it, she gestured to a series of narrow stairs. Gawen would have to stoop the whole way down, and allow himself to remain underground – a prospect of which he was not particularly fond.

"I should go first," he said.

"You'll get shot from here to next Blooming Day," Sally said. "I go first."

"I suppose these are not the most upstanding citizens in your command, then?"

She flipped her braid over her shoulder and gave him an even gaze. "Renmen needs protection and he needs anonymity. Ain't nothing like those fallen on hard times to be trusted with such things. Now follow me."

The descent was even worse than Gawen expected. Not ten steps down and the wooden stairs became slimy and moldy, creaking under his significant weight. There were no lanterns, but Sally kept walking down into the dark. Bugs skittered along the earth and rock, spider webs brushed their faces. Gawen smelled rat feces, and the lingering stink of garbage and refuse let to fester, liquefy, and become absorbed.

It was not pleasant.

But just when he was about to ask Sally how much longer they were going to continue descending, the air grew fresher; he felt the ceiling open above his head, and currents moved his hair. Ahead, the passageway gained definition as light streamed in, candle-lit by the look of it.

Torches, it turned out, were the light source. Gawen stopped behind Sally by an iron-enforced door. Sounds of discussion emanated from behind it, along with laughter, and the unmistakable sound of glasses clinking.

She knocked three times, and a grate in the middle slid open, revealing a pair of very blue eyes.

"Yes?" asked the individual.

"It's me, Gresham," Sally said. "Open up."

The eyes could not quite make out Gawen's entirety, what with his size and the general perspective.

"Who's with you?" Gresham asked.

"Gawen of Fenlie," Sally said, as if his name was a curse-word in and of itself.

Gresham started. "Are you off your saddle, Sally? You can't–" He stopped and peered at her. "Gods, you look a wreck."

But Sally shook her head, putting her hands up. "It doesn't matter. It's this or Renmen hangs."

With a reluctant sigh, Gresham opened the door. He was stout and dark, with black, shaggy hair, and a beer gut. But he had a face that looked accustomed to smiling in spite of its current scowl.

Behind Gresham, the room opened up in a haze of cheff-weed smoke and glazed eyes. The majority of those gathered were indecipherable from Territories cattle herders, but Gawen guessed they were mostly in the Asp. They sat by dark mahogany tables, and on Ardesian silk pillows. Food was provided, and some drink, but most of the people gathered around the tall, green-glass hookahs positioned around the room.

Then there were a handful of whores, impossible to miss with the layers of makeup garishly smeared across their features. He pitied women degrading themselves so.

As he stepped through the threshold, a half dozen pistols and shotguns pointed at him.

That rush. It had been years since Gawen felt it. His ears whined, his heart thudded in his chest; his arms and legs tensed, the muscles preparing for a fight even before he had time to assess the situation.

Gods, but it felt good. Like his body was pumped full of illegal essences, or the thrill of first love.

"Now, none of that," Sally Din said.

The guns lowered, some more reluctantly than others.

"Sir Gawen here is our guest," she said, striding through the crowd and making for a door on the other side. "For now."

Gawen followed Sally, aware of just how large he was in the dim, smoke-filled room. He could feel the stares on his back as he passed the patrons. But he knew, on a level buried deep for the last three years, that if they were to press him, he'd have the advantage.

The stories were true about him, after all. Even if it sounded arrogant to say so. He'd once punched a man clear through his head. He wasn't proud to be the owner of such violent acts, and that – among others – was not the sort of thing that generally made it into songs. But Gawen had seen worse odds, and left with his life.

"This way," Sally said, shoving him gently on the shoulder. "Through here."

A creaky door led to another hallway, and Gawen counted seven other doors before Sally found one and knocked.

"Who's there?" asked a rough, Queensland accent from within.

"It's me, Lee," Sally said. "I've got Gawen of Fenlie here."

Gawen's heart was still flopping around in his chest, his hands shaking. Once, those hands had crushed a Soderi's head into a pulp during the heat of battle. Once he'd taken down three cattle thieves hanging by one of his stirrups, shooting backward. Once he'd pulled down a horse with his own hands and flipped it over.

Once he had been a legend.

But there was no time to think, or regret, as the door opened and Lee Renmen stared Gawen in the eye. Renmen was long and lean, his face already lined in spite of his young age. His cheeks were sunken, covered in stubble, deep-trenched from years in the sun. Curly brown hair hung down over his ears, and a red tie was kept around his neck.

"Well, come in, then," Renmen said, opening the door wide.

The room contained barely more than a cot, a trunk, and a dresser with a water jug. And all three knights inside made for uncomfortably close company.

Renmen was most certainly smoking cheff himself, as the room reeked of it, and he was remarkably composed for a man wanted. He sat on the cot, crossed one leg over the other, and looked up expectantly.

"Sir Gawen here," Sally said, "is interested in hearing your story."

With a wide, gap-toothed smile, Renmen said, "Does he now? The Captain of the Order of the Rose wants to hear what I have to say?"

"Aye, he does," Gawen said.

"Gawen of Fenlie, the Giant of Mor, the Red Avenger," Renmen continued, enjoying the epithets. "Come all the way to speak to me? How curious."

"Curious?" asked Gawen. "I only wanted to hear–"

"I doubt the Queen approves," Renmen said.

"The Queen is not aware," Gawen said.

"You were followed?"

"No," Gawen said.

"Yeah," Sally said.

"What?" Gawen bellowed, turning on her.

Sally continued quickly. "We've probably got half a turn before we're swarmed."

"That's preposterous," Gawen said.

Sally raised one eyebrow at him. "You didn't notice the Roseguards shadowing us all the way to the warehouse?"

Gawen felt his face flush, and he turned to Renmen. "Regardless, I wish to speak with you, Sir Renmen. Or else I can apprehend you."

Renmen did not look in the least bit threatened. "Very well," he said. "I'll show you what you want to hear. Then we can proceed."

"Show me what?" Gawen asked.

Renmen didn't answer. He unbuttoned his cuffs and started rolling his stained brown shirt upward, revealing a most bizarre tattoo. It was a simple rectangle, positioned on the center of the inside of his forearm, starting at his wrist and ending at his elbow.

But his veins; gods, the veins! They were thick, stark blue against his pale skin, running like rivers and tributaries within the confines of the rectangle.

Gawen winced. "Are you sick, man?"

"Sick? Not in the least." Renmen grinned again. "This is my map. This is what I See."

"To my knowledge, Seers portend the future through visions and dreams–" Gawen paused. The Queen would not approve of such talk. So he emended, "Or they used to."

Renmen frowned. "Oh, I have dreams. I awake in the middle of the night, my arm singing with a pain like hot coals being dragged down my tendons. I see faces, hear voices. In the morning, the map is clear, written with my own blood. Roads, rivers – all marked here, on my skin, telling me where to go. I am a Blood Seer."

Looking to Sally for an ounce of sanity Gawen found no comfort. She simply stared at Renmen, her chin down, her arms folded at her chest.

"And… this map of yours, it led you here?" Gawen asked.

"It did," said Renmen. He pointed to an intersection of two veins where the skin was red. "That's here. Where we're sitting now."

"There's no way I can disprove your madness," Gawen said. Dismissing this man was far easier than accepting his ravings.

"Then I can give you more detail. In my vision, I was able to get a good view of the men I know conspiring against the Queen. One is scarred along here," Renmen said, cutting a line from the top of his jaw and down – Sir Ratliff – "another is short, carries a pair of old pistols, made sometime during the early part of Carine III's reign; grey eyes, blond beard," – Sir Crespin – "and lastly, the High Counselor Valentine himself. Though you won't see him until well after we're ambushed."

"After we're–?" Gawen tried.

Renmen continued, his eyes widening, glazing over. "I believe Valentine has been skimming money from Queen Maelys's coffers for the last fifteen years. He has made a business of information. Everything goes through him. When you get into his office, you'll find a silver key around his neck – that opens up a hidden drawer in his desk, with plenty of incriminating evidence – they are planning assassination."

"Assassination? His… wait a moment – you just get this sort of information on some cosmic roadway?" Gawen's head was pounding.

Renmen considered the words a moment before replying, "Not entirely. Sometimes I can't stop the outcome in time. This time, I can. *You* can, I should say."

"I most certainly will not," Gawen insisted.

"Oh?" Renmen asked, genuinely surprised.

"I can't compromise my position – my career," Gawen said. "Not for... this." He waved his hands to indicate Renmen.

"Come now," Sally said. "You can't tell me this job's made you so fat and happy that you're willing to compromise the very heart of yourself."

"I am still that man," Gawen said. He wanted to weep to say it, but he kept his emotions in check.

"You used to be, Gawen. But people forget. All they'll remember is a big man with a collar around his neck, and the Queen pulling the leash," Sally continued.

Gawen glared at her, trying to dispute it, but she was right.

"They're coming," Renmen said, falling back on the bed and throwing his arms over his head. "It's in your hands, now, Gawen."

Shouting, from the hall. The Roseguard had found them.

They did not bother knocking. One firm kick and the figures of Sir Ratliff and Sir Crespin emerged from the threshold. Just as Renmen had said.

The hair on Gawen's head rose, and he was covered in gooseflesh.

"Congratulations, Sir Gawen, for securing the outlaw; we were on duty, and thought you might be in trouble, when you left the castle with the woman," Ratliff said with a smirk, surveying the room. "Am I correct to assume that is your reasoning here, Captain?"

Gawen was dumb a moment before finding his words. "Yes... yes, take them into custody," he said.

Renmen caught Gawen's eye, nodded solemnly. Then he grinned like a madman.

***

It was far past the mid-night hour, and Gawen was still awake, his body a mess of nerves.

How had Renmen known about Ratliff and Crespin?

To settle his mind, Gawen went to the Roseguard quarters and found the duty log book. Ratliff and Crespin weren't even on it for that night.

They had lied to him.

Gawen went back in the ledger as far as he could. Every time Ratliff and Crespin were scheduled for duty, they had switched with another set of knights, as far back as the book went, more than a year.

They were up to something.

Gawen draped a black cape over his shoulders, and stored a total of three knives on his person, as well as two pistols and plenty of ammunition. Something told him that getting to the High Counselor's quarters would be no easy task. Valentine was not spry, but he was cunning, and would not be without protection.

But he had to know. Gawen had to treat the threat as serious, he told himself. The Queen's safety was the utmost importance.

Yet in his heart Gawen knew why: he *wanted* the fight. He *needed* to kill. Sally had challenged him, and now he had the chance to prove he was not a man of papers and protocol.

He was a knight of blood.

Gawen knew he shouldn't be walking up three flights of stairs to the High Counselor's quarters, fully armed – even as the Captain of the Rose Guard, he was pushing his limits. But he walked anyway.

He was not surprised, upon reaching the last flight of stairs – out of breath, and clutching the rail – to hear footsteps behind him.

He turned his head to the side, just to get a glimpse.

Crespin.

"Captain," Crespin said.

"Evening, Sir Crespin," Gawen said, turning fully and straightening. They'd both pulled steel.

"Oh, now, you're prepared to shoot me over the ramblings of a madman?" Crespin asked.

"You messed with the books," Gawen said.

Crespin smirked. "You finally took a look at the duty book, did you? Well, Ratliff and I have had business with the High Counselor; you're right about that. But it isn't like you think."

"Then set me straight." Gawen had to admit, as cool as he managed to keep his voice, he was thrilled to be holding a gun – loaded and ready – in his hands again. He knew he could outshoot Crespin, who was scarcely more than twenty-one and carrying antiques rather than state-of-the-art pistols. Some men and their precious guns.

"You've probably found out about the money," Crespin said, shaking his head. "And I can understand why you're mad. But you've got to know, we've been cleaning up the streets with it. The money comes from essence dealers – it's a bad thing they're doing, and we're just putting money in the right pockets."

"Robbing from essence dealers doesn't help anyone, Crespin. It means they charge more, and deal worse, and go deeper. Any idiot could figure that out," Gawen said. "No wonder crime's been on the rise."

"What would you know about that?" Crespin asked. "Not to give offense, sir, but you spend most of your time office-bound, buried in paper."

"Yes. And I *read* the papers that come across my desk. So I do know," Gawen pointed out. "Now if you'll excuse me…"

"Can't let you by." Crespin shook his head. "It's best you go back to your room, sir."

"Something is amiss, Crespin. Either you help me in this, or you–"

"What? You'll shoot me?"

Gawen felt it happening, that rage bubbling up. Just the way it had been in his earlier years, except more intense that he remembered. It had been bottled up for so long, and this time he let into it.

His vision blurred, went red around the edges. He moved, but it was as if the very center of him was pulled forward before he was fully in control, tied to an invisible force of rage and fury.

"Yes. That's right," Gawen said lowly.

Crespin did not fear him, and that was his mistake. Gawen was not even thirty-five yet, and they believed him soft, washed up. Fat and happy and buried in paperwork.

They were all wrong.

With one hand Gawen hit Crespin on the side of the head; with the other he knocked away his gun. Crespin's cheek cracked first, a satisfying and familiar feeling, and then his nose went in a splatter of blood. It was enough of an impact to send a bloody smear onto the wall.

Crespin went down. He did not move.

But Gawen did. Moving as swiftly as he could manage with his height and brawn, Gawen gained the stairs and the hallway before he was assaulted by Ratliff and three others.

"Stand down," Gawen said. "I'm your Captain, and that's an order."

One of the knights, Pestin, almost complied.

"We're not standing down," Ratliff said. "We're going to quietly escort you back to your quarters, and in the morning you'll be arraigned, I'm sure, on grounds of conspiring with Sirs Renmen and Din."

"Like the hells I will," said Gawen. "I said, stand down – that's a fecking order!"

Ratliff laughed when none of his men moved. Then he said, "Take him."

Gawen's world went wonderfully, ecstatically red. Something hit him in the shoulder, stinging, but it only egged him on. Instead of guns and knives he used his hands, his shoulders, his legs. He slammed men together, men smaller and weaker than he. He roared. He thundered. He drew darkness from all around him and sent it out again, twisting and angry and hungry for blood.

Ratliff gurgled, spitting out teeth on the ground, and the other knights were not moving.

Gawen noticed two figures at the end of the hall. One kindled a lantern: Sally and Renmen.

His vision returning to normal, Gawen coughed, grasping his shoulder. He felt the odd, puckered lump beneath his skin indicative of a bullet. Moving his arm, he didn't feel it graze bone in any way, so he was good. For now.

"How did–" Gawen gasped, shaking off the fury.

Sally breezed by him. She held the lantern up to his shoulder. "You'll need a medic, soon."

"I can survive a while more," Gawen said. He pointed to the High Counselor's door. "We need to get in."

Sally nodded. She took a pair of pistols for herself off the unconscious – and maybe dead, Gawen realized – Roseguard, and Renmen did the same.

Then she went to the High Counselor's door. But an odd look came over her face as she stood there.

"Feck," she whispered.

"What's it, love?" asked Renmen.

"Air," Sally said.

She kicked the door open, and a gust of wind followed. "Lots of it."

The windows were thrown wide, and papers circled around the room. Some were intact, while plenty of others were but shreds of confetti, twisted and burned.

The high-posted bed was empty, the cabinet drawer Renmen spoke of turned over, papers still littering the floor.

Gawen shouldered his way inside and grabbed a fistful of papers from the air, squinting to view them. Accounting. Pages. Numbers. Correspondence. Broken seals.

Renmen stood in the center of the room, eyes closed, smiling as a vortex of paper flitted about him.

"Over here," Sally said, pointing down and out the window.

Gawen glanced, and then turned away. The High Counselor was a mass of blood and bones below them, smeared across the courtyard, along with his guilt.

***

The Queen did not visit Gawen in the infirmary, but Kaythra Bav, one of her advisors, did. She was a plain woman, sturdy and yet somehow elegant. She wore long red robes, a yellow sash and turban, and she held Gawen's gaze for a few moments before she began to speak.

"How are you feeling?" she asked him.

"I've had worse," he said.

"I've no doubt. But I did not simply mean your physical state. You've been through quite a bit, made some very intriguing decisions in the last few hours."

"Sir Din and Sir Renmen?" he asked.

"Resting comfortably. Not only are Ratliff and Crespin in custody, but we've also arrested twenty knights and half a dozen essence dealers in connection. The Queen will owe you a debt of gratitude."

"She will?" he asked.

Kaythra's face was impassive. The room, Gawen noticed, was entirely empty of medics, or other patients for that matter. He'd fallen asleep to their collective cacophony, doused in vialc for the pain. But now it was silent as a morgue.

"I understand there were some unusual circumstances surrounding the knowledge you attained regarding Valentine's conspiracy," she continued, picking at the bedspread.

"Yes, but–"

"And you broke at least seven laws yesterday. Highly unusual for someone of your stature."

"Yes, except–"

"Sir Gawen, let me finish."

"Yes, High Counselor." He shut his mouth and attempted a smile.

Kaythra lifted her chin. "The Queen will not hear of any unusual circumstances. She will learn of intercepted communication you received via Renmen and Din. You are all heroes, in her eyes, but all the means were regular. *Nothing unusual.* Do you understand me?"

No doubt such news – reliant as it was on the mind of a Seer – would infuriate the Queen and put all their lives at stake. Queen Maelys was a relentless persecutor of seidcraft. What Renmen saw, how Gawen fought.

Kaythra was saving them from her fury. But why?

"Nothing unusual," he replied.

"I trust you will get back to your post soon enough. Providing you comply," Kaythra said, rising.

Gawen sighed. "Yes, I swear. I… understand, for what it's worth. But thank you; I don't know what to say."

Kaythra nodded, but continued, "And in light of your remarkable feat, the Queen wishes to grant you a boon. I suggested a house in the country perhaps? A parcel of land? Some livestock?"

There it was. Everything back to normal. The papers, the drills, the routine. A country house. Gawen knew that the routine would feel like a comfortable pair of boots, that he could slip right in and pretend nothing ever happened, pretend he had never seen the map on a madman's arms and the love for him in his woman's eyes.

Fat, happy, and pushing paper in Hartleigh.

"If it's all the same," Gawen said, "I have another request"

"Oh?" Kaythra asked. Her brows swept up to her turban.

He could not forget them. They would haunt him, even when they were gone.

"Sir Gawen?" Kaythra asked. "I am pressed for time."

Gawen took a deep breath. "I'd like to request a position among the Order of the Asp. Sir Malvin would make a good replacement for me, if the Queen should ask."

"Oh?"

"I'm not meant for a place like this…" he said, then trailed off. He held up his hands; his knuckles were split, one finger purple to the second knuckle. His hands, as they ought to be. "I thought I was. But I'm… I'm cut of a different cloth."

"That you are, Sir Gawen. I cannot argue. But the Asp are disjointed, mismanaged, and scarcely better than cattle herders. Are you certain you'd like to involve yourself with them? It would change everything."

"I could help them. Straighten them out," he said. "I have a feeling I could be a benefit to them."

Kaythra nodded. "While I can respect your choice, you will have to speak to

84

the new Captain of the Asp first."

"New Captain?" he asked.

"Sally Din has been made Captain," Kaythra said, not without a satisfied smile. "Do you think she will let you serve under her?"

Gawen chuckled, though it hurt to do so. "Oh, I've a feeling she's seen this coming."

Natania Barron is a word tinkerer with a lifelong love of things fantastic, and a soft spot for the old west. Her work has appeared in *Weird Tales, Steampunk Tales, Crossed Genres, Bull Spec*, and various anthologies; her debut novel, *Pilgrim of the Sky*, is due in December of 2011. When not venturing in imagined worlds, she can be found in North Carolina, where she lives with her family.

She can be found online at http://nataniabarron.com.

Parent Hack

Kay T. Holt

"This can't be the correct address for the campsite." Zetta frowned out the passenger side window at the seedy neighborhood and simulated a squint as the California sun flashed off her brown-irised optical sensors. "Searching the internet for an acceptable alternative. Please keep the transport running, Holmium."

The tall Guardian in the driver seat said, "Of course."

In the backseat, Nicolas and Orlando exchanged manic expressions. The kids didn't like the look of the place, either, but they knew they weren't lost. Before Zetta could finish her search, the younger boy threw open his door and dashed up the front walk of the address they'd arrived at, calling, "I'll ask for directions!"

Zetta exited the vehicle protesting, but Orlando moved faster. "Don't worry, I'll go with him." Holmium followed next, scolding his Ward in almost the same terms Zetta was lecturing Nicolas. The boys ignored their Guardians and rang the bell beside a thrice-bolted steel door.

A hidden intercom crackled, "What do you want?"

Nicolas's keen, dark eyes spotted the shine on a camera lens hidden in a crack above the door. He spoke up to it, "We're little lost orphans. Can you show us the way home?"

"Nico!" Zetta's simulated mortification was very realistic, from her wide optical sensors and posture to her tone of voice. But no sooner had she spoken than her affronted demeanor suddenly dissolved into mechanical neutrality. Holmium's disgruntled expression similarly flat-lined a split second later.

Orlando pulled Nicolas behind him and dropped into a defensive stance that was second nature after a year of mixed martial arts lessons. The strange android had stepped from behind an overgrown bougainvillea and disabled their Guardians before they'd even known it was there. "Remain calm, children. I won't hurt you." It spoke like a classic film actress, its voice a disarming combination of cultured and flinty that the boys recognized from their seventh grade film history elective but had never heard in person.

The deadbolts clicked and the door opened at last, but the woman who appeared at the threshold was instantly more threatening than the uncanny bot on the other side of the porch. She was short and skinny, but she had a gun. "Are they alone?"

"Yes, and their transport is clean of suspicious devices."

"And the bots?"

"Standard hardware and basic applications, only."

"All right, bring them to the dining room and prep them for upgrade." The hacker stepped out to let the bots file inside.

Directing Zetta and Holmium along with gentle nudges, the hacker's android asked as it passed, "What would you like for lunch?"

The hacker cocked her head and followed them in. "Lunch already? I just woke up."

"I was speaking to the children." The simulated movie star's admonishment sounded very like a Guardian addressing a difficult Ward.

The woman looked down as if seeing them for the first time. "You want to come in?" They said nothing, so she huffed, "Temperature's supposed to be in the nineties today, but you can wait out here if you want."

From deep in the house, the android snapped, "Caret!"

The hacker cringed. "Listen, this is a bad neighborhood. But inside, Caesura's cooking is the worst thing that'll happen to you. Okay?" The boys remained speechless, but their eyes followed the weapon as she gestured down the hall. Exasperated, Caret fired a stream of water into the air over their heads and tossed the squirt gun to Orlando. "Lock the door on your way in."

After she'd gone, Orlando said, "I don't like this. She's too weird."

Nicolas looked older than his twelve years as he massaged tension from his forehead with his fingertips. "Don't freak out. She's socially maladapted, but I don't think she's really dangerous."

"What about her bot? I've never even heard of a Guardian like that." He still held the squirt gun away from his body and pointed at the ground as though it held live ammunition instead of tap water.

"I don't know. It's strange enough that an adult even *has* a Guardian. I guess it makes sense for a hacker's bot to run custom applications."

"And custom hardware." Orlando smirked awkwardly under Nicolas's stare. "I've never seen a bot like hers, either."

"Pervert."

"No, I'm adjusted; you're repressed."

Nicolas massaged his face again and muttered something vaguely profane on his way into the house.

The boys found Caret and Caesura quarrelling amiably at the dining room table and Zetta and Holmium seated with them, still staring vacantly in standby mode. Caesura smiled as they entered and said, "I put a cheese pizza in the oven. What would you like to drink?"

The boys said in unison, "Just water, please."

Caret and Caesura exchanged a curious glance. "Wow, did you guys practice that?" The hacker's sneer was met with identical blank gazes from the boys. "Your email asked me to make you brothers, but I don't know what you need me for with that *Village of the Damned* thing you've got going." Caesura rolled her gray optical sensors at the hacker and went to get refreshments.

Orlando tensed at the jibe, but Nicolas was braced for sarcasm after her bad first impression. Visibly unperturbed, the younger boy asked, "How long will it take to upgrade our Guardians?"

"Twenty-four or thirty-six hours, depending on how much I sleep."

"Are you narcoleptic?" Orlando looked like he'd take that back if he could.

Caesura set his drink beside him. "Caret sleeps in a sensory deprivation tank, so her circadian rhythms have become slightly…estranged from the norm."

"It's not a tank." Caret's protest went ignored.

"That won't work. How'll we explain why they've been in standby mode for so long?"

"You won't have to. Guardians have a necessary vulnerability in their continuity. It allows them to endure long maintenance events or lengthy storage without wondering later about the lost time. I imagine it's like sleeping in a sensory deprivation tank." Caret stuck her tongue at Caesura.

"We're supposed to start back home tomorrow morning. School starts in eight days, and it took us almost a week to get here from St. Louis." Orlando didn't look very unhappy at the thought of missing the first day of school.

Nicolas shook his head. "Guardians can drive all day and night. If we sleep in the transport and don't stop for sightseeing, we could be home in less than three days." He turned to Caret. "But you still shouldn't waste our time. This is our first vacation as a real family, and nobody wants a photo album filled with shots taken outside rest area toilets."

"We're not talking about a drag-and-drop install, alright? In fact, we're not even talking about one install, but two completely custom upgrades on two highly sophisticated machines, each of which has developed a distinct set of complex parenting sub-routines. Sure, I could just scratch my rough co-parenting code on their brains and send you on your merry way, but after a few cycles, their operating systems would quarantine it like a virus, put in a maintenance call to the Workshop, and ultimately get us all busted for tampering with government property." Caret glared at the boys in turns. "I don't want to go to jail, and I know you don't want to wind up back in foster care. Maybe it's a lot better now than when I was in the system – way back before Guardians were even invented – but we all know black males your age are still the kids least likely to be adopted. You don't want me to rush this."

Nicolas pushed himself slowly to his feet before locking eyes with the hacker. "Since we all agree that successful upgrades are in everyone's best interest, I suggest you get to work. If the job is incomplete after thirty-six hours, I'll consider you in breach of contract, and cancel payment." With that, he left the room, left the house, and seemed to take all the breath in the place with him.

After a painfully protracted moment, Caesura punctured the tension by silently excusing herself to check on the pizza. Caret sighed as she pulled a wireless keyboard from her pocket and stretched the film out on the tabletop. "What the hell is up with that kid? Is he going on thirteen or thirty?"

Orlando snapped, "There's nothing wrong with Nico."

"Hey, you don't have to protect him from me. I'm just the criminal he hired to brainwash your Guardians." She didn't look at him, but at the gigantic computer screen that had appeared across a wide section of wallpaper above his right shoulder.

"It's not like that – the hack is just a formality. We'd still find a way to be brothers even if you couldn't make our family units fit together."

"Oh? And will you still be brothers when you're all grown-up and he doesn't need you anymore? What'll you do with yourself then?"

"I can take care of myself."

"Obviously. And anyone else who comes along."

Orlando slammed his palms on the table, causing Caret's keyboard to lose its grip and recoil onto itself. "You're just jealous because you don't have a family!"

She barely spared him a glance. "Yes, and you're just insecure because you can't tell the difference between being needed and being wanted."

As Orlando stormed out, he heard Caesura ask Caret, "Why do you have to be such a bitch?" He didn't hear the hacker's muttered reply, but the bot's remark brought him up short at the front door. He'd never heard an android swear before.

Outside, Nicolas sat on the hood of the transport, hunched miserably over his handheld. Orlando had learned better than to disturb him when he was crying, so the would-be older brother angled across the driveway and up the block toward the dilapidated convenience store on the corner. What Caret said had stung, but as abrasive as she was, nobody could cut him up quite like Nicolas when he was upset.

The clerk at the store gave him a cursory squint through the inches of bulletproof Plex between them before returning his focus to his grimy handheld. Once upon a time, that would have been Orlando's signal to boost a small fortune's worth of junk food and make a getaway, but that was before Holmium found his stash and offered him a deal: If Orlando quit stealing, he could finally take martial arts lessons. Backslide, and there would be no more lessons for a year. Orlando had been vigilant ever since, but now a familiar guilty chill prickled his skin.

Unlike some Wards, Orlando had taken to his Guardian right away. Holmium's simulated sense of humor was right up his alley; the clever bot would even feign clumsiness to get a laugh out of Orlando. Last Christmas, Holmium had surprised him with an acoustic guitar as a reward for improvement at school. Orlando understood his Guardian was just a machine and that its personality was really nothing more than the product of incredibly adaptive programming. He knew Holmium wouldn't be aware of any changes the hacker made, but he was the only good dad Orlando ever had. As he browsed the snack aisle, he couldn't help feeling that the fact that Guardians weren't human didn't make betraying their trust any less of a betrayal.

***

Nicolas heard Orlando leaving and turned to watch him walk to the convenience store. He wondered if he would steal something while Holmium was in standby mode. He didn't think it was important either way, but it would be interesting see what Orlando would do, left to his own devices.

Nicolas couldn't stop thinking about what *he* would do. How easy it would be to disable the GPS device in his handheld and run away while everyone else was distracted. Sitting there, he remembered the last time he'd run. No pressure to achieve all the time, and nobody around to be 'so disappointed' in him when he inevitably screwed everything up.

His last foster parents had pulled him out of sixth grade and signed him up for online college courses. They would never shut up about how much potential he had, but they had no idea what he was really capable of. When Child Safety officers finally tracked him down after four months, Nicolas refused to explain how he'd managed to get from the Midwest to the Mediterranean without being spotted by any public surveillance systems.

After that, they'd put a tracker in his handheld and put him in Zetta's care. A perfect Guardian for imperfect Nicolas. She kept their apartment tidy in spite of his worst efforts and she was never late picking him up from school. He loved her cooking. But he hated her for making him feel like the broken one.

No matter what Caret thought, Child Safety would never send Nicolas back into foster care. If he screwed things up too badly with Zetta, he'd find himself in a correctional facility for troubled youth. He knew that, yet here he was, 'tampering with government property'. He stared at his reflection in the blank screen of his handheld until he finally stopped crying. Then he scrubbed his face with the inside of his t-shirt and went back inside the hacker's house.

He could hear Caret and Caesura squabbling in the dining room. Some code-talk about cooperation protocols and identity compensations. He intentionally squeaked his shoe on the hallway tile; adults hated being snuck up on.

Caesura peeked around the corner and smiled to see him. "I kept your pizza warm. Sure I can't interest you in a little fresh squeezed 'lemorange' juice? I make it myself."

"Thanks. That sounds nice." Nicolas sat across the table from Caret (keeping his back turned on the code scrolling across her giant computer screen) but waited to speak to her until he heard the juicer buzz to life in the kitchen. "Sorry I snapped. I usually have better self-control."

Caret gave him a wry look. "You lie so sweet, I almost don't care that you're trying to manipulate me. For what it's worth, I'm sorry you're socially maladjusted, too."

Nicolas ground his teeth.

"You break things."

"You don't know anything about me. My records are sealed."

Her eyes rolled. "If you wanted to keep secrets, then you shouldn't have hired someone to hack your parent."

"She's not my–"

"But I didn't have to read Zetta's mind to figure you out. As cold as you pretend to be, you practically broadcast your issues." Now her smile was sad and real. "Anyway, it takes one to know one."

It was all Nicolas could do to sit still. He was so comfortable feeling misunderstood that the present circumstances were almost painful.

"I know you're even smarter than you act. I'm pretty sure you're only paying for my services because you're afraid of what you might do if you let yourself figure out how Guardians operate." Her gaze drifted toward the kitchen and her sad smile drifted further into gloom. "I admire your restraint."

"I don't want to hurt anyone. I just..." He massaged his face to banish the tension.

"Hey, you don't have to explain yourself to me. Or anyone. But get yourself a damn hobby before you get yourself locked up, okay?" He nodded miserably and Caret stood up and stretched. "I'm going out for a smoke. Don't touch anything while I'm gone."

A minute later, Caesura arrived with his pizza and juice. "Is she gone? I thought I was going to have to squeeze every fruit in the house before it was all clear in here."

Nicolas went from confused to worried as the bot seated herself across the table from him and started typing code at incredible speed. "What are you doing?"

"Caret's not the only hacker in the house, you know."

He dashed around the table. "Stop! She'll think it was me!"

"Relax. I'm only adding a few lines to Zetta's personality sim-ware."

"What will it do to her?"

"The engineers at the Workshop gave her a face like yours and filled her head with every psychological trick in the book, but they forgot something important." Her fingers were a blur, but Nicolas knew that if he stopped her now, Zetta's system would fail.

When she finished – it felt like an hour had passed, but it was probably only a minute or two later – he gazed up at the new code speeding smoothly through Zetta's processors. He couldn't help being impressed by its intricacy. "What...?"

Caesura turned him away from the monitor and captured his starry gaze with twinkling optical sensors of her own. "Nobody's flawless, Nico. And nobody should be."

"You broke her?"

"Just a little. Enough for you to love her." Her sad smile looked familiar. "Don't tell Caret."

***

Orlando returned to find Nicolas had gone inside and Caret had come out.

He hoped the latter wasn't due to the former. "Hey." She made room for him on the step and he sat. After a huge drag on her cigarette, she offered it to him. "No thanks."

She made a point of exhaling away from him. "Kid, you are so wholesome I want to get a cavity just to balance out the universe. If you tell me you're a vegetarian, I may have to kill myself."

"Uh…"

"Really? You don't even laugh at bad jokes?"

He pulled a packaged snack from his convenience store bag and offered it to her. "Broccoli-puff?"

Caret cracked up. By the time she gasped to a stop, her cigarette had burned down to the filter. She managed, "Oh, man. I'd make you promise to only use your powers for good, but I guess that's a foregone conclusion," before the giggles overtook her again. He sat back on his hands and enjoyed the break in tension.

After a while, she caught her breath and lit another cigarette. "I bet the girls in school just love you. The boys, too, probably."

Orlando reddened, but shrugged past the awkwardness. "I guess. Not teachers, though."

"And your Guardian?"

"Nah, Holmium's cool." His blush deepened. "Caesura's pretty cool, too. Did you build her yourself?"

Caret eyed him a minute. "Yeah. You thinking of a career at the Workshop?"

"No, Nico's the tech genius. I'm on an athletic track." He shrugged again. "I'm just curious."

"Oh?"

"I mean, you made her, but it's not like she's your daughter. And she acts kind of like your Guardian, but…not."

"Uh-huh."

"The way you guys squabble, it's like you built yourself a sister. Or a girlfriend." He laughed.

Caret didn't. She finished her cigarette in one long pull before finally saying, "That's some astute shit, coming from the jock in the family."

"Wait – what part?"

She stood and offered him a hand up. "That thing I said about only using your powers for good? Remember that the next time you're 'just curious'. Not everyone is as gracious as me." Orlando followed her silently back inside; he had no idea what to say to that.

Caesura and Nicolas were laughing at something on his handheld when Caret and Orlando entered the dining room. Caesura waved the others over, "Have you seen this video? There's a cat riding around on a Guardian!" She smiled brightly at Caret. "Can we have a cat?"

"Nope."

"Spoilsport."

Caret stuck out her tongue, sat at her keyboard and started entering commands again. The others had barely loaded another cat video for Caesura before the hacker said, "There. Done."

The kids gaped at her. "But you said... What happened to 'thirty-six hours'?"

"I lied. I just needed time to find out if I could trust you with so much incriminating code."

"I knew you were good. I can always tell." Caesura hugged a boy tightly in each arm, to everyone's obvious surprise. "Congratulations, brothers."

A matched set of clicks and whirrs drew Nicolas's and Orlando's attention as their Guardians restarted. Holmium cycled up first and smiled. "Thanks for directions. I think a sunset beach party sounds like the perfect way to celebrate the halfway-point on our cross-country trek."

"You'll get some great shots for your photo album, I'm sure." Caesura stopped hugging the boys and started clearing the table.

Zetta cycled up next. "I hate to impose anymore than we already have, but would you mind if the boys use your facilities before we're on our way?"

"Feel free," Caret said with a nod down the hall for their benefit.

When it was his turn, Nicolas used eyeliner to write a credit transfer code on the mirror. He and Orlando had been saving their government stipend for months to pay for the hack, but he didn't think he could slip Caret the code with the Guardians watching.

Everyone was out front by the time he finished; Orlando was helping Caesura carry a jumbo picnic basket out to the transport. "Did I miss something?"

"Your brother invited us to come along, and your parents said yes." Caret's expression was unfathomable.

Oh... "Was that supposed to happen?"

"How would I know? It's your family."

He wondered if she expected him to protest getting more than he asked for, but this didn't feel like a bad deal. "Are you coming?"

She nodded. "Caesura insists."

"She works fast."

Caret grinned down at him. "Don't I know it, kid."

Kay T. Holt is co-founder and editor of Crossed Genres Publications and runs the Science in My Fiction Blog. She also writes weekly for the Geek Mom blog. Her fiction has been published in *M-Brane SF*, and the anthologies *Rigor Amortis* (Edge, 2010), *Beauty Has Her Way* (Dark Quest, 2011) and *Space Tramps* (Flying Pen, 2011). She lives outside Boston with her giant husband, their genius child, and two monstrous cats. She loves science and art, and uses both in her writing.

Her personal blog is http://subvertthespace.com/kayholt.

The Hero Industry

Jean Johnson

It's really not that difficult to stage a kidnapping on Mars. There are plenty of mining facilities, new and old, for caves in which to stash people, and I suppose the self-contained atmospheric modules in each hotel room can be tampered with just enough to vent an anesthetizing agent of some sort. All I know is, right after we arrived and were officially welcomed by the government, we went to our hotel rooms. I showered and turned in for the night, and woke up with a minty-metallic taste in my mouth, bound hand and foot in my pajamas on a rough cot in a stone-carved room somewhere in the Martian equivalent of nowhere.

After shaking off the muzzy-headedness of the drugs, I looked around, saw that I was alone, bound, in some sort of storage room with a flush-fitted metal door, no window…no water, no waste facilities, no food. There were two ventilation ducts, one up high to the left of the door, one down low to the right of it, but a baby would've had trouble crawling through them. They caused a small draft to circulate around the room, but it was a warm one, so I wasn't in danger of freezing. Diode strips crossed the ceiling in four lines, illuminating the otherwise bare chamber.

Now, in the DDC, Department of Diplomatic Corps, they do cover the possibility of kidnappings and so forth – it's standard instruction for all government officials – and the key thing to remember is to stay calm, observe, and think.

So, I realized that either I was going to die, given the lack of amenities – which is not exactly conducive to staying calm, I'll admit – or that I was under observation, since it would make no sense to light up the room a murder victim was being stored in, unless someone was watching me to see when the drugs wore off. Particularly on a world like Mars, where every erg of power is precious. Since I'm naturally an optimistic person, I chose the latter viewpoint.

Sitting up – which was a bit of a struggle, but manageable – I looked around the room, smiled, and said, "Well, you certainly have my attention, whoever you are. I'm ready to listen whenever you're ready to talk. But please don't take too long. I'll eventually need to use the bathroom, and maybe a drink of water would be nice? It's much more pleasant to listen when one is comfortable, wouldn't you agree?"

And then I waited, still smiling lightly, politely. And waited. And waited. And got bored, so I started working on the binder tape used on my wrists and

94

ankles. That's an advantage when being kidnapped on Mars; things like metal handcuffs are all accounted for, but binder tape is cheap and nobody really notices how much of it goes missing. The key is to be patient, of course, so it doesn't get bunched up and become impossible to tear. That, and to have at least a couple of long fingernails handy for making the first puncture-cut.

Not long after I got my hands and legs free, when I was sitting there, playing with the ball of mangled tape, the door opened. In stepped two...hmm...I guess someone else would call them terrorist types. They were clad in bulky loose clothes of indeterminate age and color, sort of beige-ish green like overused army surplus, and their heads and faces were covered in scarves. They even had sunglasses on, how cliché! And, of course, they were carrying guns.

Naturally, I gave them a big, friendly smile and asked very cheerfully, "Hello, there! How are you doing, today?"

That stopped them in their tracks. I immediately went on the attack, taking advantage of their confusion.

"Did you have a good weekend?" I asked. "I was hoping to catch the big game back home, with the Red Rockets versus the Bay Blasters, but I was lagged from the flight and had to go to bed early. Did either of you catch the score?

"Uhh..." one of them replied. He was the taller of the two, his clothes a little paler overall.

I fixed him with a hopeful look – raising the brows and such – and pressed, "So what was it? Who won?"

"The...Rockets won. 6 to 3?" The taller fellow glanced at the shorter one. "Wasn't it 6 to 3?"

"Shh!" the shorter one hissed, and I got the impression it was a she under all those layers of cloth. "Don't tell her that!"

"Let me guess, you're a Blasters fan?" I asked, re-seizing the initiative. This part is key in negotiations: Keep the other side slightly off-balance, disarm them with pleasantries, and control the conversation with mixtures of sympathy and questions. "You know, I was starting to root for them, too? I'm actually more of a Satellites fan, truth be told, but Rockets versus Blasters looked like it was going to be great. And Jeff Cheung is such a great center, and their goalie this year practically defies gravity! What was your favorite part of the game? The best play of the night?"

"Well, I really liked the–"

"–Don't talk to her like that!" short and female hissed again. "She's our prisoner, not our pal!"

"Maybe you shouldn't talk to *him* like that?" I asked, giving her a pointed look of my own. "Look, for whatever reason I'm here, whatever you might want from me, we can do this the *easy* way, or we can do this the *hard* way."

...And at that point I had to jab my thumbnail into my palm to keep from laughing, because from the way short and female jerked back, it looked like I'd just stolen her lines out from under her. I can let myself laugh about it now, but back then, I knew one false twitch would ruin everything I was trying to do. So instead, I spread my hands, then clasped them.

"Personally, if I were you, I'd pick the easy way. You're that much more likely to get whatever it is you want. Now, since you insist on getting down to business, rather than discuss the game, we might as well get down to it. What's the name of your group, and what are your demands?"

They looked at each other, taken aback by my question.

"You *do* have a name, don't you? Clearly, you're organized," I pointed out. "You obviously have superiors you'll be reporting all of this to, and undoubtedly your organization has an agenda of some sort. Goals which you wish to accomplish, and which you are hoping will be furthered by kidnapping me. So let's introduce ourselves. Hi, I'm Marcia Cowbell, member of the Department of Diplomatic Corps. Who are you, and what are your goals?"

They sort of shuffled a bit, then the short one puffed up a bit. "We are proud members of the Free Mars Movement. We are sick and tired of you Terrans ignoring us and our suffering! We will destroy your foul, corrupt government and install a new one by the people of Mars, for the people of Mars!"

Tall and male puffed up as well. "That's right! No more fat, foreign governors! No more bribes and corruption! And *you* are going to be our ticket to the peoples of all the planets finally taking notice of what's going wrong, here!"

"You're right, I am," I agreed firmly, deflating them a bit with surprise at my calm acceptance of their claims. My mind was racing, though. "But…not quite in the way you were originally thinking I'd help. Instead, as soon as it is convenient for your leadership to get down here, they and I are going to have a lovely chat about how to *really* get this revolution of anti-corruption and self-government started. After all, that *is* why I and my colleagues from the DDC came here," I reminded them. "We're here to help you find a way out of the problems you're in – and do ask your leaders to hurry. The more time they waste, the worse their position will get. Not better, as you might've thought."

They looked at each other. I knew because they actually turned toward each other, not because I could see their eyes behind their sunglasses. I decided to press the point a little while they were thinking about what I'd just said.

"Look, anyone else you go to, they're just going to see a bunch of lawless, criminal kidnappers. They'll refuse, by your actions, to see that you have a legitimate problem that needs a legitimate, long-lasting solution. Which you do. With anyone else, you'd get a pat, pre-rehearsed answer, one filled with outrage and resistance, and that'll get you nowhere, guaranteed," I warned Tall and Short. I touched my chest briefly before clasping my hands again. "With *me*, you won't get pre-set answers. At the moment, I'm not offended by what you've done. I think you have rightful, just concerns, and I want to see them fully addressed. With me, particularly since I am still willing to listen, you'll get suggested solutions that will actually work. *If* applied correctly. And *if* you can open your ears and actually listen to what I'll have to say.

"Now, go talk to your leaders, and bring them down here so we can can have a nice, productive chat. Or arrange for me to go meet them, your choice. In the meantime, a bathroom break and a glass of water sometime soon would be very lovely," I added, finishing with a light, friendly smile.

They kinda looked at each other again, then Short muttered something about needing to get new orders. She and Tall backed out of the room, locking the door behind them. So there I sat, having no flying clue what I was going to talk to their leaders about, if I got the chance to do so. Which meant I had to start thinking in a big hurry. But since I was fairly sure I was being watched – probably from a camera tucked into the lights, or maybe in the vent ducts – I kept my expression polite and pleasant, and just idly played with my tape-ball while I thought. And thought. And thought...

The biggest problem was, we'd been kidnapped. I had to presume I wasn't the only one missing. And kidnapping came with several problems. First off, the government would treat these radicals as criminals...which, admittedly, they technically were. However right or just their cause was, kidnapping was kidnapping, and a major crime. They would be vilified, their cause trampled in the mud, their needs overlooked, their rights discarded. And I couldn't come out as a spokeswoman for them without having the old Stockholm Syndrome smeared across my actions, labeling me a brainwash victim.

No, I knew they had made a huge mistake in kidnapping us. The news media and the government and the people would paint them the villains in this mess, not the victims. Society doesn't root for the villains. Underdogs, yes, but not villains. We want the good guys to win. We want heroes to look up to and support, people who do the *right* thing when a situation goes wrong...and that, *that* was what gave me the idea. Thinking that thought right there.

What I needed to do was to turn these faceless villains into heroes. Somehow. That was the tricky part. So as I sat there in my flannel pajama suit, growing hungry and thirsty and in need of a bathroom and a toothbrush and a fresh change of clothes, I plotted. And plotted. And plotted.

After another hour or so, I had reviewed what villains were, what heroes were, how to define the differences that made each of them appealing or repulsive, and figured out the best chance these Free Marsies had at turning this bad situation into a brilliant public relations campaign to get interplanetary attention – and more important, interplanetary support – behind their cause.

I even had time to rehearse what I needed to say. This was a good thing, because Short finally came back, this time with two new scarf-wrapped, sunglasses-sporting figures, one male and one female. They certainly stood with a lot more authority than Short and Tall had carried themselves, though I wasn't sure if these were the actual leaders of the movement, or just higher-ups. Either way, I sat up on the bed and smiled.

"Hello, there! I'm glad you came to see me," I told them. "I take it you're higher-ups in the Free Mars Movement? Possibly even lieutenants in the organization?"

They didn't even glance at each other. The male spoke. "Something like that. You seem rather...pleasant...for someone who's been kidnapped."

"Well, I'm not brain-damaged, if that's what you're asking," I retorted dryly, giving him a sardonic look. "Ironically, your choice of kidnap victims were the very people sent to *help* you. Specifically, the DDC sent us here to help *you*, not the Mars government. Now admittedly, you have been a bit…mm…*over*-eager in arranging this meeting with myself, and quite possibly my colleagues if you snatched them up, too…but nothing has happened to me so far to change my mind about being willing to work with you and help you resolve the problems at hand.

"Unless, of course, you decide you'd rather be a fool and throw away the opportunity I'm about to present to you. The choice, of course, is yours…but a wise man at the very least would listen to what I have to say." I shrugged, leaving it in his hands. "If you're smart enough to pull off all of *this*, then you're smart enough to see an even better opportunity when it becomes available. The only question is, *are* you smart enough to reach for it? I'd certainly like to think so."

"That depends on what kind of 'opportunity' it is," Tall, Pale, and Lieutenant-ish countered.

I'd expected some resistance, so despite his flat tone, I took it as a willingness to at least listen. I nodded at the foot of the cot.

"Have a seat." When he didn't move, I shrugged – the important thing in these types of negotiations is to remain polite and pleasant, so an attempt at courtesy never hurts – and I went on. "You have three big problems. The biggest one of all is the trouble you're experiencing here on Mars. Now, we won't get into the whys of all of that right now; the important thing to remember about your problems with the Martian government is that you've been having a very hard time getting the truth out to the rest of the worlds so things will finally get fixed. The government controls the broadcast equipment, and the government is corrupt, so on and so forth…right?"

"Right." He folded his arms across his chest, not exactly an encouraging sign. Thanks to his sunglasses in the way, making me wonder if it was a dress code or something, I didn't know whether or not he rolled his eyes, too. I continued anyway, keeping my expression open and light.

"So…if you'll forgive me for putting it this way…you've decided to pull a publicity stunt. Kidnap one or more government officials, and both the government and the media are pretty much obligated to look into the matter. As soon as word gets out – presuming you didn't kidnap all of my colleagues, the rest will be yelling everything to their superiors back home as soon as they realize some of us are gone – you'll finally have media attention. Which is great…up to a point.

"That's where the second problem starts, however," I cautioned him and his companion. The second woman hadn't said a word yet, nor had Short, the female guard from earlier. I could only tell the two women apart because the first one had a lighter green scarf covering her face and hair, and the second, newest arrival had obviously feminine curves under the loose folds of her clothes. Still, thanks to her scarf and glasses, and the stiff way she held her body, I had no clue what the new woman was thinking.

"What problem is that?" Tall Lieutenant finally asked me.

"The problem is, kidnapping will always – *always* – be seen as an act of villainy, when what you *need* is for people to see you as heroes." I quickly held up my hand as he drew in a breath to retort. "*Yes*, you needed the media attention. *Yes*, this was probably the most effective way you could get it. I don't deny any of these things. But what you need to do *now* is turn around public opinion on this whole matter before it snowballs beyond all control. That's where I come in. Because I have the solution to your *third* problem, and it will most definitely help you fix the first two as well."

Short Lieutenant Woman snatched a pistol from somewhere and aimed it at my head. "Why shouldn't I just kill you, right here, right now? You think you can come in, telling *us* what to do?"

Up until that point, I'd never had a gun pointed at my head. I think my heart stopped beating for about two or three seconds. But it was odd. I wasn't actually scared. Maybe it was because the surreality of the moment, or because too much was on the line, but somehow I stayed calm. *At least now I have some clue of what she's thinking...*

"The moment you pull that trigger," I stated as calmly as I could, "your cause will be associated with a murder. *Any* cause associated with a murder will be vilified and decried, and your entire purpose *for* kidnapping me, the freedom and civil rights of your fellow Martians, will be tainted *permanently* with the stains of my blood. You will destroy *any* hope of sympathy and support from offworlders.

"I'm not saying this to save my life," I added bluntly. "I have no control over whether or not you do choose to shoot me in the end. I'm saying this because *history* has proven it, young lady. Over, and over, and over. *Any* death of your kidnappees, or maiming, or other serious injury, and your cause will be shot down just as *dead* right alongside me. Is that what you want?

"*Think*, woman," I ordered her when the gun didn't move. "Which is more important? Your anger at me, because you know I'm right? Or your anger at the situation here on Mars? Not which angers you *more*, but which is more *important*."

Her arm hesitated, trembled, then started to lower just as the man at her side murmured, "...Put it down."

I didn't let myself breathe a sigh of relief, not even after she tucked it away in the folds of her layers of shirts. Instead, I did my best to hold her gaze – a difficult task, thanks to those sunglasses. "It may irritate you that I'm right. You may even be feeling a bit of despair right now because you know people are going to look at this kidnapping effort as the actions of villains, rather than normally honest people being pushed to the edge by worse atrocities, however subtle by comparison. That despair may be feeding your anger, making everything worse. But I'll ask you take a deep breath, let it out, and listen to the third problem you have. *And* my solution for it."

She folded her arms and didn't take a deep breath, but didn't protest either. She also didn't leave.

"So. What is our third problem, and what is its solution?" Tall Lieutenant prompted me.

"You need to turn your cause from an act of villainy to an act of heroism. Now that you *have* the media's attention...or you soon will, since I don't know how long I've been out," I added in an aside, "you've already accomplished the task of shocking people awake to the realities of your first problem. But as I said, they won't root for a villain. They will root for an underdog, but not a villainous one.

"So. You need to *create* a hero, one strongly associated with your cause, but eloquent enough to convince everyone that he or she is just as appalled by the kidnappings as the average citizen will be, elsewhere," I told them, the tall male and the two females, both the lieutenant and the listening guard at the door. "And then, you run with it."

Short Lieutenant cocked her head and shook it. "...I don't get it."

"Neither do I," her companion admitted. "Explain."

"It's going to take someone incredibly brave. Someone so brave, they're willing to allow their *face* to be shown – hear me out," I added as they started and their postures shifted to something less than pleased with that idea. I held up my hand, warding off any protests. "As I said, people *will* root for an underdog, but even more, they will root for a *hero*. And a heroic underdog? It's the perfect pairing to get people to cheer you on.

"If you look at this situation we're in, we have the perfect, villainous crime. 'Oh, dear god in heaven, someone's been kidnapped, that poor, poor woman who was sent to help the Marsies!' Or whoever," I dismissed, flicking a hand. "Either way, you've set up the perfect live-action drama. You are capturing peoples' attention. That's great. But you need to *hold* that attention, and hold it in a light that's favorable toward you.

"So, now we need a hero to step into the scene. A 'hero' who will effect a rescue of the kidnappees – staged or otherwise, all it has to do is look and feel real. What we need is someone dashing enough to swoop in and cart the victims to safety," I told my listening captors. "Preferably depositing them on the media's doorstep, rather than the government's, so the government cannot hush up this whole matter.

"And then this hero needs to be both brave enough and eloquent enough to say, 'I, too, am suffering the same plight as my fellow Martians. I, too, long for freedom from government corruption and its oppression of our sovereign rights! *But*, I do *not* agree with what my fellow sufferers have done. We Martians are honorable men and women, and *this* sort of injustice must not be allowed to take place. Our cause is too important!'

"...Or words to that effect, so on and so forth," I finished, shrugging. "The exact speech can be written up later, polished and practiced over and over until our prospective hero gets it right. It *will* need to be practiced, too, because whoever it is will have to be very careful to not let their passion for the cause overwhelm their tongue and have them blurting out the *wrong* things. This is very much a public relations problem at this point, and thus has to be handled very carefully. Luckily for you, I have written more than a few speeches in my day, and I know how to manipulate the media in your favor. *If* you actually *want* the media on your side, that is. Once you have the media, you'll have everyone who watches it."

"So, what, you're expecting to be the first kidnapping victim we set free?" Lieutenant asked me, lifting his kerchief-hidden chin. "We have three more of you. We left the Asian woman alone, so she could call her office and make a lot of noise. Which she's finally doing."

I blinked and frowned at him. "Oh, goodness, no! I need to be on hand up until the very last minute, to make sure all of this gets pulled off smoothly. You see, that's the hidden *fourth* problem. All of this has to be kept so tightly hushed up that not a word of it leaks out. My other three colleagues must *never* know their rescues were staged and not real. If people find out this was faked, that'll taint your cause as well. No, I fully expect to be the last one rescued. That's so I can be on hand with you Marsies to help make sure whoever gets picked to be the Hero of the Free Mars Movement has the wit, the charm, and the acting ability to pull it all off."

"How do we know *you* won't go running to the media, once you're free?" Short Lieutenant countered, her tone skeptical.

I gave her a sardonic look. "Because it would ruin *my* career if it got out that I colluded with my kidnappers? Remember, this *started* as a very real kidnapping...and I'm offering to defraud my own government, in helping you. I'm offering my assistance because I *did* come here with the intention of helping you fix your first problem. You've managed with your second problem, this kidnapping, to convince me just how bad things must be, if you're willing to risk prison time and possibly being shot down by government agents just to get the word out there, but in doing so, you've almost completely shot down your whole cause. Since I did come here to help you, and I've only been inconvenienced a little bit so far, I'm still willing to help you dig your way out of the deeper troubles you're now in.

"I'm not the uncaring villain you're trying to paint me. Work *with* me, and I will help you get your real problems known. All the publicity you can handle, and all the backing from the people. You know I'm right," I added lightly. "Galling as it is, you know I am right. Make up your minds quickly. For one, I really do have to use the bathroom, and for another, it's going to take hours to find the right 'Hero' for your organization. Someone brave enough to show their face – because the people *need* to see who the hero is, so they can better identify with and rally behind them – and someone smart enough not to let their passion torpedo your cause with the wrong kind of speeches."

They looked at each other. Finally, Lieutenant Man sighed. "...You're right. It *is* galling. But you're also right. Those who forget the lessons of the past are doomed to failure, and our cause is too important to be allowed to fail. I'll find you a suitable hero – ladies, escort her to the bathroom. Give the others restroom privileges, too. And something to eat and drink. One at a time, under guard. It'll help our cause if we're not unduly cruel, even if we're currently the 'villains' as she puts it."

"Find me two or three candidates, so we can pick the best representative possible, but not more than three at most, or word will get out," I suggested as he turned to leave. "They should be smart enough to grasp what they'll need to do, they should be charming enough to pull it off, but not too cocky or they'll go too far off the set speech and ruin things. Oh, and they should be relatively handsome or pretty, depending on the gender. It's a sad fact, but they will get all the more attention if they *look* as handsome and heroic as they act. Remember, what you need now is some serious, positive publicity to counteract the negativity of this kidnapping. *Then* we can focus the media on the real troubles plaguing the people of Mars."

"…Right." Turning, he left the room. My two female captors gestured for me to get to my feet. Which I was grateful to do.

***

So. That's how it began. I finally got "rescued" about three weeks later, the last of the four kidnapees. And it took a couple of months for the media storm to die down, and a few more for the real work on reforming Martian government to dig in and start working. At that point, I was sent back home to relax and resume my more local, Earth-bound duties.

About a year and a half after that, I was kidnapped again, this time by an environmental group. I woke up in a wooden hut on an island and my captors were already there, watching me.

Apparently, one of the organization's members had a cousin on Mars who had been involved in the Free Mars Movement – I think it was the first female guard, if I remember right – and she had confessed to her cousin that the rescue and subsequent positive media storm had been a bit more organized than it looked, and that I'd had a role in it. So *this* cousin had the wild-hair idea of pulling off the same stunt, but since she didn't know the exact details of how we'd gotten the incident on Mars to look so real, there was nothing to be done but kidnap *me* and have me teach *her* radical group how to get positive media attention.

And yes, that's pretty much how my third kidnapping went, too, and why it happened. The *fourth* one, however…well, that one went a little differently.

The fourth one took place at my house, in the middle of the night. I woke up as they entered my room, snapped on the bedside light, gave them all a dirty look and said, "Listen, you idiots. If you people *keep* kidnapping me, over and over, *someone* is bound to take notice! Now put your guns away, pull out your notepads, and take down the following instructions:

"You will choose *two* of your people to approach me during the *daylight hours*, like a pair of *normal* guests coming to visit me, and you will *act* like normal guests, coming and going. We will sit down in my living room, we will *discuss* your situation like civilized people, and I will consider giving you the information you need at that time. Got that? *Good.*

"Now take yourselves right back out again and let me get some sleep – and *don't* let anyone see you leaving, either. If you idiots aren't more careful, you're not only going to expose everything to the media and ruin your chances at some positive attention, you'll ruin it for all the *other* groups I've helped...and they will come after *you* for ruining everything! Now go away, and come back in the morning!"

At which point, I snapped out the light and flopped back onto my pillow...and pretty much held my breath until I heard them leave. I'll admit I didn't get much sleep the rest of that night, but they did come back during daylight hours, nice and polite, exactly as I'd ordered. After that point? Well...that's where things started getting a bit legally sticky for me. They couldn't keep kidnapping *me*, after all. The third time had already drawn almost too much media attention for our efforts to survive scrutiny.

I tried very strongly after that to steer my 'visitors' away from kidnappings, because they were getting a bit too predictable...but then they came up with even *crazier* ideas. Like bank robberies and art heists. At times, it's taken every ounce of cleverness I can scrape up to keep them from veering straight toward incurable public relations disasters. I've even taken on staff to help me manage all the different requests I've been getting.

In a way, it's kind of ironic. I spend my free time helping revolutionaries attempt to change the world...but at the same time, I've spawned a revolution *among* the revolutions out there. It's no longer the same business it used to be.

You could even say that I've created a new employment field: The hero industry.

Jean Johnson is a highly praised, multiple-book bestselling author (including the NY Times Bestsellers List), producing both fantasy romance and military science fiction. When she's not busy dodging either plot-bunnies or people who try to pin her solely into one genre or the other, she can be found practicing her evil mad scientist laugh (because it's all about standards, you know) somewhere near Seattle. But don't panic, she's mostly harmless. She can be found at www.JeanJohnson.net.

FLICKA
CAT RAMBO

"Son of a bitch, here they come," Steve said, looking at the SUV coming down the street, gray as the Idaho fall sky above it. "The whole herd." He jostled Roy, hard enough to hurt.

"Cut it out," Roy said. They were putting up signs advertising specials, plastering them with thick wheat glue on the side of the tiny town's only grocery store. Three kilos of veggie burgers, and you got the buns free. Seitan, $4.99 a kilo. And a rarity – milk, actual milk, for the few gourmands in the town.

"The whole herd," Steve repeated. He spat into the gravel, leaving a wet, dust-edged star.

But when the vehicle pulled up before the grocery store, it disgorged only two people. The first was unmodified, a standard issue human in nondescript rancher's clothing.

The other, a slim, teenaged girl, showed modified features: enormous, liquid brown equine eyes; blonde, glossy hair, heavy as the silk thread Roy's mother embroidered with, drawn up in a pony tail and tied with blue ribbon; a long, aquiline nose dominating a face that was, despite the incongruous angles, beautiful. Her skin was sun-burnished bronze. The jeans that clung to her limbs had been tailored to accommodate the tail, golden strands matching her ponytail. Her unshod feet were hooves, fetlocked with gold.

The older man, neatly goateed in salt and pepper, entered the store without paying attention to Steve or Roy. The girl paused to look at them.

"Hey," Roy said, not sure what to say. "Heya, I'm Roy."

Her eyes shifted to regard Steve expectantly.

"Don't ponies talk?" Steve sneered. He turned his back and ripped down a handful of old, tattered signs for gum and bread and Healthy Choice frozen dinners. Two blue magic markers lay like a slashed x across a white paper pad at his feet.

A scarlet tinge crept into the girl's brown cheeks.

"I do talk. I'm Flicka," she said to Roy. She paused a moment longer then wheeled and went into the store.

"Man, that was cold," Roy said.

"She's a freak. No ass or tits, just all hair. That tail makes me sick to my stomach. They're a bunch of freaks." Steve spat again, this time off the porch's side towards the ice-rimmed puddles of the parking lot and the SUV's tires.

Roy grunted, trying to pry the lid off a can of paint.

"I was reading about it in a skin mag. Some look like regular humans. I guess they're the masters or something. Then the rest are modded like fairy ponies. One had this two-colored mane. And most of them had hooves and tails. Waste of air," he added. "Gen-modded freaks and alternative family structures." He spat again.

"More and more people are getting gen-mods."

"It's unnatural. It's against the Lord's will."

Roy let that lapse into silence. He knew better than try to argue Biblical matters with Steve. He also knew Steve was aware of Roy's atheism but chose to let the subject lie, in order to keep hanging out with Roy. There weren't that many boys their age in the town.

The pair came out. The older man had a plastic bag in either hand. The girl carried a hot chocolate and drank from it as he unlocked the truck. The store clerk Ian followed them, carrying bags and helping put them in the car before he returned to Steve and Roy. He was a couple of years younger than they, and treated them with a combination of respect and scorn mixed with a touch of hero-worship.

"Is he her father?" Roy asked Ian.

The boy shook his head. "No, she's his niece, I think. She said her father's name is Blaze."

"One of the horses?"

"Yeah, he's the lead stallion."

"So how's all that work?" Roy asked. "They gen-mod all the kids like that?"

"Yeah. There's some big legal case about how far you can gen-mod your kid, the guy said they're mentioned in it."

The staples crunched in rapid succession into the plastic siding as Steve put up a sign advertising frozen fish sticks at 12.99 a kilo.

"Fucking freaks," he repeated under his breath.

***

After dinner, halfway through their latest book, Roy and his mother debated whether the next should be fiction or nonfiction, but it was Elsa's turn to choose and she opted for a recently released biography of Lincoln.

"Blah, history," Roy said, gagging.

She smiled and patted his shoulder as she rose to put the book away.

He was lucky, he thought, to have the coolest mother in Boomville, a rural town where white supremacists and hippies had settled in an uneasy détente. Elsa had broken away from the former group after a relationship with Chip Starfire, a representative of the latter. Elsa had left Chip in turn as well, and now she and her son, the product of that union, lived at the town's edge.

The study in which they sat was Roy's favorite room: an old but comfortable sofa lined one wall and bookcases the others. Most of the families in

Boomville eschewed television for political reasons, the hippies for its corporate and worldly ties, the survivalists for its constant propaganda and softening influences. It made them an odd demographic. Roy sometimes wondered if there were other little enclaves of non-television states throughout the country, but he suspected they were few and far between.

"Hey, I saw a couple of those new people today," he said.

"The ones that bought the DeMille place?"

"Horsey people. I don't understand all the details, but they're a Neo-family."

"That's what I heard. All the rage on the West Coast. Are you tempted to join them?" she teased. "You always loved horses."

He ignored the question. "They freaked Steve out."

"Because of the gen-mods? Or the Neo-family?"

"Both, but more of the first, I think."

She shrugged. "The Cummings family has always lived strictly by the Bible."

"Ian didn't seem to have any trouble with them."

"Ian was brought up in a commune. They probably seem glamorous to him."

Roy liked looking at his mother, at the straight cut Aryan features, and wondering what about her had appealed to his scruffy father. Her hair fell in glossy, regular blond waves around eyes the faded blue of thrift-store denim. "Is that the voice of experience?"

"Ian and you have grown up in the same backgrounds – no TV, tiny town, little hope of getting out. Don't the new people glitter for you, no matter how strange you find them?"

He remembered the spill of Flicka's mane, the wide brown eyes. "Yes," he admitted. "I'm worried, though. Steve really does hate them, and I guess the rest of the Cummings will too. And the other survivalist families. Grandmom and Grandpop."

Elsa grimaced at the mention of her parents. "Well, they hate everyone," she pointed out.

"True. True. I'm turning in, Mom. Night."

In his bedroom, Roy went to the window and looked out at the pines. Snowflakes drifted down from the sky, benedictive kisses on the landscape. Darkness hovered over the mountains, white-capped shadows hunched against the sky. He turned on his music player and picked up a carving knife and a block of wood as the first meditative cello notes floated out.

He was working on chess pieces made from blistered maple. He figured he would match them with pieces of darker ironwood when ready to complete the set, and then make a board from alternating squares, inlaid in a ruddier wood framework. Although he worked slowly, his chess sets sold well when completed; he was laying away enough money, bit by bit, to pay for college in a year or two. Better a few years late than never.

He carved the knight with Flicka's face, exaggerated eyes, the long nose,

and incorporated the spill of hair, mane-like down the back. She held a wand – a ?
riding crop, he decided at the last minute, and added the details. *tool*?

He smoothed patches with a burr to before using fine-grained sandpaper to
bring out the wood's grain. The watery brown lines across paler beige tangled
along the curve of the figurine's hair and marked the hands like old scars. Wood-
scented dust accumulated on his clothes as he worked.

***

He blocked the remainder of the maple pieces the next morning, then
decided to take a walk in the hour before noon to stretch out the kinks in his
back. He turned towards the DeMille place; he liked to walk Waverly Road to
see what knots or limbs had fallen from the cedars and boxwoods along it.

The newcomers had installed a gate where the access road met the main
road, an airy, gilded plastic conceit with rearing lions on either side. He took his
sketchpad from his jacket pocket and roughed out the lines, thinking they might
be used for his rook.

"Hello," a voice said behind him. Startled, he turned to find Flicka. She
giggled, watching his face. She wore a blue windbreaker and jeans. Her hooves
left round marks in the snow.

"Scared me," he said.

"What are you drawing? Can I look?"

He was reminded of a fawn, of some woodland creature as she drew close
enough to look at the paper. The shy hesitation was born of... innocence, he
thought, and reconsidered as her hand rested on his sleeve, steadying it and
turning the pad towards her.

"The gate! It's really good. Will you draw me?"

"I'd love to," he admitted.

"Here and now?"

So while she posed beneath the gate, lips pursed in an attempt at a sultry
smile that ended up collapsing into giggles, he sketched her.

"Come in and meet everyone, so they can see the pictures." She pulled him
after her.

The recently renovated house smelled of plastic and cleaning solution. The
kitchen was a hubbub of women and children, and the clop of their hooves on the
floor an impromptu drum dance. They exclaimed happily to see him and pressed
food and drink on him.

The pictures were admired, and he was installed at the round table in the
middle of the room, drinking coffee and drawing the baby placed on the table in
front of him. It blinked sleepily at him, its tail tightly braided and tied to a cord
around its waist, up and out of the diaper. Roseate ringlets fell in pink-tinted curls
around its face. Its hooves gleamed like mother of pearl and its eyes were flower
pupilled like a goat's. Roy remembered a cartoon he'd seen long ago, *Fantasia*,
and the centaurs and fauns that had danced in it.

He gave up on getting all the names. Petunia was Flicka's mother, so he tried to keep that straight. The rest were a whirl of Columbine, and Starchild, and Vanilla, and Quickhoof, and Quixote.

A silence came into the room as another man entered, and Roy realized from the beard and broad shoulders this must be Blaze. He rose, putting the pencil and pad out of the baby's reach.

"Pleased to meet you, sir," he began, proffering his hand.

Blaze advanced and took the hand in both of his, holding onto it as he peered into Roy's face.

"One of the local boys," he said. He had a wide, grizzled face, as though it had undergone no modification, but his hair was pulled back, exposing pointed ears. Like the others, he was hooved and tailed. "The Montgomerys are away, looking at a new person who wants to join our herd, or I would introduce you. You will have to come back again another time."

The words were gracious, but the tension in Blaze's shoulders as he glanced at Flicka made Roy feel uneasy. "Another time," he agreed, gathering his drawing materials.

Blaze walked him down to the gate.

"You think me overprotective, perhaps," he said, breaking silence for the first time as they reached the structure.

"No, no. I just came up to say hello, sir."

"I am the stallion," Blaze said. "I protect my wives and the children of those wives. Flicka is my oldest child, but she is still very young."

Message received loud and clear, Roy thought, but he felt obliged to speak up. "This is a small community," he said. "People are used to each other and each other's ways. It'll take a while for them to get used to you. The more sociable you are – at least this is my opinion, sir – but the more sociable you are, the more quickly everyone will acclimate to each other."

Blaze studied him. "Maturely spoken," he said dryly.

But when Roy made an impatient gesture to open the gate, Blaze swung it open and said in apology, "I've angered you, but I don't mean to. I am used to rash young men, and you seem to have a better head on your shoulders than most."

Roy nodded. As he kept down Waverly Road, he could feel Blaze standing beneath the golden arabesques, but when he stooped to pick up a whorled knot of cedar and cast a glance backwards, the other man was gone.

***

Steve called the next day. "Headed into Couer D'Alene to pick up supplies, do you want to go?"

They drove along pine-bristled hills. Steve's foot on the truck's accelerator was heavy. Roy looked out over the vista of hills, watching for eagles.

"How's business?" Steve asked.

"Not bad," Roy said. "Working on a new set right now."

"How much you got built up so far for college?"

"About 10K."

"So a while yet before you hit the magic number. You think about investing some, get a better return?"

"What are you suggesting?"

"I have an idea for a business. On the Internet like yours, but it'll sell stuffed animals."

"Stuffed animals? Like teddy bears?"

"No, no. Taxidermied animals. Squirrels and elk and stuff."

"Do you think there's a market for that kind of thing?"

"Yeah, people want them for their living rooms. They pretend like they shot them."

" So what's the investment?"

Steve leveled a finger at Roy. "You pay for me to take taxidermy lessons over in Couer D'Alene, I take them and start stuffing things and sell them on Ebay."

"How much are the lessons?"

"5K."

"That's a crap-ton of money," Roy said. "Man, I'd need to think about it."

"Yeah, all right."

They drove along in silence.

"I broke up with Ginger," Steve said, looking forward at the road.

"I'm sorry to hear that," Roy said automatically. Ginger and Steve had been an on again, off again couple for eight years through high school and beyond.

"She said this was it, no marriage, then no relationship. She wants to explore other options, she said."

"And how does that make you feel?" Roy's normal strategy when dealing with unexpected emotional confidences was to channel his hippie father.

"I told her if she would just wait a little while longer, I'd make it all up to her. But she said she wants children, she thinks it's the most important experience in a woman's life, and she wants to do it soon."

"She could do that out of wedlock."

"No child of mine is going to be a bastard."

"Technically I'm a bastard."

"Yeah, and look how you turned out." Steve socked him on the shoulder.

"Ow."

In Couer D'Alene, Roy helped load groceries into a cart and then the truck.

"Anywhere you want to go?" Steve asked.

"I want to stop in the bookstore and pick up some stuff for my mom."

Steve rolled his eyes. "All right, I'm going to check out music while you're doing that."

In the bookstore, Steve picked through the volumes with careful patience before buying the biography of Lincoln.

As he paid for them, the door jangled behind him.

"Can I help you, young man?" the clerk asked, staring over Roy's shoulder. Roy turned to see Steve there, hair awry and a bruise on his cheek.

"He's with me," Roy said, and pushed the rest of the money at her before taking Steve's arm to step outside. "Jesus, what happened?" He tilted Steve's chin back to look at the damage, and Steve passively let him manipulate his head.

"Saw a bunch of those horse kids at the music store," he said. "They were bragging on something and I told them to shut it. That girl came over and got in my face, so I told her to fuck off and pushed her. She hit me." He grinned. "Good punch on her."

"Idiot," Roy said.

Blaze came up towards them on the sidewalk, flanked by Flicka and four other teens.

"I believe my daughter has injured you. The gen-mods give her certain advantages in a fight, and she knows better than to strike people."

"Naw, it's okay, Pops," Steve said. He grinned at Flicka, but she stood stone-faced. Roy couldn't catch her eye.

Blaze glanced behind Roy, frowning, and Roy turned.

Mr. Montgomery stood there. He wore stiff new Western clothes, from high-heeled Ropers on his feet to a wide brimmed hat atop his head.

Trying to fit in, maybe, Roy thought.

"What's happening here?" Anger edged Montgomery's voice

"Flicka struck a boy," Blaze said.

Montgomery's gaze was wintry. "Indeed? That's bad, Flicka, very bad. We don't attack humans."

"Yes, sir." Her voice was quiet.

"She was provoked," Roy said.

"And you would be?"

"Roy Allston."

"Don't interfere with another man's family, Mr. Allston. I am this herd's master. And I will decide who was provoked. Let us go."

He turned on his heel and they followed. Blaze looked back, his expression unreadable, and nodded to Roy.

"You think that girl likes me?" Steve asked.

"Which girl?"

"Princess Pony."

"I don't think she likes you at all."

"You just want to get into her pants first. Fucking abomination."

"Make up your mind, man, are you hot for her or is she the next sign of the Apocalypse?" Roy said.

"What I thought was sometimes girls will do that thing, that slapping thing, when they like you. Ginger slaps me all the freaking time. Or she used to, before we broke up."

They pulled in front of the grocery store and Roy helped Steve unload the groceries, but his fingers itched to get at his chess set.

***

He made Montgomery into the king, and used another view of Flicka, this time with eyes downcast and angry, crowned with a spikey-edged crown for the queen. The bishops were Flicka's mother and aunt, and the pawns ten versions of the chubby baby, hair tumbling around its shoulders. It took almost all the maple, only a chunk sized for a single piece or possibly two well-designed ones left over.

The task took him well into the evening, and when his mother urged him to dinner, he shook his head. She'd seen him in similar creative throes before, so she brought a tray up to his room with a grilled cheese sandwich and a soy shake, which sat achieving thermal equilibrium on his desk.

He carved the people of Boomville into the ironwood: his grandparents, crowned and frowning as the king and queen, Chip and Ian as bishops, Steve as a heavy-armed rook. As he picked up each piece, he wondered whether or not to put his own face on it. He stared into the mirror, thinking where to begin, but in the end, each face that emerged under the knife's able flicker was someone else's. Even his mother appeared as a knight, an item in her hand that could have been a box of myrrh, or equally easily, a cheese sandwich.

It was his best set yet. He smiled, thinking of Flicka's reaction. He left the set out, standing in four neat lines on the table, and examined it for flaws while he ate the lukewarm dinner. He fell into bed and exhausted slumber, drained of some force only replenishable in his dreams.

***

The next morning he stowed the pieces away in a slotted case and carried it under one arm to the DeMille place. As he caught sight of the edge of the property and the gaudy gate, he saw sunlight dance and scatter across the snowy ground as it shook.

Steve and Flicka struggled against the opposite side. Steve had the girl by both wrists, pulling her too close against him to kick. She stamped downward, but her hoof skidded off his heavy black boot.

From where Roy stood, they looked like fighting dolls. He couldn't see the expression on Steve's face, blocked out by the fall of golden hair that was the back of Flicka's head.

He ran towards them, picking his way along the icy road, but before he could reach them, he saw a third figure step out from the underbrush. Blaze, pulling at Steve's shoulder, making him release Flicka.

Roy got to the gate just as Steve pushed Blaze away and half turned to Flicka, struggling with the gate. It swung open, knocking the case from his arms, scattering chess pieces like shrapnel. Flicka burst through even as Blaze punched

Steve in the stomach and he doubled over.

Roy fell back, Flicka atop him in a tangle of limbs that, the back of his mind thought, would have been delicious at any other moment. He rolled her aside and made his way to his knees.

Blaze and Steve were fighting in deadly earnest now. The older man's nose dripped blood, and Steve favored an arm. As Roy reached to open the gate, an uppercut from Blaze sent Steve reeling backward, arms windmilling, to thud dully to the ground without moving.

Sobbing, Flicka pulled at Roy from behind, and he turned, awkwardly soothing her, aware of Blaze's eyes from the other side of the gate. He looked up. Blaze turned away to stoop beside Steve and clasp his throat between thumb and forefinger.

"Dead," he said after a moment.

Flicka wailed louder in Roy's arms and he stroked her hair, smelling its floral fragrance. The gate squeaked as Blaze came out.

"I need to call the police. Roy, would you take Flicka up to the house?"

He disentangled her but she insisted on helping him gather the chessmen before they went. It was a lengthy search. By the time the patrol car pulled up, they had found all but one of them, the knight Flicka, vanished in the ice-glazed, thorny tangles of blackberry.

***

That afternoon, Roy took up his last piece of blistered maple and carved a replacement knight.

He gave it a horse's tail, and hooves that supported the slender leg columns, brown striations like veins over the polished surface. It wore a crown that could come on and off, a tiny circle salvaged from the last scraps of black ironwood.

Its face, large-eyed and long-nosed, was recognizably his own.

Cat Rambo lives and writes in the Pacific Northwest. Among the places her work has appeared are *Asimov's*, *Weird Tales*, and Tor.com. Her collection, *Eyes Like Sky and Coal and Moonlight*, was an Endeavor Award finalist in 2010. Find her website at http://www.kittywumpus.net/blog.

SEED

SHANNA GERMAIN

Clark has come with his cherries again. Carrying them in his ungloved hands, their skins touching his skin.

I take them delicately and without flinching, as I have been taught, my bare palms cupped for his offering, his dark red fruits tumbling into my hands. They are too much, too visceral, their blooded curves beckoning my tongue in a way that is not for polite company. Not even polite, paid company.

"Thank you, Clark," I say, now that his cherries are in my hands, and I can look away from them, to his face. He likes it when we address him by first name. Proper address – last, home, first – make his ruddy cheeks go more red and plump, like his cherries. Smind Kaja Meira says this means he is embarrassed or angered. So we must never call him Tupelo Oklahawma Clark, only ever Clark, and we must let him dump his cherries into the bowl of our cupped hands until they overflow, and, if we can help it, we must not show our own embarrassment at their round, sweet scent against our noses.

"My pleasure, Sallie Kaja Arana," he says. The words come off his tongue slow and careful, and I know he has worked hard to memorize my whole name, even if he doesn't have the accents right.

"Just Arana," I say. "If it pleases you."

"It does," he says. And then like always, as if he's tasting my name in his mouth, a sound that makes me shiver and flush. "Arana."

I think he is a pretty man, although I don't know if that's true by his own people's standards. Big-bellied in a way that signifies his fecundity. Pale, barely pinkened skin that shows he spends much time in the common spaces. He wears many layers, his outfit cuts across him in funny places, belts at waist and ankle – but all of that serves to show more of his girth and weight, and perhaps that is the purpose. Still, I like him best of all when he is naked as the rest of us, just his skin and body, no artifices between us.

"Please make yourself at home," I say. Clark is already doing just that, but it's important to follow decorum, to say the thing that we wish for our clients. Even the ones who pay with such high, personal prices as bright red cherries for something we should gladly give away for free. Smind Kaja Meira says this is the way of things, that one person's food is another person's lying with, and we should take what he offers and be grateful.

I prefer it, truly, to our own men, the skinny, boney ones who pay us in

113

monies so that they may eat with us, so they may enter our private kitchenette spaces and feed us our own bits of day-old meat and scavenged berries. The way they watch my mouth chew and swallow, commanding me at their bidding. "Open your mouth," they say. "Let me see your tongue, your teeth. I want to watch you bite this. Now this. Swallow, oh the gods, swallow. Yes." Their bare hands touching my lips, their fingers tasting the secret inner places of my mouth. In exchange for this great and private thing, our own men try to shill us, to never pay in foods but always in the small, plain monies of the worlds, hardly worth a loaf of bread, a piece of dead fish.

Last year, one of the men took advantage of Gardin Kaja Kalliara while in her kitchenette, stuffing her mouth with quail bread until she could take no more, holding her against the table and force-feeding her from his own mouth, pieces chewed by his own teeth even after she'd said no and no again. We girls of Kaja's house do many things in our kitchenettes, things that would embarrass our great mothers if they knew, but to be forced, to eat from the mouth of another? No. Never. Smind Kaja Meira threw the man out, but it was too late. Gardin Kaja Kalliara had eaten her last meal at the hands of a gluttonist, a gorgist, the worst kind of rapist. We mourned her as we should a sister – returning each to our private kitchenettes the hour after her death, grieving for four days and four nights, putting out half our foodstuffs to share with her in a final breadbreak before she left for the aboveworld. But she never came to eat.

I don't care what the dissenters say; Smind Kaja Meira is right to advertise the House of Kaja to the men of Clark's kind, who pay us with what matters to share something freely given. Even if it embarrasses me so that I flush and blush and stammer.

"Make yourself comfortable," I say again to Clark, and there is something soft in my voice, because I mean it all the more after having thought of our own men, and what they want from me, from all of us.

"I will," Clark says. "Thank you."

It is odd to be standing here, just me and Clark in the common space. Usually there are many of us, but food has been scarce of late, and the other girls are out picking berries from the bottom of the hollow or scavenging scraps of meat from the leavings of yesterday's lion-killers.

"The other girls will be here soon." I try to keep the bowl of my hands still, so the cherries don't shift and draw attention to themselves.

"I don't care about the other girls, Arana." Clark has eyes of a color I've never seen before – only once in an elaborately wrapped piece of candy that tasted of mint leaves and winter breath – and each time he looks at me with his pale blue gaze, I don't know where to put my mind.

"I'll just take these to my quarters," I say, lifting the cherries closer to my mouth. So close that I can smell them, their pungent sweetness. The odor makes my mouth water, makes my stomach constrict with want. I cannot control it, and my head ducks slightly, until my lips nearly brush the fruits.

Clark barely notices, begins to untie his shoes, but I realize what I've done.

"Forgive me," I say, my own voice choked. "Forgive me."

He looks up, his head cocked to the side, uncertain, his fingers stilled on their laces. "Arana?" he says. It is all question, one that I cannot answer.

It isn't polite to leave Clark there by himself, without responding, but I have no choice. I can't believe I've done such a thing, brought food to my mouth in the presence of a semi-stranger, a client, an other, in the public place of the great room. The cherries are making me crazy, singing their scent-song to my mouth and belly.

I scurry toward the privacy of my kitchenette, the one place that is mine and mine alone in this whole big house of common rooms, dropping a few cherries along the way, but I don't bend to pick them up. I tell myself I will come back later, properly gloved, and pluck them from the hallway.

I shut the kitchenette door, leaning against it, my breath short and quick. The cherries roll from my fingers into the washbasin. I run cool water over them and over my wrists. I let my forehead drop to the side of the sink and get another whiff of the cherries, their pungent ripe perfume.

Clark is waiting for me back in the common room, probably beginning the slow take-off of his clothing, the way he does, folding the pieces carefully off to the side. I should not eat these cherries, not even one. I should not lick them the way that I am doing, should not be sinking my teeth into this one's stretched skin, letting its insides enter my mouth, fresh and sweet. But I cannot help it. It is done, and the thing is on my tongue and I am chewing and chewing and swallowing.

My body swells and puffs, the way my blood rises sugared and sweet inside me, surging into the heat of my cheeks and the pit of my belly. I try to keep the pleasure down, not let it take over me, but it is hard and I cry out, soft, a mew that echoes around the basin. My hands tighten on the basin, hold on hard while my breath sinks and swims, sinks and swims, and I spit the seed from my teeth into the basin with a clatter.

Clark, I think. Clark has paid me in cherries and now I must leave them here, these beautiful round secret things and I must go and lie with him in the common space. I like to lie with him, as I like to lie with any who come – this is the secret of us, the one we hide so that we can eat. But the cherries. I think I like the cherries, the private place of them breaking open in my teeth, I like that best of all.

***

"Was that good for you, Arana?" Clark asks after and I nod. It is funny how they ask that, men of Clark's kind. Lying with is always good, always pleasurable, for us.

Usually, I like this part too, the after, resting among the pillows and the bodies, feeling everyone return to normal. But today it is, has remained, just the two of us. Something that has never happened before. Lying with is something

115

you do with community, in the community places. But the girls have not come back, and it is just Clark and I here, our breaths quiet, his question breaking the stillness.

He takes my hand in his, and I twine my fingers to his in return. Our hands, our way of touching, this is all we are, this is what we do. Smind Kaja Meira says that other cultures eat together the way we lie with, that they gather in common rooms and feed in front of one another, gorging orgies of food and drink. I would not believe her, but it is Smind Kaja Meira, and she does not lie.

Smind Kaja Meira works hard to prepare us for our clients. First, she chooses us carefully, from the time we are old enough to eat alone, and then we are trained in many things: food care and preparation, together-eating, lips and tongue and swallow skills. Most of us also receive additional trainings: medical, cultural, historical, languages, hunting, defense. I am good with heavy pans and small kitchen knives – sometimes men come to me, not to eat, but to have me throw small, sharp blades into cutting boards they hold in front of their chests, and I never miss – but I have not been trained in culture. Smind Kaja Meira says I do not have the mind for it, and she is probably right. Still, I wonder sometimes, if all she says she knows is true, or if she sometimes makes it up, to help us attempt to understand the worlds.

Clark's flat palm runs up and down my side.

"Why do you never eat what I bring you?" Clark asks. "You always run off with it. Do you not like it?"

Where is Smind Kaja Meira? She should be here to answer questions like these. That is why she is house mistress here at Kaja – her smooth talk, her understanding of what men of Clark's kind really want to hear when they ask things like this. The sun slants sideways through the open spaces, and I think how she should be back from now, how all the girls should be back by now, and I feel the first stirrings of concern on my belly.

I smile at Clark, as I've been taught. Smind Kaja Meira says men of his kind like to know they're good at lying with, just as men of our kind like to know they're good at eating with, the private things we do in our kitchenettes.

"I like it very much," I say. And I mean both the lying with and the cherries.

He smiles back, his face pretty pink like heated salmon, his teeth shimmery as scales. It would not do to admit that I have the desire to lick them. We do not touch mouths during lying with, not ever.

"Then we could do this again," he says. "Without the others?"

Our bodies are melded together, sticky from heat and grunt.

"Many girls, many pleasures is what Kaja offers," I say. "I am sorry my sisters are not here for you today." This is the other thing about Clark's kind of men – they want all of us at once, the more the better. That, Smind Kaja Meira says, is why they like us, why they pay us so well. Because we lie with in groups. She didn't say so, but she gave the impression that Clark's kind always lies with one-on-one or alone. I would like to ask him if this is true, but I do not think it is my place.

Clark rolls me over, so that I'm above him, my hands on his big, doughy belly. He is fuzzy like an animal there, in his upside-down bowl of soft flesh. "The other girls are nice, but I only care for you, Arana," he says. "I only want you."

There are his eyes beneath me, looking up into mine, mint and breath. He reaches up and touches my lip. Just for a moment. And I let him. Just for a moment.

This thing I am feeling does not have words. Not any words that I know of. I do not care to lie with him alone on purpose – I miss the mix and roll of the other girls, of watching their bodies move about Clark and myself – but his fingers are touching the gate to my most private of places, they are softly splitting it, and I am letting him.

The image that comes next is unbidden, shameful. Leading Clark alone, unpaid, back to my kitchenette, opening my mouth to his fingers lifting a cherry, taking the fruit between my teeth. The fruit and his fingers, my teeth and tongue. Showing him the insides of me. I want to hold a cherry up to his mouth, watch his lips open around it, see the skin split and spill fruit onto his tongue. Taste the food as it mingles with his breath.

"Arana?" he says. He shifts beneath me and I pull my mouth from his touch.

"I'm sorry, Clark. That is not possible." I can see from his face, the way it pinkens again, that he thinks I am talking about lying with, but I am talking about this thing I see, this desire that makes my mouth water so much it is hard to taste the words around it.

He starts to say something, but the door to the house opens to a whirr of girls and voices, Smind Kaja Meira's oddly loud among them.

"Careful with her," she says. And there, being laid on the golden pillows, is Alphie Kaja Therese, her pale skin scored with red stripes as though lion-marked, her long blond curls filled with blood. She is young among us, with a laugh like copper bells, but is one of Smind Kaja Meira's favored. I cannot see her face, but I can hear her, small mews of pain and fear rising from her. The girls with care training begin to tend to her, quick and efficient. The others stay back out of the way or scurry down the hallway toward their private spaces.

"What happened?" This is what Clark and I ask at the same time, and in voicing it, it somehow brings us closer together, not in a touching way, but in something else.

Ever the mistress, Smind Kaja Meira's gaze slides to us and her face takes on a calm smoothness. She puts her hands together, back-to-back, in a signal of benediction.

"I am sorry for the disturbance, Clark," she says. "Please forgive me, but one of our girls is injured and we must close the house. Only for a day or two, at most."

He rises with a big push, his weight lifting and leaving a blank space beside me. "I understand," he says. "What can I do?"

There is a brief moment of silence while Smind Kaja Meira considers his offer. She seems about to say something, and then says only, "Nothing, yet. But perhaps in the future. I am grateful for your offer. Now you must go."

I don't see him leave. I am standing and coming around to Alphie Kaja Therese, to the side of her. I am staring at face, at the blood that cuts her skin into pale bits, the teeth that show, pinkened and exposed, where her lips should be.

***

"Who has done this, Smind Kaja Meira?" This is the question we all want an answer to. But for once, the mistress of our house has no answers. Or if she has them, she does not give them to us. We talk rumors about the lack of foodstuffs as of late, the wrath of neighboring houses who dislike Smind Kaja Meira's focus on men of Clark's kind. Some talk rumors about men of Clark's kind, but I do not join in those. Clark's kind of men are confusing, but I don't think they'd do such a thing.

"I know who has done this," says Zeern Kaja Steph. She is a small thing, bird-boned with dark hair and black eyes. She is culture-trained and often tells us tales from her classes with Smind Kaja Meira.

"Who?" we say. "Who?"

She lowers her voice. "Our own men. It is our own men."

"No," we say, and "No," again. But once she says that, as soon as her mouth opens and she puts the words into the world, she cannot take them back. And I cannot stop thinking of them.

The house is still closed, and for this I am glad. I do not want to take our own men back into my kitchenette. I don't want to eat – alone or in private. I don't even want to see Clark, his sweet-bowled belly, his mint eyes.

We are all busy doing what we can. With the doors closed for business, there is little money or foodstuffs crossing our threshold, and so the food-skilled must go gathering for all of us now, a job that is both coveted and feared. They go in groups of three, two for finding foodstuffs, one for protection. There have been no other attacks, but the girls who are foodseers say there is something metallic in the water, something bitter in the late summer grayberries that portend danger on the horizon, and so we are ever watchful.

I am one of the ones who guards the house now, patrolling the common spaces with my small, sharp knives held carefully in my fist, or standing at the door, asking who goes there and what their business is.

The healer-trained care for Alphie Kaja Therese day and night, washing the new blood from her face and hair, slathering her with poultices and herbs and bandages. She refuses to eat, shamed that she must be hand-fed by one of the other girls, right in the middle of the common room, for all to see. We have drawn cloths up around her face to give her some semblance of privacy, but still she says no. To force her would be against all we are and yet if she does not eat, she will die.

Smind Kaja Meira sends me to beg of her to eat. The others have already done so, others with more power of persuasion, more skills in communication. I do not know what I can do that the others cannot. Still, I am made for duty. And so I slide under the white cloths that surround her, sit at her side. I cannot look into her face, the empty space where her lips should be, the way her teeth and gums show through the gap of her mouth. I cannot look at her at all, lest my stomach roll and give way, and for a long time, I am shamed into silence by my own selfishness.

"Please, Alphie Kaja Therese," I say. "You must eat or you will not live."

Her words back are slurred and half-formed. Her tongue, too, was cut. Not from her mouth, but enough so I can hear her testing it, trying out its new shape as she speaks. "Like this?" she says. "Like this?"

"I don't know what you mean." Even though I do. How could I not? She could live, yes, but every day with her private places exposed for all to see. Men of our kind will watch her from the corners of their eyes and mouth-call, children will pantomime a drooling, gaping maw, women will say nothing but will turn their eyes away, in fear and in secret shame that they are suddenly glad again for their full lips, their closed mouths. She will be out of a job, out of a house. She will become two-named.

"Sallie Kaja Arana," she says, and she says it slow and careful, in a way that reminds me of Clark, and I suddenly miss his cherries, pouring from his skin into mine. "Look at me."

I look. It is all I can do. Her golden eyes close so that I can't look into them anymore, and my gaze moves down, toward that gaping place of her mouth. I am violating her even by my looking, and yet she has asked me to, and I must honor her request. A dozen teeth I can see, through the wide gap of healing skin. Her pale pink gums, the way they make half-moons around her teeth to hold them in. The red of her tongue as she speaks.

"Please." She takes me by the wrist, pushes her thumb into my veins with a sharp exhale of breath. My hand falls open, revealing the set of small knives there. "Please," she says. Her eyes open like golden apples, a sweet shine.

"No," I say.

She thinks I mean no to what she is asking. But that is not what I mean.

"Not with knives," I say. "Not with those." Knives are for throwing at men. Men who pay, and who hold cutting boards in front of their vital spaces as game. Men who don't pay and take lips and mouths that are not theirs as sport. Knives, these simple, sharp tools, these are not for Kaja's girls. These are not for us.

I ask the forbidden question: "What are your favorite foodstuffs?"

Silence and silence. I have overstepped, and I feel the pain for it, knives without knives threading my pulse.

Alphie Kaja Therese keeps hold of my wrist for a long time without saying anything. When she pulls me toward her, I lean in, my ear against her exposed places as she whispers her list.

***

119

I have no way to get a hold of Clark, and so I must find the foodstuffs on my own, the herbs too. I go out alone, against all rules, because what Alphie Kaja Therese asks is both private and forbidden. I carry my knives in my fist and my heart in my mouth, and I gather what is needed. I occasionally see groups of girls – two and one, scrounging and gathering – but they are easy to avoid. I see men of our own kind, too, alone mostly. I expect to be scared of them, or angered about Alphie Kaja Therese. But my knives stay in my palms and I find I am mostly tired from what I am about to do.

Alphie Kaja Therese deserves a feast, a private thing she makes alone and eats alone, in the privacy of her kitchenette. Instead, I gather what little of her list I am able to find. Tomatoes bought off a pathside vendor for the last of my monies, dug asparagus sprouts, mushrooms from beneath the moonwise tree. The herbs must be bought, and I have nothing but Clark's remaining cherries to trade. I take them, gloved, as I should, to the apothek and hope she will give me two things in return: the herbs I need and silence. In the end, she does, but there is the understanding that I am still in her debt. I have promised her the next food to come into my hands from Clark, whatever it might be. Of course, I have not seen him since that night, so I can only hope he will return, that he has not found another house to take him in.

I prepare the food carefully, small container and gentle movements, and carry it to Alphie Kaja Therese in the midst of day, when most are out gathering and patrolling. I slip beneath the cloths and sit at her side. She is sitting up, reading from a book of philosophies, which surprises me for some reason. Perhaps it is because she looks so healthy and well, except for the red wound that dominates her face.

"Sallie Kaja Arana," she says. And although her lips are healing and her tongue is healing, she still says my name funny and I still cannot look at her mouth. "Where have you been?"

"I'm sorry I took so long," I say.

"I've just missed you," she says.

"I brought what you asked." I put the food container on the cushion next to her. "I will go so you can partake in privacy, as you should."

She puts her hand to my wrist, a pale fluttery thing. "I cannnot," she says. "Smind Kaja Meira says I am to be found a home in Kyotti. I shall be Alphie Kyotti Therese."

"Kyotti? The call house?" A shudder ripples through me. I want to suppress it, that and the sound of my voice, but both come through, rise into me. Smind Kaja Meira has told us of this place, where girls dance, their lips held open with metal bars and bits of wire. Where the two-mouthed open, gaping and aching, in time to music. I did not believe Smind Kaja Meira, but now I know it must be true. "No."

"Oh, yes. Smind Kaja Meira says she has lined it up." Her speech is much faster now, truer. "I shall lie on a pillow all day and they will pay to see my mouth, even as I sit. And I shall have my own kitchenette and no one shall ever make me feed them again." Her voice has taken on a far-away sound, low and oddly off-key and she isn't looking at me.

"Alphie Kaja Therese, you can't." Even as I say it, I know she can. She asked for death, and I have given her the chance to make that happen. Now she has asked for a second life, and Smind Kaja Meira has given her the chance to make that happen.

"Please do not tell Smind Kaja Meira," she says. "I did not tell her I asked for a last meal."

I nod – it is as much promise as my mouth will allow – and take the food away with me, dumping it into the waste of my kitchenette. The red-green juice of tomatoes and herbs, the fresh, dead scent of it as it drains away.

***

I am not the one who finds Alphie Kaja Therese, and I am ashamed for how glad I am of that. It is one of the other girls, scavenging, who comes upon her, face-up, floating along the moonstream. Cut with a hundred knives. Or by a hundred men. Or by one knife and a hundred cuts.

"It is our men," say the girls. Or they say other things. That it was Clark's kind of men. That she had taken her own life. I throw my knives against the walls of my kitchenette. Again. Again. Until my hands tingle and my tongue is dried to the insides of my mouth.

Smind Kaja Meira calls me to her private kitchenette. I have never been before, and I wait outside, unsure whether to knock or stand silent. Finally, she comes to the door on her own, as if she had known I was there.

"Come in," she says.

Her space smells of herbs and mushrooms and a clean that I cannot name. I avert my eyes from her private things, the utensils and fruits, and keep watch on my own belly, the pale skin of it bowing in and out as I listen. Even so, from the corner of my eye, I see her own knives glitter, sharp and silent, as she peels the soft golden skin from a hand-held pear, a hundred small, sharp cuts.

"I am sorry for our loss," I say, just to say something.

"As am I." Smind Kaja Meira stands, leaning her hip to her counter. Her movements are casual, at ease, as though she is alone here and unashamed. "But I have need of you now. Will you take Alphie Kaja Therese's place in the ranks?"

It is a question, but not a question at all. There is no need for me to even answer, beyond a formality, or to ask what that entails. I am for serving, and until she says otherwise, I am for serving Smind Kaja Meira. There is no other way to be.

"Of course," I say.

"You will find her murderer – it is our own men, I swear of it – and you will cut their lips out. Yes?"

Again, there is only one answer for a question from Smind Kaja Meira. Besides, it is what I want to do anyway. What my knives are for. Cutting. And

121

revenge.

"Yes."

"And you will not speak of that again," she says. "No one is to know your role."

And no one does, not even as I track down the men who say they did not kill our sister, even as I take their lips and tongue so they may not plead their false innocence again.

***

As soon as the house re-opens, Clark returns. He is one of the first. I am on door duty, and so it is easy to see him. He wears his usual attire, although the belt cuts less deeply and his top hangs over him with more movement, as though he is less able to fill it than he was once. Two peaches nestle in his big palm. Their soft curves make my mouth ache and water.

In normal times, we would all be in our kitchenettes, making half of our food for Alphie Kaja Therese, helping her trip to the aboveworld. But these are not normal times. We are reopening, and I do not know if I am glad or anguished to see Clark standing at the door.

"Who goes there and what is your business with the House of Kaja?" I ask through the door, even though I can see it is him, Clark, the man I once thought of feeding from my own mouth. The very thought of it makes my cheeks heat with shame and want.

"I'm Clark," he says. "Don't you know me?"

His forehead wrinkles into waves and I don't need Smind Kaja Meira or anyone to tell me this means he has been made sad by what I have said. His face rises to mine, that mint-candy gaze, and I don't know where to put my stomach, this quieting in my belly.

"I know you," I say.

His face changes and pinkens, his lips open in a soft smile that shows me his shiny teeth. Then it slips away, into the opposite shape.

"I heard about your..." He stumbles over the word. "...Sister. I'm sorry. She deserved better."

"She did."

We are quiet a long time, him on one side of the door with his peaches, me on the other side of the door with my knives.

"I brought you something," Clark says. "You don't have to be with me. You can have it."

He holds the fruit out and when he smiles, he smiles big and full so that I can see his teeth. This is what Smind Kaja Meira wants for us. Men of Clark's kind and not men of our own.

I step outside the door, my feet on the outside ground for the first time in weeks. The gate shuts behind me with a clang.

Clark offers me one of his peaches, and I take it, skin on skin on skin, his hand to my hand. It is heavy and fuzzed, like the curve of his belly. With my knife, I cut a slice clean from the peach, and I think of skin falling open. I think of lips cut away, and I think of the work my hands will do, have done.

The juice runs down my wrist, to the elbow. A sticky trail.

There is no circus, I think, and I don't know where that thought came from. I do not like it, I do not want it, but now it is out, and I cannot take it back or let it go. It may have been our men who maimed Alphie Kaja Therese, but I know it was not our men who killed her. I think of Smind Kaja Meira's convictions, of her small paring knife and its perfect skin-slice. I think of my promise, how I am to cut the lips from those who killed my sister. I think I will find pleasure in it.

But first, there is Clark and his peaches.

"Eat with me," I say.

Clark dips his head at my request. He knows no hesitation. He knows not what I ask. And yet, he bows his head, the back of his neck pale and soft. His lips brush the sticky sweet skins of fruit and of me, and then he takes the soft peels of us into his mouth.

Shanna Germain is a plucker of cherries, a juicer of peaches and a sucker for pretty words. Her stories, essays and poems have appeared in places like *Absinthe Literary Review, Best American Erotica, Hint Fiction, Pank Magazine, Storyglossia, The Little Death of Crossed Genres* and more. Visit her in her own little world at www.shannagermain.com.

Scrapheap Angel
RJ Astruc & Deirdre M. Murphy

The first paperclip is mine.

I give it to Akash during our 10:15 RMB – Regulation Mandated Break. He's at the water cooler, gulping from a plastic cup, his eyes buggy from screen-glare. Patches of sweat darken the underarms of his kurta, because the air-con's broken down (again) and no one in accounting will tell us the cost-code for mechanical repair.

He looks pretty miserable, even though he's only been at work for five hours – two less than me. But then I grew up without luxuries like air-con, so the heat of Kashal City doesn't bother me so much. City-born guys like Akash can't handle it, though: they wilt as soon as the thermometer rolls over forty.

I come 'round beside him, take a cup, and fill it from the cooler. The little filter makes a peep noise when it decides I've had enough.

"Hi," says Akash.

At first I don't realise he's spoken to me. I mean I realise but I don't quite *parse* it, because no one talks at work. We all know each other's names, of course – we see them on our call sheets and on the stats graph – but we don't make casual chit-chat like you see employees do on television. It's not that we're unfriendly; it just seems like a waste of energy.

Akash is looking at me now, though, so I can't *not* say Hi.

"Hi."

"How's your day been, madam," says Akash. "I trust you are well."

It sounds like he's reading from a script, and then I realise he *is* – it's Casual Opening 45, which we normally we use for virtual reception desks. I grin; I can't help myself.

"Indeed sir. Could I interest you perhaps in an upgrade to a better office?" I say, in my Phone Voice. "One with a maintenance department?"

"Thank you madam," says Akash. "Please authorise my transaction."

I make the chirping sound that the credit-checker does while it's processing, and mime passing my swipe card across the autoteller. I don't have a swipe card though, just a paperclip I've been fiddling with all morning, bending and unbending it until now it's shapeless and seconds from breaking apart.

Akash is about to speak, but something dark comes into his face when he sees the paperclip.

"Ah, god, Claire," he says, sagging.

124

"Akash?"

He takes the paperclip from my hands and holds it in his palm. His lips are moving at the corners, like he's struggling to hold something in or maybe spit something out. It's awful to watch him. Like he's been broken, irreversibly, and I *don't even know why.*

"Akash? Akash? Are you okay?" I ask, but he's already walking away.

***

It's a nice view from up here. Contact Centre 98 is on the hundred and seventy-first floor of the Tzim Complex. You look out the window and you can see clouds: the top of our tower rises above them like a mountain peak. The elevator ride each morning takes two minutes. Some of the girls on my usual shift use the time to finish doing their make-up, checking their reflection in the shiny metal door.

I sit in G desk, which is formally known as Contact Centre 98. There are always ten other people on at G, although I don't see the same people every day – it depends on what shifts we've been rostered to. Akash's shift usually starts a few hours before I leave and finishes a few hours before I get back.

I have to say that before the paper clip incident, I hadn't really noticed Akash. He was just another face on the G: at once familiar and at the same time utterly, utterly foreign. I'd seen him every day for *years* but I couldn't have told you if he was married, if he had children, if he came from a rich family or a poor one like mine.

But after that day I start to notice him.

At first it's because I feel sorry for him. The heat isn't getting any less – we're in the middle of summer, and in summer in Kashal City you can cook on the pavement. Kids have to go running inside before they burn the soles of their feet. Despite our long hours indoors, poor city-boy Akash is starting to get sunburn on the rims of his ears and his nose.

One afternoon I catch Akash playing with paperclips. He's clicking them together as he talks, his pale fingers moving quick like a woman braiding her hair. I crane over and see there's a nest of them building on top of his desk. He's twisted and tweaked them into strange shapes, and he's added some other things – parts of a copier, maybe?

I can't work out what he's doing – but I do know that if those *are* parts of a copier, stolen parts of a copier, Akash is going to be in serious trouble.

We have a RMB together from 3:10PM to 3:25PM, so I get a chance to ask him about it. I don't know how to start the conversation, but as we're alone in the break room for a moment, I figure I can be blunt. "Those things in with the paperclips," I ask, as he's looking through the cupboards. "You didn't steal them, did you?"

He laughs. "Of course not. They were in the bin."

The bin is where they put the stuff that they can't sell to recyclers or send to the free dump. Employees can take what they want, 'cause it saves having to pay disposal costs.

Relieved, I nod. But I still can't help wondering if his sudden paperclip obsession is somehow my fault. "Did I upset you that day?" I ask. "I'm sorry if I did. I didn't mean to."

"No. I'm not upset. Just…"

Akash frowns. He's looking at a picture on the wall – it's one of the posters our supervisors put up every few months about the dangers of going out in the city alone.

"Just what?" I prompt.

"Have you ever thought of getting out of here?"

"What? Quitting my job?" I shake my head. "No. Never."

"Really never? Not even when you've had to use Casual Opening 20 on sixty callers in a row? When you're starting to feel like you might as well be a robot?"

I grimace. "Okay. Sometimes. But then I remind myself how great it is here. We get free meals, and free hospital services, and subsidised rent. My cousin works for Jupiter Monitoring, and they have to buy their food from a cafeteria. *And* she has a bad back from her desk chair. *And* they only get a three minute RMB every three hours, which is probably not even legal–"

"Claire," says Akash. He sounds tired, and maybe also a little bit bored. "I think there's more to life than a fifteen minute RMB."

That makes me angry. I'm not often angry, and in truth I'm only angry *now* because he's right.

***

I went to Kashal City because Kashal City has Opportunities. You want a job, you want to make big international dollar-credits, you go to Kashal City. Kashal City has vid-theatres, black museums, and the night life is legendary. Politicians, ambassadors, Bollywood stars, all the big names... they come here to party.

But you need cash to live large in Kashal City, and I used up all mine surviving until I got this job. Most of my pay still goes towards paying off my old debts: to my school, my landlord, my bank, and the money I send home to my parents each month. And I don't have much time, either. I take whatever hours my supervisors can give me, no matter how erratic. It means I'm tired all the time, but you've got to survive, don't you?

I've heard some people say that making us work like this is *taking advantage*. But I don't think that's true. A corporation has got to turn a profit, doesn't it? And it's not as if we don't get paid a fair amount. And we get lots of benefits.

I've always wanted to travel, to really see the world, but I do think that I'm happy here, too. After all, I'm much better off, and my family back home is much better off too.

And I don't like to complain.

***

Akash is building something out of twisted paperclips and broken bits of computers and worn-out printer parts.

It's getting bigger.

After a month it's big enough to attract attention. Our supervisors start coming by just to look at it. Even one of our third tier bosses has been in. I suspect they want to get rid of it... but apparently it's good for attendance. People have started turning up for their shift a half hour early, just so they can watch him build while they work.

Akash won't talk about the *thing* when our supervisors are around. But he takes questions when they're not, and the phones are slow. Everyone wants to know if it's a statue – an angel, maybe, or some kind of bird? But Akash says it isn't. "It's not art," he says. "It's a dream."

One day one of the girls on D desk asked him if it was Shiva. Akash laughed at that. "No, not Shiva," he told her. "These parts are done with that part of the cycle."

"Then–"

"And not any other god, either," he added quickly, looking pointedly over her shoulder. A supervisor had just gotten off the elevator. We all rushed back to our own desks. Akash tapped his phone, though there was no light to indicate an incoming call, and started Casual Opening 20.

When the supervisor came toward his desk, Akash stopped mid-word and then said, "I am very sorry, madam, you have a wrong number. Yes, I assure you, we do not make pizza here. Have a nice day."

The supervisor walked past without comment.

When she was gone, Akash said, to no one in particular, "Dreams are important. Don't forget that."

Akash has started talking like that a lot. In a mad way, I mean. It reminds me of the poor mad men who sit about outside Kashal City Station with their begging bowls out, babbling on about gods.

But at least he does his job well, even if he's always fiddling with stuff while he's on the phone.

***

The D desk girl, the one who asked about Shiva, is the first to bring something bright for her desk. It's just flowers, but people smile when they see them. Then other people start decorating their desks, too. A man from accounting brings in a tall narrow bookshelf and a collection of tiny airplanes. Someone else has tiny dolls.

127

One of the girls from G desk brings in a bare branch. As she takes her calls she fills her hands with bright origami paper, making crane after crane, and hanging each one neatly on the branch.

As Akash's 'dream' grows, he starts spending more time on it. It doesn't matter much at first, because he's good on the phones – he's quicker than even me to pick up the calls as they come through. But then he gets distracted by this tweak of metal or this paper attachment, and he misses the calls. We have to scrabble to cover him; and our productivity stats start dropping.

We don't *want* to get angry at Akash. We all like him by this point. We like the way he's managed to make our workplace feel somehow *fun,* as well as productive. But it's hard enough to keep up with all the calls with everyone working: we can't do our jobs *and* his at the same time.

On our shared RMB – I admit I've started taking my breaks with him on purpose – I tell him about the stats.

"We're not looking good," I say. "You're pulling us down."

He blinks at me. As if for a moment he doesn't even know what I'm talking about. "We're still making our targets, Claire," he says. He sounds almost flippant, as if the stats don't matter to him at all.

"That's not the point. We're doing *your* work. We're really struggling..."

But he's not even looking at me anymore. He's looking back toward G desk, and his sculpture of wires and circuit boards.

Longingly.

I throw up my hands. "Well, don't let me keep you from it," I say sarcastically.

"Don't you have anything you want out of life?" Akash asks. "Don't you have a goal, a vision, something that's bigger than–"

"Oh shut up," I say, and I go back to the phones, even though I have three RMB minutes left.

***

Every six months we have a stats meeting. That's when the big boss comes in to tell us if we've achieved our targets, and what our new targets are. Contact Centre 98 usually reaches its targets – we're not like Contact Centre 60 or Reception 04.

This time we're even *more* determined than usual to be the best, to prove to our supervisors that our decorations improved productivity. Akash might be a lost cause at this point, too busy poking about on his project to pay the phones any mind, but the rest of us have picked up speed. Since my talk with Akash, our stats have pulled out of their nosedive and are steadily rising.

The personalisation of our desks has made us feel like more of a team, too. I figure it's because we know more about each other. We're not just G desk any more. We're Adit-the-plane-guy, and Jamilla-with-the-dolls, and Yuki-the-origami-girl, and Melanie, who likes old records and black and white movies, and so on. I'm Claire, Claire-with-the-travel-bug. My desk is covered with pictures of places I dream of seeing – theatre ads and pictures cut out of travel magazines.

We go into the meeting room and sit down, all of the workers of the hundred and seventy-first floor, not just G desk. A supervisor starts things with Casual Opening No. 17. The meeting goes forward, each supervisor taking a turn, and for the first time I realize it's a standard script, like our phone conversations. I watch as most of the workers nod as if they were hearing something new or inspiring. I realize these meetings are the closest thing to drama most of us ever see.

The big boss arrives right on cue, to go over the productivity numbers, and hand out the coveted Productivity Award. She starts with Formal Opening No. 12. As I listen, I realize her speech is just as scripted as the supervisor's. First, she talks about problems some teams are having, and how they should fix them. She doesn't name the groups, but you can see who it is in people's faces.

We sit and listen, politely applauding once the boss gets to the groups whose productivity is worth naming. I start fiddling when she gets to the final two. Did we make it to first? I know if Akash had been pulling his weight, we'd have made it for sure.

D desk is allowed to take a bow, so I know we made it. But first we applaud politely for D desk.

Then it's our moment. The boss smiles, flashing white teeth. "And our top producers this period, G desk, who will have the right to take 20 minute RMBs on Mondays and Fridays for this six-month, so long as they continue to exceed quota".

I realize I'm grinning a little, and try to smooth my face into a professional expression as I stand up. The polite applause starts. Then laughter booms from the back of the room. It's a strange, rough sound, and it takes me a minute to realize it's Akash. He walks forward, a too-large coat over his shoulders, hanging down to his knees. He is moving smoothly, confidently. He looks different, somehow. He looks – fine.

The boss shifts to a different script. "What's the meaning of this?"

Akash strides forward to stand by the huge windows at the front of the room. "There's more to life than RMBs!" He snaps the shades upward, and sunlight pours in.

"What?" The supervisor is confused.

He looks at her sadly, then turns to us. "You should all remember that there's more to life than RMBs. It's important."

The boss frowns at him. "You're out of order–" She stops, because he's dropped the coat to the ground. He's wearing his sculpture, a gleaming patchwork robe that covers him neck to shoes.

He turns and gestures wildly, the structure on his back smashing into one of the huge, reinforced windows, which shatters like a car's windshield, a huge star radiating out from the point of impact. As if nothing had happened, he repeats,

129

"Dreams are important!"

Our jaws drop open and he laughs, flexing his fingers to show glittering edges, which he pokes through the edges of the glass, slicing through the plastic holding the shards of glass together. The remains of the window hang limply from the frame, and he sits down..

He looks at us from his precarious seat, and I feel like he's staring directly into my eyes. "When I say dreams are important, you all just look at me."

The big boss gapes at him.

Akash nods to her. "Like that. So, instead, I'm going to show you." He spreads his arms and leans outward. A glittering collage of paperclips and miscellaneous parts fills the space between his arms and his body, and there's an old calculator in his hand.

Their eyes wide, the boss and the supervisor step toward him. But before they can grab him, Akash pushes a button on the calculator and with a wiggle of his hips he slides out of the window.

We all rush to the windows, G desk first, being already on our feet, but everyone follows, even Contact Centre 60 and Reception 04. I suppose we are all imagining we will see a distant spot of red on the ground, though logically I know we're too high to see something the size of a person down that far.

But as we reach the window, Akash rises in the air and flies by the windows, grinning at us from about 20 feet away. His lips move, but the noise of his machine and the wind drowns out his words. Then he turns and soars toward the sun, and we lose sight of him in the glare.

***

Our supervisors gave us one day to remove all extraneous objects – that's how they put it – from our work areas. They're trying to get things back to normal, as if Akash never lived here, never turned their cast-offs into a flying machine.

If you came into our office, you'd think that we weren't any different from any other Contact Centre. But I see the change in people's eyes, in the way they look out the windows. The accounting department finally got the air-con fixed, and no one cares. We open the windows anyway. Yuki folded one last crane and gave it to me before handing in her resignation. And Melanie left to work in Bollywood.

Me? Well, security's still important. But by scrimping and saving, I've managed to build up a little money. And Kashal City is calling. Whatever is going on in the streets can't be as dangerous as diving off the hundred and seventy-first floor dressed like a scrap-heap angel.

I may not be able to fly, but I think it's time I started to live a little.

RJ Astruc has appeared in *Strange Horizons, Abyss & Apex, Midnight Echo* and like a bajillion other magazines. Her latest books are *Harmonica + Gig* (science fiction) and *A Festival of Skeletons* (fantasy). You can read her out of copyright fiction online at www.rachelastruc.com.

Deirdre Murphy grew up reading mythology and speculative fiction. Her love of the far, strange places of the imagination influences her creative work. She has stories and poetry in venues including *MZB's Fantasy Magazine, Crossed Genres, With Painted Words, The Best of FridayFlash Volume One, Magicking in Traffic* and the Torn World anthology *Family Ties & Torn Skies.* She is one of the primary creators of Torn World, a shared science fantasy world that includes fiction, poetry, art, and worldbuilding at www.tornworld.net.

You can find her musings about life, creativity, and publishing at wylddandelyon.livejournal.com.

The Dragon's Bargain
C. A. Young

Tylat cradled a cup of warm wine in his hand and nestled more deeply into his cloak. The days spent traveling with the caravan had worn on them all, and the damp evening chill had an unpleasant way of sinking into his bones. The sky was full-dark now save for the eerie aurora that hung around the dragon's peak, and the caravan's central fire blotted out the rocky path that passed for a main road this far into the mountains.

"The road is narrow enough that we'll be on foot tomorrow," Cathe said as she joined him at the fire. Her weapons as well as her smile glinted in the firelight, and Tylat gave her a polite nod in return. Take away the royal crest on her armor or the gem studded hilt of her sword and he might have mistaken her for any young soldier instead of the Farwellan princess.

"I suppose they'll keep camp here and send us up with a guard or two each," Tylat ventured, then turned to Alair who sat a bit further away. He was barely a boy, fifteen at most if his smooth cheeks were anything to judge by. "What do you think?"

Alair's gaze didn't leave the fire. "I think they'll only send guards because they think we'll run away."

"That is what you Abroni royals do, isn't it? Run?" Cathe grinned at the boy and refilled her cup. Apparently her appearance wasn't the only thing she had in common with the soldiers of Farwall.

"When it's expeditious, yes. Other times we crush our enemies," Alair said, sharp enough that Tylat had trouble stifling a smile of his own. The boy was fierce in his pride if nothing else. "And what do you think of all of this?"

"Besides the matter of my tent being richly appointed more for my elder brother Mithat's return trip than it is for me?" Tylat scratched his chin and tilted his head to the side as if to ponder. "I think that if I were the sort of dragon who would accept second-born royals in exchange for their elder siblings I'd take advantage of the opportunity to eat six heirs instead of three."

Cathe barked out a laugh and clapped Tylat on the shoulder. Alair's expression, though, crumpled. Tylat wondered how much of the boy's confidence had depended on believing that his sacrifice was somehow meaningful. Considering that the other ransom the dragon had been prepared to accept was the entirety each nation's treasury, Tylat could sympathize.

Without a word he stood, refilled Alair's cup with the last of the wine, and excused himself to his tent.

***

In the morning Galen, the caravan leader, confirmed that the camp would hold position and send only the few of them ahead on foot. Tylat tried to take his breakfast alone in his tent, but between various members of his guard and the caravan coming in to brief him on various logistics and the camp chaplain's attempts to counsel him on his impending doom, he despaired of having any peace at all prior to his final one.

Eventually he shooed off even his own servants and sat down to drink what was left of his (now lukewarm) tea. No sooner had he raised the cup to his lips when a wiry messenger in Farwellan livery was escorted in.

"Oh good. Another interruption."

"I apologize, Highness," the young woman said and bowed low. "Her Highness the Princess Cathe ordered me to give you this." She passed him a battered scrap of paper, folded over twice and sealed.

Tylat cracked the wax in half and read the single line written there:

"I have a plan."

"Tell your princess to come to me before we depart," Tylat said and waved the messenger away. When she was gone, he dropped the note in his lantern and let it burn to ash. When Cathe pushed back the tent flap a few minutes later, dressed in full armor save for the helmet she carried under one arm, Tylat did not bother to stand.

"Is there some strange Farwellan custom that forbids a peaceful breakfast for the condemned, or is this just a fortunate coincidence?"

"The boy tried to escape after you retired last night. Now that you've told him our efforts could be in vain he's afraid, and he doesn't want to die."

"Of course he doesn't want to die." Irritated, Tylat poured out the rest of his tea. "And it's not my fault that we're trapped in a bad bargain."

"Well, you're not exactly improving matters."

Tylat gave Cathe a bemused smile. "Oh, of course. When three nations' armies are deemed insufficient against a single foe, I often decide to take matters into my own hands. What are you suggesting? That I slay the dragon for the benefit of some brat who doesn't have the honor to do his duty? I see now why Farwall's military is so successful. You're insane."

"I prefer to think of it as knowing my enemy," Cathe said. She put her helmet down on a nearby couch and produced a bundle of papers from her pack. "Tell me, Tylat, what do you think would happen to our siblings if the dragon observed three full armies marching on it?"

He considered the question. "Dragons are legalistic when it serves their purposes. A frontal assault would constitute a breach of covenant."

"Exactly. It isn't an issue of force. The problem is that sending the armies is simply the most expensive way for each nation to fail to get what it wants."

133

"Whereas paying the dragon is the most expensive path to success, and exchanging potentially troublesome lesser heirs is the most convenient of the three options on the table," Tylat conceded. "What I fail to understand is what benefit the dragon gets out of such a deal."

"You said it yourself last night. Six heirs to eat instead of three? The whole island is already in uproar. That would be a catastrophe."

"So the whole object is to toy with us?"

"What else? If the dragon can steal three royal heirs from three separate capitals in the same night, it could certainly have plucked us up as well if it had wanted us," Cathe said, and sat down next to her helmet. The wood of the couch creaked under the weight of her armor. "It could have taken anyone. If the beast wants material gain, it needs only to take what it likes. The dragon is more like a cat with a field mouse. Who and what it eats is less important than the game."

"But that returns us to our original problem. There are only three of us, and the dragon is powerful enough that we're here purely as an amusement. I can't dispute the logic of why fighting back against this thing is good, but I'm mystified as to how we could possibly accomplish it."

Cathe handed Tylat the papers. "I see your tutors have led you to expect them to teach you everything you need to know. Fortunately, mine did not."

He untied the bundle and shuffled through the papers. Rough drawings of dragons with lurid red organs were scrawled across pages, as were folk tales with notes in the margins, and what looked like an ancient battlefield account.

Tylat handed it back. "Surely you don't expect me to believe you compiled all this."

"I don't expect you to believe anything except that I refuse to go into an enemy's house without knowing him. And with these, I think I know how we might use the element of surprise to our advantage. Can you imagine the honors we'll have when all six of us return instead of just our elder siblings?"

"I can imagine that the tents might be a bit more crowded," he joked, "but I'm intrigued by the possibility."

"Good. Then I will tell you what I told Alair, which is that the family sword I'm carrying is both ancient and carries a great enchantment. I believe that I can, given the element of surprise, use that enchantment to kill the dragon, but that you'll need to trust me. Let me go in first, when the time comes. Let Alair go second. We'll meet in the dragon's chamber and celebrate our victory there."

"And if I arrive in the chamber and discover a perfectly contented dragon waiting to feast on my entrails?" Tylat said as he watched Cathe rise and gather her things.

"Well, then I suppose we're reduced to our original plan after all," she replied, and left him to consider the possibilities.

***

The hike from the caravan camp to the dragon's mountain fortress was rough going. Dead scrub blocked the path and had to be cut away, and the rotten roots left the ground loose and hard to traverse. Alair in particular struggled, as the Abroni guard had tied his hands and refused to unbind him for fear he'd try and escape a second time. The ground grew more barren the nearer to the peak they came, and the air changed too as they ascended into the haze that wreathed the mountain's peak. Tylat covered his face against the miasma of carrion and sulfur stink.

They arrived at the dragon's massive stair just before sunset. The contours of the scorched stone were hard to make out in the failing light, but lanterns burned along the path and marked the way to a pair of great metal doors set into the mountainside.

Cathe turned and faced the guards. "We will go one at a time to ensure the dragon's honesty. When my brother Corin arrives here, send Alair and wait for his sister. Tylat shall go last. If our siblings do not appear you'll know that the dragon has defaulted on its bargain, and to return to camp and send the message to gather the armies."

One of the Farwellan guards stepped forward as if to accompany her, but Cathe warned him away with a dark look and a hand on the grip of her sword.

Tylat watched her ascend into the haze and only just saw her vanish into the great doors. When she was gone, he sat down beside Alair.

"You shouldn't have run away," he said quietly.

Alair's mouth twisted like he'd bitten down on something rotten. "I hope the dragon makes you watch while it rips your entrails from your body," he said, and spat at Tylat's face.

With a slow swipe of his sleeve, Tylat wiped the spittle away and stood. "Abrona had better hope I don't live to remember you said that."

***

Less than an hour later, Corin emerged. Filthy and naked, he burst from the fortress and stumbled down the mountain stair nearly at a dead run. Tylat watched the Farwellan soldiers wrap the Crown Prince of Farwall in their cloaks with such interest that he nearly missed it when one of the Abroni guards brought Alair to his feet and began to haul him bodily up the stair.

"I'll go under my own power or not at all!" the boy shouted, but the soldier ignored him. The other guard from Abrona turned away, and Tylat thought he saw a trace of shame in the soldier's expression. Whether that was at his prince's behavior or the fact that they were feeding a boy to a dragon Tylat couldn't be certain.

When the crown princess arrived, much quicker than Corin had, Tylat didn't bother to wait for her to arrive among her guards before he began his walk up the now-dark stair. Instead, he fixed his eyes on what little he could see of the fortress and followed the lanterns. He remembered the sickly glow he'd watched the night before from camp, and knowing he was within it now was oddly satisfying. What a pity that Mithat had always been less inclined to wonder at the world. Yet another thing his brother would appreciate less, he supposed.

The heavy black doors parted inward with a groan as he approached. They opened just wide enough for him to pass. A hot burst of rancid air hit him, and he clutched at the cloth that already covered his nose and mouth and tried not to gag as he entered.

Inside, a pair of hulking guards stood posted on either side of the doors. They paid Tylat no attention as he got his bearings and let his eyes adjust to the brighter interior of the fortress. Intricate designs, some merely geometric but others suggestive of strange figures, lined the stone walls that opened into a vast passageway that was more an underground canyon than a corridor. A path fit for a dragon, he supposed.

Tylat started across the chamber toward the path, but heard his brother Mithat cry out as one of the dragon's monstrous guardians dragged him out of the shadows.

"Tylat! By all the Seven Ladies, get me out of this place!" Like the prince of Farwall and the princess of Abrona, Mithat was stripped and filthy. He was also shackled at the wrists and ankles, and wore a heavy iron collar as well. By the look of him, the dragon's accommodations had been less than comfortable. He was bruised and dirty, but more disgraced than wounded.

Tylat regarded his brother with as much detachment as he could manage. "Are you aware of the bargain the dragon has made?"

Mithat's expression blanked briefly as he opened his mouth, and then closed it again. He seemed at a loss, as if he were searching for the right response.

"I've just traveled for a fortnight through the wilderness in a caravan intended for you, brother. I watched our mother weep for days before the dragon sent its messengers, and she chose to buy your life with me instead of gold. Under the circumstances I think it's within my rights to wonder if you knew what you were begging for."

"I'm sorry," Mithat said, but looked away, clearly unable to meet his brother's gaze.

Tylat considered, just for a moment, stabbing his brother in the guts. Instead, he turned away and walked down the dragon's path. He heard, after a few moments of descent, the clatter of chains on stone and the slap of bare feet running away.

As he descended, he wondered if their mother would mourn him the way she had Mithat. He doubted it.

The dragon's chamber was beyond stifling, and Tylat nearly had to shield his eyes at the brightness of it. Steady gouts of flame jetted up from shining black stone bowls. The floor and the walls were made of mirrored bronze and jet, and the ceiling was studded with gems.

Only the shreds of Cathe's armor bore witness to whatever valiant failure she'd suffered. There was less of Alair; only a few scraps of hair and fabric remained.

"And here's the third brave one, come to sacrifice himself for the kingdom of Idris," the dragon purred, then paused and sniffed the air. "Except what's this? The stink of disappointment? How curious. Don't tell me you'd conspired with the daughter of Farwall to end me before my time."

"Of course I conspired. I dislike your bargain."

"So I see. And yet here you are anyway when you could have slain your brother instead. Is your honor so ingrained, or have you decided to try and finish what your northern friend tried and failed to start?"

Tylat smiled. "Well, when you put it that way, I suppose could offer you a better deal."

The beast shifted a little. It peered down at Tylat and tilted its long head to one side. "What could you possibly offer me besides amusement or a meal?"

"An army. A kingdom. Three kingdoms if you lend me your soldiers."

"All things I could take easily," the dragon said and raised its claw as if to strike.

"But not in the manner I offer them!" Tylat shouted with an edge of fear in his voice. "Give me the power to rule in your name. Vulgar mastery doesn't suit you, but with your support I could make you the secret master of the world."

"Ambitious," the dragon said and rested its massive foot on the stone again. "I suppose, if a royal child of some kingdom or other thought to make that kind of bargain I would have to consider it."

"A pity, really, that you are not the first."

Tylat spun and opened his mouth to shout surprise, but was cut short by the sword that ran him through. He clutched at the blade in disbelief as he looked up at Cathe's grinning face. She stood in her padded dressing gear, bloodied not by her own injuries, but by his, and probably Alair's as well. "You treacherous bitch."

"There's no treachery where there is no allegiance," Cathe said, and shoved him off her sword with a booted foot. He crumpled to the floor at her feet. "What a pity for Idris that you did not know your enemy."

She turned away toward the dragon's path. It was a credit to the beast's mercy that he never saw her reach it.

C.A. Young's short work and poetry has appeared in Crossed Genres magazine, as well as anthologies like Coscom Entertainment's *Vicious Verses and Reanimated Rhymes*, Fae Publishing's *Idol Musings*, and Circlet Press's *Like Butterflies in Iron*. His first novella, *The World in a Thimble*, appears in Candlemark & Gleam's *(re)Visions: Alice*.

You can find him at www.dimlightarchive.com.

A Tiny Grayness in the Dark
Wendy N. Wagner

I am just waking up and beginning to feel fear choking in my throat when the man with black wings finally takes me out of the box. I don't know how long I've been in there – it's the longest time so far, longer than a day. Long enough to sleep and wake up again inside that horrible blackness. My arms and legs are stiff and pins-and-needled as he lifts me out and holds me at his eye level. He's that strong.

He stares at me, in his usual unblinking way, and then rings the bell that calls Bone Woman. He won't have to wait long. She can move pretty fast even if her walk is jerky. He doesn't loosen his grip on me a second. He just stares. His eyes are like gleaming blue stones in his pale face, bright as haunt-lights.

Bone Woman turns on the hose and flushes my vomit out of the box. After he puts me down, she sprays me clean. I shiver. It's always cold, getting clean, but it's not as bad as the box. It doesn't even come close.

Then the man with the black wings leaves. Bone Woman pulls off my old nightgown and bandages. They are rank with sweat and pee and puke. I can't look at them. I just stand there, skin goose-bumpy all over, and I don't want to look at her either. Without the familiar squeeze of the bandages, my shoulder blades feel strange. The skin isn't used to the feeling of air.

She runs the hose over me again and lets me dry myself with a big sheet of linen. It somehow smells like stones warmed in the sunshine. I love that smell. I hold the sheet to my nose and try to breathe sunshine into me. I even close my eyes, working hard to draw up a memory of the sun on stones. I can remember a picnic once, someplace with sunshine, a long time ago. Bone Woman still had all her skin then. Now I can feel her fingers like sticks as they grip my shoulder, winding the bandages tight, tight. The fresh bandages are warm and stiff.

It's always hard to breathe at first, she binds my shoulders and ribs so tight. It takes the fabric a few hours to work itself around my shape and start to feel good. But still – it's better to struggle to breathe than feel the cold air on my stinging shoulder blades. The bandages are something I've grown used to, come to accept as another part of growing up. They are for my own good.

I know I should try to smile at Bone Woman. It isn't easy. She's tied her jaw on today, but she didn't quite get it lined up first, and the dry yellow teeth hang over each other like untended tombstones. If I have to be a skeleton when I grow up, I hope I can do a better job keeping myself together.

She pats my shoulder and we walk into the house. It's always good to be inside again, where thick curtains block out the orange glow of the Pit and the dust is kept away. We spend a lot of time sweeping and mopping. The Pit's dust settles on everything and works its way through the tiniest of gaps around the doors and windows. Its constant grit rubs at the skin and stings the eyes.

I wash my hands and shuffle into the kitchen, feeling the cool smooth floor under my toes. They are beginning to feel normal again. Even my brain is working the box out of itself, pushing out the darkness, shaking out the suffocating closeness of it. I walk up to the stove, where my school clothes wait. Everything is cozy and warm and I take my time putting on the uniform. Bone Woman puts porridge and milk on the table. My socks feel soft over my knees.

There aren't any sounds in the house except the sound of my feet as I cross to the table, and then the sound of my spoon moving in my bowl. I can't remember when Bone Woman stopped breathing. I don't think the man with the black wings ever did.

***

The best thing about school is all the voices. I walk up to the big black iron gates and the sound of kids shouting and singing and laughing is like a wave crashing over me. All of them talk so fast, like they're trying to cram as many words into their day as possible. I do it, too. It feels good.

The man with black wings talks, too, sometimes. Like all the winged men, he doesn't need to breathe, but he still has a voice. As he rambles on and on, he shows me pictures of above-world things: mountains, trees. Men with smooth, unwinged backs riding horses across yellow fields. They're the kind of pictures they show us in school in classes like Modern Human Living. I like them, these pictures. They make something sing inside of me. It's the part of me that cries the loudest when he puts me in the box.

None of the other kids understand about the box. It sounds like nothing to them, and sometimes I am a little ashamed that I am so afraid of it. They ask me if there is ever blood. If it's ever left a scar. Today I try to explain again. They listen.

"So ... are there spiders?" Vincent always tries to help. Today his left cheek is swollen, with a patch of tiny white dots across his cheek bone. Sometimes they wiggle. I think they're maggots. He says whatever they are, they're worse than spider eggs by about a thousand times. But his fingers are bandaged together so he can't pick them out. Nobody else wants to touch them.

I shake my head. His niceness makes it worse, somehow.

"It's not like a box can hurt you," Alicia snorts. Her hands are bandaged, too. "Not like fire sticks."

Naomi doesn't say anything, but the word *fire* makes her twitch. Her skirt gets wet around her crotch, too. She's already pissed herself once this morning. However her parents designed her homework, it must be a lot worse than the box.

139

At least I'm not scared once I'm out of it.

She makes a little sound to herself and I look at her. I think all the not-scared parts of Naomi are broken.

***

That afternoon, in the middle of Spiritual Development, two skeletons in white nurses' dresses come into our classroom. A lot of skeletons are shabby, their bones barely animated after a few years of life in the workforce, but these women are well-preserved, their haunt-lights red as the Pit's own glow. They must love their jobs to keep their lights so bright. They stop at Mrs. Grayson's desk.

Everybody looks around, eyes real big but as quiet as they can be. We've seen the nurses before. They come for the kids who are ready to graduate and go to work, big kids in the eighth or ninth grade. Except that kindergartener last year whose stitches pulled out during PE and started spraying blood everywhere. The teachers explained that he went to the Pit. To the Visitors Center, where the human souls go for Ultimate Development.

I hold my breath, just like everybody else. My shoulder blades itch so bad I want to throw myself on the floor and rub my back across the carpet, but I manage to hold myself perfectly still. I have to dig my fingernails into my skin to do it. That always helps. If I grow up and lose all my skin, it will probably be hard to resist anything.

The skeletons are up at Mrs. Grayson's desk a long time, whispering in her leathery ear. Even her horns look like they're frowning. But she doesn't say anything. She just points her long black claw in Naomi's direction.

No one is surprised when the skeletons lift her by the arms and carry her out of the room, and she only makes her little sad noise a few times. But she leaves a trail of yellow pee all the way out the front doors.

***

I walk home with Vincent. Usually, he's really funny and we laugh all the way, but today he is quiet, mostly rubbing at his face. His hands are more like mitts than hands, all bandaged up like that. I watch him scrub at his bumpy cheek and then rub on his forehead. There are red spots above his eyebrows like two tiny horns, and they get redder as he rubs them.

He suddenly stops. There's no reason to; he just stands there scuffing his foot in the red dust of the road, looking at me. And rubbing his face. "Is your father a wing-man or a horn-man?"

I stare at him.

"Or something else? A gargoyle, like Mrs. Grayson? Or one of those shiny worm things that puke out fire? What do you think he does all day?"

He's talking fast. Faster than normal, even, which is pretty fast for a kid.

We're not supposed to talk about our parents. About what we'll become when we're old enough to graduate from school. We all start out the same, as cute and human as the kids in our textbooks. But as we get older, that little bit of human rubs off or gets trained out of us, and the shape of our souls shines out.

We're meant to scare humans. We're meant to drive out the weakness that keeps them bound to their sins. It makes sense that our souls have cruel shapes.

I can't take my eyes off those raw red bumps on his head. Vincent seems too young to have spots like that. They're sort of gross.

I'm staring so hard at the bumps that it takes me a minute to realize he's crying. The tears bead up along the bottoms of his eyes and he doesn't make any sound as they splash off his face. I put my hand on his shoulder. It's hot and bony for just a second before he jerks away.

"Did you see her face when they took her? Naomi? I ain't never seen anybody so scared before." He's careful not to meet my eyes, fixing his attention off into the waste lands. "Who do you think will develop her soul? Your dad, maybe? Mine?"

I can't answer. I try not to look at his forehead or wonder how much longer till the nurses come for him. I just shake my head.

He swipes the tears off his cheeks with a rough swipe of his arm. "I gotta go. My mom's waiting for me."

He runs all the way to the front gate of his house, where a skeleton, his mom, I guess, opens the gate and leads him inside. It's a nice house, a lot bigger than ours. His dad must be really good at his job.

***

It isn't easy to stop thinking about Naomi and Vincent, but I manage until the man with black wings comes home from work. He brings with him the stink of brimstone and cooked meat, and he spends a long, long time washing in the bathroom. The smell stays in there. The bathroom always smells like the Pit. Like suffering. It makes me think of Naomi. Once she's developed, who knows where her spirit will go? That's one question they won't even let us *ask* at school.

I set the table and Bone Woman lays out meat, bread, vegetables. I miss the sounds she used to make. I miss her voice. It's like living with a stranger now. A fleshless, voiceless stranger with my mother's candle-flicker in her empty eye sockets. It's hard to meet her gaze as she puts scoops of everything on my plate. I'm pretty sure her light is getting softer, and she's looked more fragile every day.

Of course we eat in silence. Ever since the first day of kindergarten, ever since the box began, dinner has been a quick and quiet affair. I hunch as close to my plate as I can so I don't have to look either of them in the face. It's been five years, but it's not long enough to make me forgive them.

The first day of school was the worst. My kindergarten teacher explained it as she passed out coloring sheets of the Ten Commandments. School would prepare us for life, for work. There would be homework every night. Our parents

141

would help us with it.

I remember screaming that night. Shouting for them from inside that close-squeezed darkness. *Mom! Dad! Daddy, please!*

I don't say anything anymore. And I don't call them "mom" and "dad," either.

With my head down, I chew my meat. I sip my milk. It is not easy. Bending like this tightens the bandages across my shoulders and ribs until they cut into my skin. My shoulder blades burn with every breath, every bite.

The sound of fabric snapping is as loud as a scream.

My parents stare at me. Bone Woman's eyes widen, their haunt-lights flaring within. The man with the black wings covers her hand with his, his whole face stretched with horror.

I want to cry. My back feels so good, so free I can hardly take it. I want to tear off my clothes and run through a waterfall. I want to dance. But I'm stuck here, in this chair, looking at them look at me as if I am the most terrifying thing they've ever seen.

Then he stands up so hard and fast that his chair topples over. He's mumbling to himself. I can't understand his words even as he grabs my shirt collar and rips my shirt right down the back. There is a wonderful sensation of stretching. Unfurling. I can't hold back a happy sigh. It is better than moving after a day in the box.

He drops my shirt collar and cups his hands around my face, looking down at me. Black liquid pools in the corners of his eyes, runs down his cheeks. It's not until they splash down on his shirt, like Vincent's tears this afternoon, that I understand he can cry.

Finally his mumbling becomes words. "I thought we had more time. You're just ten years old, a child. My baby." He brushes moisture from his cheek as he stares at me. "Verna, you know what we need."

She is already moving out of the dining room, her tendons snapping and popping around her exposed joints. I have never seen her move so fast. Her haunt-lights brighten the hallway for a moment as she runs toward their bedroom.

"Come on," he says. He helps me out of my school shirt, unwinds the shreds of torn fabric from my ribs. Bone Woman – Verna, my mother – appears at his elbow with the kind of shirt winged men wear, all white stretchy fabric with long slits in the back. She fiddles with the openings for a while, adjusting everything to her liking. His face is still unreadable, its usual marble-white smeared with drying tears. He is like a statue in one of those filthy Italian cities I've seen in photographs.

Verna throws one of his big gray cloaks over me and they each take a hand. They are walking very fast. We go out the back gate and cross into the barren space behind the house.

No one is allowed to come here. The only time I've ever set foot in this black and gray desert was that day when I was very young, long ago when Bone Woman was still just Verna, the light of her eyes as bright as the chirping songs she sang to me during the day. Long ago when my father would hold her very tightly and cry into her hair some nights, and only made me look inside the box, not stay in it. I was very young when we packed the picnic basket and crept through the wasteland.

For the first time in years, I actually want to be with my parents. They are leading me away from the Pit, out of our dark and nasty little town with its sulfurous air and acid rain, taking me to the edge of the world. The wasteland is forbidden, but I am glad to be in it.

We hurry up the hill and I realize how small our world is. The wall around the under-world begins right here, its unscalable gray surface stretching into the boundless darkness of the sky. The only light is the faint ugly glow of the Pit's flames.

Father points up. Up there, so high above our heads, there is a tiny grayness in the dark.

"Do you remember?" His face is very serious. "The picnic. The cemetery."

Of course I remember. I might have been very little, but I couldn't forget that trip through the wasteland and then up through the sky. How could I forget that flight, higher and ever higher in his arms, feeling safe but nervous as we moved up toward the black lid of the under-world, straight to that little gray patch? How could I forget being pushed through the opening, first me, then my mother, and last father, all of us rolling and laughing on the floor of that decrepit mausoleum?

It was the best day of my life. The day we all sat on the sun-warmed stones, our eyes running with tears at the strong and burning brightness all around us.

"Sunlight," I whisper. I had felt it just that once, but I could never forget it.

Bone Woman pulls me into her arms. There is nothing soft about her hug and I realize that the lights in her eye sockets look smaller. Even her crooked-tombstone teeth look drier and looser in their sockets. She's almost burned out her life spark, but she's waited for this one moment, rationing her strength for this trip. I feel the tears start up in my eyes.

"I don't know if I can do it."

She taps her fingertips to my lips. It's the closest she can get to saying *Don't be afraid*, and I know it. I kiss the dry strip of muscle over her cheekbone.

He looks nervous. "You have to go, little one. You have to go now." He pulls me into his arms and squeezes me, hard.

We would all be in trouble if we were caught out here in the forbidden zone. We would be sent straight to the Visitors Center. We might not be human, but our souls could still be developed. It would hurt desperately.

I bury my face in his shirt. It's like I'm a little girl again. His little girl. "I don't want to leave you."

He kisses my forehead. "I showed you the world once. I showed you the sun." His wings flap, stirring dust. "This entire place is like the black box. Don't you see?"

He stretches his arms, shaping the whole dark expanse of the world. The

143

gray wall around everything, the ugly stain of the Pit. The dust, settling on us even as we stand there. I cling harder to him.

"Go! Do you want them to take you to the Pit? Do you want to live your life like I have?"

He is trembling. My father, who never shows his feelings, is shaking with emotion.

Verna lays a hand on his wing, steadying it. She reaches a finger into her eye socket and lifts out the tiny spark within. She sets it on my lips. The flame tingles and then scurries inside me. I can feel it as warm as courage inside my belly.

They say in school that to become a good tormentor, the kind of tormentor who can really help free a soul from its sins, you must be tormented. That's why we have homework; that's why Vincent's father puts spiders beneath his son's skin, and that's why there are always burns on Alicia's body. All that suffering is supposed to break down what is human-like inside you and slough it away. It's supposed to get you ready for life developing spirits down in the Pit.

I never stopped to wonder how the parents felt about homework or if anyone ever asked them if they even wanted to work in the Pit.

I think of my father's face, so blank and hard every time he took me out of the box. He's never once complained about work or my homework. But he's never hurt me like any of the other kids have been hurt. Instead, he's put me in the box, small and dark and shut off from anything good.

"This whole under-world is my black box," he whispers into my hair.

His breath is like wind warmed by the sun, and I think of that magical day we sat in the cemetery and ate our lunch, laughing, happy, a family. It was the best day of my life. The most alive day of my life. No one else I know has ever felt like that.

My heart clenches as I understand how much my father loves me, and why he chose the box, and why first, he showed me the sun.

I hug him tight. I kiss his hard face. I kiss my mother on her dead mouth.

And then I stretch my new black wings and fly for the hole in the roof of the under-world. Out of the box.

Wendy N. Wagner grew up next door to a cemetery, and credits the locale with her fascination with all things dark and eerie. Her short fiction has appeared in *Beneath Ceaseless Skies* and the anthologies *Armored* (forthcoming), *The Way of the Wizard* and *Rigor Amortis*. She is also an assistant editor at *Fantasy Magazine*. Wendy makes her home in Portland, Oregon, and blogs about words, food, and apocalypse preparation at http://operabuffo.blogspot.com.

RECEIVED WITHOUT CONTENT
TIMOTHY T. MURPHY

For two weeks, Daniel had been making a serious effort to get home before his mother so he could check the mail in private. "Dude, what are you waiting for, anyway?" his best friend Adam asked him one Thursday as Daniel was rifling through a stack of junk mail and bills.

"Ha! This!" Daniel shouted, pulling an envelope out from between the leaves of the Daily Shopper. He handed it to Adam and practically skipped back inside to the apartment.

It looked like a shipping envelope from a box with one clear side showing nothing but a plain slab of cardboard. It was addressed from the Barkman Foundation, and had a sticker from the Postal Service that said "Received Without Content."

"So, what's the big deal? It's just a piece of cardboard. Looks like somebody cut it out of a box or something."

"That's what you're supposed to think," Daniel told him. He dropped the rest of the mail forgotten onto the coffee table and took the envelope from Adam as they walked back to Daniel's bedroom. He sat at his computer and tore the envelope open.

While surfing to The Barkman Foundation's website, Daniel showed Adam the other side of the cardboard. "See?"

Adam just shrugged. "It's dirty. So what?" Daniel just kept smiling.

According to the website, The Barkman Foundation was a scholarship foundation. There were pictures of teenagers and colleges, links to all kinds of advice, sample S.A.T. Tests, study guides... the works. "All fake." Daniel told Adam. He logged in to the site and a pop-up appeareds asking if he wanted to register something called a Loki Card. When he clicked "Yes", a window popped up for his webcam and asked him to hold his Loki Card under it.

Daniel held the slab of cardboard out as the instructions told him – flat in his hand with the 'dirty' side up. For a moment, the computer screen only showed the cardboard and Daniel's smiling face, but then hurdy-gurdy music started to play and an animated clown car rose up out of the cardboard on the screen. Several brightly colored clowns climbed out and started to perform. There were jugglers, unicycle riders, a dancing bear, pie-throwers, and a whole troupe of acrobatic clowns all running around each other in a riot of circus feats.

"Okay," Adam told him, "that's pretty cool. Why's it on a piece of

145

cardboard?"

The window suddenly closed and a new pop-up appeared that said, *"Congratulations, Daniel! You have successfully registered your Loki Card! Welcome to the fight against the Re-engineered Youth! For too long, the rich have run our society and gathered up all the finer things in life only for themselves. Now, advancements in nanotechnology available only to the privileged families among us have given their teens an unfair advantage in information, education, health, fitness, and beauty. The nation's rich are rapidly broadening the gap between us and them, but on November the 8th, ordinary teens like you across America fight back.*

"A re-engineered teen can see the display rising from the card right inside their heads as you saw it on the webcam. The microscopic nanotechnology embedded in their visual cortex reads the code like the webcam does and translates it into visual information for them. This is just one of the many advantages their nanotechnology gives them over you. Here, we turn that advantage against them. Hidden in the card's display is a very special code. It's an administration code, so they won't be able to see it, but their nan-packs will process it in the background. In moments, every bit of nanotech in their bodies will shut down completely. Some will be able to initiate a restart with their smartphones, but most will be forced to get replacement packs.

"On November the 8th, at about Noon EST, place your Loki Card where any group of re-engineered teens will see it. We assure you, this will not harm any of them, but for the weeks that it will take to receive, grow, and program new nan-packs, they will be forced to live and go to school as we do. The playing field will be even, for once, and we will spread awareness of the growing gaps in our educational system!

"Welcome to the battle!" - BlueJeanRebel

"Dude, are you serious?" Adam asked as he finished reading it. Daniel was putting the Loki Card in his backpack with a wide grin on his face. "That thing is like a weapon, or something?"

"It's not a weapon," Daniel said. "It's a tool."

"Are you kidding? It's going to hurt somebody!"

Daniel shushed him as they heard the front door open. Daniel closed his browser quickly, and they went into the living room where his mom was kicking off her shoes and stumbling into the kitchen with a load of grocery bags in her hands. "Boys, could you put all this away?" she asked, running for her bedroom. "Appleseeds called on my way home. They're short-staffed and need a server tonight."

By the time they got the groceries stored away, Mom was scurrying back in her Appleseeds uniform. "Sorry, Honey, but you're going to have to scrounge for dinner."

"Oh, hey Mom!" Daniel called as she was picking up her keys and purse. "I'm going to need some money for the field trip tomorrow. Please?"

"For what?"

"For lunch. We're going to be at the zoo for lunch period, so we're eating there."

She sighed and said, "I'm sorry, honey, but you're going to have to take a lunch."

"Aw, c'mon, Mom..."

"No, Daniel. I'm sorry, but it's expensive to eat there, and we don't have the cash for it right now."

"But you work three jobs."

"I work three part-time jobs and none pays very well."

"I'm going to be the only kid there toting his own lunch," Daniel said, sulking.

She scoffed. "No, you're not." She rushed out the door shouting, "I love you!" and left them alone again.

"Dude," Adam told him, "you know I can spot you a few bucks tomorrow, right?"

"It's not the same thing." Daniel said, popping the top off a can of Spaghetti-O's. "Thanks, though."

"You're not serious about using that Loki thing tomorrow, are you?"

"Do you know how my mom lost her job?" Daniel asked as he started the microwave.

"No, but..."

"She was an I.T. tech for Shanghai Games. She was really good at it, too. Suddenly, one day, they announced that they were doing a little restructuring and any technician that didn't have nanotechnology by a certain date was going to be let go. Well, thanks to all the medical bills my dad left behind, my mom couldn't afford any nanotech, so she was fired. Now, she can't find a job in I.T. without it. That's why she's working all these crappy jobs with a Masters Degree. Me? I want to go into computer animation. Think I'm going to get it without any nanotech?"

"Well, maybe."

"Do you know how much that stuff costs? I looked into it, you know. A basic nan-pack for one teenager costs more than most cars. Most places offer twenty-year loans for them with really high interest rates."

"So, take out a loan and don't get a car."

"With what money? I need a job in my chosen field before I can get the nanotech that I need to get a job in my chosen field. Heck, I won't even be able to get the college education I need for the job without the nanotech."

"Yeah, but do you have to take it out on somebody else?"

"Oh, come on. All of the school's quarterbacks for five years in a row have been re-engineered, and so have the last three Homecoming Queens. Four sophomores placed for Varsity Cheer, this year, and they were all re-engineered, too."

"This is about Jessica Noonan, isn't it?" Adam said.

"No, it is not about Jess!" Jessica Noonan was one of the four new cheerleaders. Rumor had it her family had won some major court settlement years before and now they were the richest family in town. Sure enough, Jess was re-engineered. She'd always been beautiful, though, and had never seemed to notice Daniel was alive.

"As soon as these guys are fourteen, their families buy them all the nanotech they need and it makes them healthier, prettier, smarter, helps them train in sports better, and gives them access to information faster. I've got to compete against all the other computer geeks for a tiny number of scholarships, and the re-engineered guys are starting out with a huge advantage." He pulled his Spaghetti-O's from the microwave, stuck a spoon in it and walked to the couch. "It's like the site said. Rich people suck up all the good stuff for themselves and leave the rest of us in the dirt. I'm tired of it."

"All right," Adam said as Daniel flopped back onto the couch and reached for the remote. "I've got to head home. Just, please don't bring that thing to the zoo tomorrow, okay? Teenagers didn't make the world this way."

"Yeah, sure," Daniel said, but he didn't seem very convinced.

***

The next morning as they were filing in through the gates at the zoo, Adam spotted the Loki Card in Daniel's inside jacket pocket.

"Dude!" he whispered, slapping Daniel on the arm. "What are you doing with that thing here?"

Daniel looked around to be sure no one had heard and whispered back, "I told you, man, it's not going to hurt anyone, just kick them down a few notches for a couple of weeks. That's all."

"Yeah famous last words, and there are only about a thousand things that can go wrong with this stunt."

"I'm not going to get arrested, all right? I know what I'm doing."

They walked through most of the tour in silence, listening to Ms. Page giving her biodiversity lecture. The zoo had special glasses with ear-buds so that ordinary people could view the 3-D displays. They usually cost twenty bucks to rent, but they let Ms. Page's class use them for free.

Daniel spent a lot of the time looking at the displays, but most of it watching Jessica. She and Allyson, Holly, and Tiffany – the other sophomore cheerleaders – were wearing their uniforms of scarlet and gold today. Even among the beautiful people Jess was the really beautiful one, with her bright blond hair, powder blue eyes, and bronze skin. He almost hoped she didn't get caught by the Loki Card.

They had a moment to look around in the butterfly pavilion, and he saw her and the other cheerleaders bent over a display, ooh-ing and aw-ing at it, smiling. The other three took off for another display, and Jessica stood smiling at that same one, slowly waving her hand over the glass. Hesitantly, he stepped up beside her and looked into the display. There was a "loading" screen, and then he

148

saw a 3-D movie showing metamorphosis. "Is this how you see the world all the time?"

She glanced at him, smiling, and said, "Basically, yeah."

"Must be nice," he said.

She shrugged. "It's all right. My nan-pack is older, though, so it takes me a moment to load some stuff like this."

"What, your tech is older? Your dad doesn't really strike me as the type to go cheap. No offense."

She frowned, crinkling her nose and looked back down at the display. "It's a long story. I don't like to talk about it."

"Well, still," he said, "it's nanotech. I'd give anything to be able to have it, myself."

"And I'd give it all up to be a natural-born genius like you," she told him.

Daniel did a double-take. "Excuse me?"

"Oh, come on. I know you're on the Dean's List too. And I've seen those movies you made on YouTube. They were pretty cool."

"You did?"

"The whole school did. You're good."

He could feel himself starting to blush. "Uh, thanks." He followed her on autopilot to another display. "I want to do it in college."

"You definitely should," she said, smiling back at him again.

"Not likely without any nanotech."

She shrugged and said, "It's getting cheaper and cheaper every year, though." She looked him in the eyes and said, "Talent like yours, I'll bet you could get a grant for some." Her friends called to her and she turned to follow them, but not before waving back at him. "Think about it!"

"Yeah, sure," he said to no one. "Like that's going to happen."

It was almost time for lunch. He told Ms. Page that he needed to use the bathroom and ran ahead to the food court. They had reserved a bunch of tables for the class to use, so Daniel casually walked past them and dropped the Loki Card on a random chair when no one was looking. Then he waited for the rest of the class to catch up.

The first thing Adam did when he got there was look in Daniel's pocket. He gave him a disapproving scowl, but bought him lunch anyway. "Where is it?" he asked as they sat down at an empty table.

Daniel pointed his thumb over his shoulder and said, "I just tossed it on a chair over there."

Adam looked over Daniel's shoulder. "Well, congratulations," he said in a sarcastic tone. "The computer geeks are all sitting there. None of them will ever talk to you again."

Daniel glanced back and saw that, as he'd hoped, his rival re-engineered computer geeks were sitting down and one of them – Tommy – had just picked the card up off the chair and flipped it over.

"Sweet!" they heard Tommy call out. "Check this out, guys!" Everybody at the table leaned in close to see it. There were cries of, "Whoa! Cool!" before Jessica called, "What are you looking at, guys?"

Daniel turned around again to see Jessica and her friends all gathering around the card, too. "Oh, even better." Adam told him. "Now you're never going to be able to get a date."

He watched Jessica smiling down at the card for a moment and almost tried to think of a way to pull her away from it. "It's all right." he said finally. "No one's gonna know it was me, or anything."

Suddenly, the computer guys gave a confused blink and jerk of their heads. "Whoa," Tommy said. "It just stopped."

"What do you mean?" Allyson asked. "Like the clip was over?" She was still looking at the card.

"No, I mean it just went dead. It's just code. How can it just go dead like that?" The other geeks were looking just as confused as he was. Daniel fought back a smile as they looked around, trying to figure out the trouble.

"I don't know what you're talking about," Allyson said, still watching the card. "It's working for... wait." She blinked a few times at the card. "It just stopped."

"See?" Tommy said.

Tiffany called out, "Hey, guys? My music quit on me." She was pulling out her smartphone and tapping at it with her thumb. "What the hell?"

Another of the geeks, Kim, was staring out into the distance. "Crap." she said. "All the displays are off, too."

Daniel faced his table again, unable to hold back the grin on his face, as Tommy was saying, "That's not possible." Adam had his eyes squarely on his meal, ignoring Daniel.

Daniel was about to say something when someone behind him screamed, "Jess!"

He spun in time to see Jessica fall backwards, shaking all over. Allyson caught her and lowered her to the ground, and Jessica went into full-blown violent convulsions. "Oh, Jesus!" Allyson was shouting. "It's not the displays! That thing shut off our nan-packs!"

"Oh my God!" Tiffany half-screamed. "What do we do?"

"But... but..." Daniel stood up confused and staring as all the other students in the class gathered close. A few of them pulled out their smartphones to call 911. "...it can't hurt them. They promised."

Allyson was holding Jessica's hands as Jessica convulsed and made wet gurgling choking noises. Holly had both her hands under Jessica's head, wincing as Jessica slammed her head down onto them again and again.

"I don't know, dude," Adam said faintly, coming beside him to watch. "She looks pretty hurt to me."

"Get out her smartphone!" Allyson shrieked at Tiffany. "Run the restart! Quick!"

Tiffany fumbled in Jessica's bag for the phone and started tapping wildly at the screen as Ms. Page came running on to the scene. Tommy quickly explained to Ms. Page about the card and everyone's nan-packs shutting down. Jessica continued to convulse and Allyson finally turned to Tiffany and screamed, "Come on!"

"I'm trying!" Tiffany shouted back. "It says her nan-pack isn't responding!"

Jessica's convulsions slowed and she began to heave her chest as her head fell to one side. With a weak lurch, she sprayed her lunch out onto the concrete and down her cheek, and her body went slack.

She wasn't blinking.

"No!" Allyson cried. She pressed her fingers into Jessica's neck and said, "Her heart stopped!" She ripped open the front of Jessica's top as Holly bent down to blow a couple of breaths into Jessica's mouth.

"This isn't supposed to happen." Daniel whispered weakly to Adam who, was standing and watching in horrified silence. Daniel pulled out his smartphone and tapped for the Barkman Foundation's website. All he got was a 404 error. *Website not found.* "What the hell?"

Allyson was rocking up and down, pumping her hands onto Jessica's chest and screaming at Tiffany, "Where's her pen?"

"I can't find it!" Tiffany shouted back, rummaging through Jessica's pack in a panic.

Daniel pulled up the Twitter feed for the Foundation.

Jason563 What the h*** is going on?
TeganTildar They just hauled off one of my classmates in an ambulance. #WTF!
PinkUzi These cards are killing people! Where the hell is BJR?

"No," Daniel whispered. "Oh, god, no." He looked up at the scene playing out in front of him.

People were standing around watching, some crying as Allyson and Holly gave Jessica CPR. Ms. Page was calling 911 and was saying something about a 'pacemaker pad.' Tiffany upended Jessica's pack, dumping out all the contents screaming, "Where the fuck is it?" Books and pencils and make-up and slips of paper went flying and bouncing away as Tiffany shook the bag violently.

All the while, Jessica just lay there with her eyes open and still.

"There!" Tiffany screamed, reaching for a cylinder the size of a pen that was rolling away from her.

"Give it here!" Allyson shouted. She took the 'pen,' using her fingers to count the spaces between Jessica's ribs. She clicked the end of the device and an electronic whine started as a long needle popped out of the end. She took a couple of quick bracing breaths, tears streaming down her cheeks, and then lifted the needle over her head and stabbed it into Jessica's chest.

"Oh, god!" someone gasped as the device made a blast of air and a high-pitched squeal. Allyson pulled it back out of Jessica's chest and threw it aside. Holly blew two more breaths into Jessica's mouth, and the two of them went back to CPR.

All Daniel could do was watch. The Twitter feed on his phone just kept spewing the same panicky crap over and over, so he shut it off.

Lights and sirens came. The EMTs hit Jessica with a pair of defibrillator pads and threw some sort of big electric gauze pad over her chest. The police asked questions while the EMTs worked. Allyson waved the Loki Card, shouting the whole story at the officers. They stuffed it away without looking at it. Daniel realized that the police and the EMTs must have nanotech too and thanked every god he could think of he hadn't hurt one of them.

They rolled Jessica away on a gurney with an EMT holding the pad steady on her chest, and Ms. Page started making calls. Allyson went on the ambulance with Jessica, and someone finally asked Holly what had happened.

"Somebody hid a code in that piece of cardboard," she answered sniffling. "It was some kind of root-kit that shut down all our nan-packs somehow."

"That shouldn't have done that to Jessica," Tommy whined.

"But Jessica is a 'Nixis Baby'," Holly told him.

"A what?"

"Nixis was a brand of nanotech from years and years ago. They had a serious design flaw that no one caught until it was too late. Jess's mom had a Nixis nan-pack before she got pregnant with Jess, and it passed right along Jess's umbilical cord and infused itself into Jess's system in the womb."

"Hang on," Tommy said, "I think I remember this, now. Weren't there like lots of stillbirths and really bad birth defects and stuff?"

Holly nodded. "Jess got really lucky. She survived, but the nanotech embedded itself in her system and took over her development when she was just into her second trimester. Her parents told us that Jess never had the chance to develop certain functions on her own, like an immune system or some of her neurotransmitter production, or even the signals that make her heart beat. The nanotech does all of that for her, whether she likes it or not, so she was basically born on life support. It makes her really pretty and really smart, but if it shuts down, then so does she."

"Who would do this?" Tiffany cried. She was sitting on the ground by the pile of books and papers, putting them back in Jessica's pack. "Who would do something like this?" She let the pack fall back to the ground and collapsed in sobs.

The bus came. Someone helped Tiffany pick up the rest of Jess's things and half-carried her to her seat. Daniel had just stood there staring off where the ambulance had gone, so Adam took him by the arm and quietly guided him to a seat in the very back of the bus. Everyone switched their seatback screens to CNN and found that they were in the middle of the story already.

"So far at this hour, a confirmed sixteen dead across America and dozens more on life support in what looks like a co-ordinated attack against Re-engineered Americans. No group has come forward to claim responsibility yet, and authorities are asking that anyone with information contact their local police..."

Daniel pulled up the Twitter feed on his smartphone again. No one knew what to do, and they were all talking about not squealing and not going to jail for murder. He just sat there in a cold sweat, watching them all whine and tried hard not to be sick. Adam didn't say anything, but he did put his hand on Daniel's shoulder.

***

The school sent them all home. Daniel's mom took the night off and made him dinner, asking all sorts of questions and trying to make him feel better. He just sat there on the couch numbly, watching the news as the death toll went up to twenty-five. He kept waiting for BlueJeanRebel or someone to say it was all a big mistake, a joke gone all wrong, but it never happened.

Hours later, while he was still sitting there, his mother sat next to him and said, "The school called, Honey. Jessica's on life support, but it looks like she's going to be okay."

"Really?" his throat rasped. He distantly noticed that his cheeks were hot and sore.

"Yeah. Apparently, she had a sort of medical pen that had a spare culture of her nans for this sort of emergency."

"I saw it. Allyson had to stab her in the chest with it."

"Yeah, I suppose you did. Well, they have to do a lot of work, now, and she's going to be in Intensive Care for a few weeks while the emergency pack grows to replace her old system, but she'll be okay. They say she might even walk away without any brain damage."

"Brain damage?" That did it. He scurried for the waste-paper basket and threw up, then fell onto his hands and knees and wept like a baby.

His mom tried to put her arms around him, but he shrugged her off. He sat back against the couch and watched the screen roll out the names of the dead and the hurt. Same old shit, he realized. Someone got an advantage, someone got mad, someone got used, someone got hurt. It wasn't glorious. It wasn't funny. It was just another day.

"I'm sorry, Mom," he whispered, and pulled out his smartphone. His mother looked on, confused, as he dialed the police. He couldn't look her in the eyes as he said, "I need to confess."

Timothy T. Murphy writes in Science Fiction and Fantasy. He grew up in small town Iowa and has lived in England, upstate New York, and Albuquerque. In Albuquerque, he missed the color green, and in England, he missed the sound of thunder. He has returned to the Mid-West and now lives in Omaha, Nebraska.

To Sleep With Pachamama
Caleb Jordan Schulz

Dirt caked the leg bone like a rotting sock. Augusto Cabesa De Vaca brushed off the bone and tucked it into the back pocket of his overalls. He stood up, his head just clearing the edge of the grave. Sunlight struck his eyes when he brushed his shaggy black hair off his forehead. He shielded his eyes with his hand and looked across the graveyard, past the barren fields and the gallows where purple-faced men hung, to the Amazon jungle. Gigantic trees towered like skyscrapers, their leaves spreading out like a green ocean.

Augusto's eyes shifted to the pile of bones between him and the next open grave.

"I think we should get paid by the bone," he said.

Waira Del Toro, his workmate and friend, peeked out of the grave. Dirt smeared her cheeks and forehead.

"That wouldn't be fair. You'd just grab all the hands and feet first. And I'd get stuck with leftovers like the pelvis." Waira held up a clunky pelvis bone.

Augusto lifted up a spine. "You could have this. There's a lot of segments."

"You think they'd count as individual bones?"

"Don't see why not." Augusto shook the column which rattled like a gruesome windchime.

Waira tossed the pelvis out of the grave. "Got another one almost done?"

"Almost. Just looking for the skull."

Augusto resumed his digging, and soon found a hard lump about the right size. He pulled at the hard dirt until his fingers revealed the back of a skull. He brushed more dirt away, but stopped when his fingers touched on something other than bone. Augusto peered closely and saw that the face of the skull was covered by a mask. It was of darkened metal, with carved-out eye sockets, a mouth, and grooves for the eyebrows and nose.

A wave of thrill washed over him and Augusto instantly knew the mask was special. He tucked the skull-mask under the crook of his arm and climbed out of the grave, struggling to pull his short, heavy frame upward. He sat on an overturned bucket, which groaned under his weight.

A minute later, Waira emerged with a skull of her own and sat next to Augusto. Waira was short and lean, with a wide face and searching eyes. Her cacao-hued skin was lighter than his, the color of the dark soil around them.

When Waira offered him their shared liter of water, Augusto showed her the skull-mask. Her eyes went wide.

"You found that just laying down there?" she asked.

"Well, I dug it up. Have you ever seen anything like it?"

Waira shook her head. She ran a finger along the mask's etchings. "It's beautiful."

"Isn't it? I never knew they buried the dead with masks."

"Me either. It's too bad you'll have to get rid of it."

Augusto frowned. "It's only a small mask. They won't care if I keep it."

Waira raised an eyebrow. "You're foolish if you think that."

Augusto knew she was right. He had to turn it over to the salvagers. Everything manmade went to the salvagers. It had been that way for decades. Ever since humanity began migrating to the space stations orbiting Earth and to the colonies on the moon and Mars, the law was to cleanse the Earth. The United Federation of Earth Nations had agreed to clean up their mess as a final apology for turning the world unbearably hot and polluted, with few remaining resources.

Each country was responsible for uprooting anything manmade – roads, buildings, electrical wires – anything, including human skeletons. The goal was to recreate the Earth as it was before humans had run havoc across it. A great sweeping vista of restored terrain would be left in its place: plains and mountains, hills and valleys, rivers and lakes And perhaps in time the Earth would become livable again. Perhaps the fish would repopulate and the crops return. Perhaps the droughts would lessen, the rains lose their acid, and the floods return to normal. Perhaps then, hundreds or thousands of years from now, humanity might return.

Augusto kicked a rock. "Maybe I could take the mask with me when my time here is done and I am sent into space?"

"You think you'll be sent into space? You're Quechan."

Augusto didn't have the heart to argue because her words were true. His Quechan heritage – and hers as well – would keep them on the Earth as long as possible. Quechan people had lived in the Andes and the Amazon basin for longer than recorded history. But despite their people's long history, they occupied the bottom rung of the social ladder. When other Bolivianos were ferried up into space, it was the Quechans who were left behind to clean up.

"Let's get back to work," said Waira, tossing her skull into a nearby wheelbarrow.

Augusto looked at his skull-mask. "What should I do with this?"

Waira shrugged. "Separate them. Put the skull in the barrow and the mask in the scrap pile."

He weighed the skull in his hand. "It doesn't seem right. What will they care about one small mask? It's not as if we can we can remove *everything* from the Earth anyway."

"Maybe, but it's not up to you, is it?"

"Of course not. But it's a ridiculous idea in the first place – removing all evidence of mankind. An idea by fanatics. Anyone with common sense..."

"Be quiet!" Waira looked around. "Or do you want to get us in trouble?

There's nothing you can do about it. They're in charge, not you, so just get rid of the thing."

Augusto sighed and began prying at the seam between the bone and the metal when a siren pierced the air. Augusto's eyes went wide and he immediately dropped the skull. He looked around, expecting soldiers to come running toward him, but when none came he knew something else was amiss. The long, slow alarm was so loud that it hurt their ears. After several minutes, a tinny voice blast through the air.

"All workers assemble immediately in Bolivar Plaza! All workers assemble immediately in Bolivar Plaza!"

Augusto and Waira exchanged a look. Augusto tossed the skull-mask into the grave where he'd found it. Together, they crossed the graveyard, littered with gaping holes, and walked across the open field toward what had once been the beautiful Bolivar Plaza, but was now a patch of earth where the three men hung from the gallows.

A crowd had gathered by the time they arrived. Hundreds of workers, grimy from a twelve-hour shift, massed before the raised platform. On it stood Project Leader Tzinia Mogoñon, a tall woman with dark, pulled-back hair and long, needle-like fingers. Next to her stood two burly guards in dark blue uniforms. Between the guards stood a squat man with dark skin and hair. His clothes were soiled with dirt and his face clotted with blood.

Tzinia scanned the crowd before addressing them in a commanding alto tone, "Today our security was threatened. A man ignored the rules of the United Federation of Earth Nations. His crime? Desecration of the Earth. The punishment for this is death."

She gestured to the guards next to her. The guards pushed the prisoner next to the already hanging men where an empty noose hung. They looped the rope around his neck and secured it tight before backing away.

"Any last words?" asked Tzinia.

The man stood with his head held high and his back straight. "I die with Pachamama."

Tzinia nodded to the guards and one of them yanked on a crude lever. The floor beneath the prisoner dropped away and the man fell. The rope went taut and within moments the man stopped jerking.

"Take this lesson with you," said Tzinia. "Dismissed."

People quickly moved away from the gruesome sight. Most were silent, and the few that talked, did so in murmurs. Augusto walked with his head down. Waira was next to him. She didn't want to disturb him, but needed to ask a question.

"Augusto," she whispered. "Your Quechan is better than mine. What did he say? What does Pachamama mean?"

Augusto kept his eyes on the ground. "He said 'I die with Mother Earth'."

***

Waira yanked up on the ribcage. The ribs bent under the pressure and one of them snapped off in her hand. Waira tucked the rib in her back pocket and wrestled again with the ribs. She heaved, her back muscles tensing, and then the ribs pulled free, spraying dirt everywhere. Waira spat dirt and set the ribcage up out of the grave. She climbed out and counted the bones, making sure she was missing nothing. Augusto was already sitting on his bucket, staring out across the field. Waira joined him.

"How are we supposed to know if we got all the bones?" asked Waira. "I mean – what if we dig up a man with one leg and keep looking – but this man only had one leg when he was buried?"

Augusto shrugged.

Waira followed her friend's line of sight, across the graveyard toward the gallows.

"You shouldn't stare at corpses so much," said Waira.

"I'm just getting prepared."

"Well, help me with these bones, and we'll get there even sooner."

Augusto reluctantly picked up the bones with Waira and dumped them in the wheelbarrow. They hefted the wheelbarrows and left the graveyard, and approached the gallows slowly. Something about the recently executed man made Augusto and Waira act with more reverence.

They went to the first of the other three men. The man's body swung back and forth in the breeze like a decrepit pendulum. His swollen, purple face was bent forward. Waira propped up a small step ladder next to the corpse as Augusto grabbed hold of the corpse's legs and lifted. Waira climbed the step ladder, and pulled at the noose around the neck, loosening it until she could pull it off. The body slumped in Augusto's arms and let out a peal of gas.

"Oh God," gasped Augusto. He heaved the body into the wheelbarrow and jogged a little ways away. "That's the worst thing I've ever smelled."

Waira had also put some distance between herself and the body. She held a handkerchief over her nose and mouth. "Yeah… it's like rotting chicken and sharp cheese."

"I don't see why we have to clean up the bodies," said Augusto.

"I guess they don't distinguish between digging up bodies and taking them down." Waira waved him toward the gallows. "Let's get this over with."

With covered noses, they hurried to take down the corpses and put them in the wheelbarrows. Once finished, they hefted them away from the gruesome structures. Augusto's muscles strained to hold up the heavy wheelbarrow. Bones were piled several feet high and it was all he could do to keep the barrow steady. Beside him, Waira struggled as well. Together, they trundled the bones across a wide field, away from the barracks, toward the jungle.

Before the jungle, just beyond the perimeter, was a squat, mud brick furnace. Leading to it, from the perimeter's interior, ran a wide conveyor belt. They stopped at the belt and began to heap the corpses onto it as it inched forward.

They watched the first corpse get ferried along, until the belt stopped beneath a metallic globe. The globe pulsed a green light over the body before the belt started up again, promptly dumping the body into the furnace's orange maw. The fires roared and smoke plumed skyward.

Waira frowned. "Do you think it's right – burning their bones?" she asked without taking her eyes from the orange glow.

"It's better to be buried."

"Why?"

"Because we're a part of the Earth. We can demolish our cathedrals, our fountains, uproot the roads and cobblestones – but it doesn't mean we weren't a part of the Earth."

"We were part of it, and we wrecked it."

"Look – I'm not arguing that we screwed up. I'm just saying that obliterating everything we constructed doesn't make sense."

"How so?"

Augusto pointed at the jungle. "Think of those trees – at first there's just a few, but soon there are a few more. Soon there is a thicket, and maybe they grow where flowers once were. The flowers are pushed away, but they survive, maybe growing where grass once grew. Life moves. Even the soil – pushed by the tree roots – can alter the flow of a stream. Humans may have changed things, but that doesn't mean we're not a part of the Earth."

"And because we're part of the Earth, we should be buried?"

"If we're going to take away everything we're done to the planet, the least we can do is leave our ancestors' bones in the ground."

"What if, instead of burning them, we just send the bones up into space and built orbiting cemeteries?"

"That's billions and billions of skeletons going into space. We're clogging Earth's atmosphere bad enough by living there. Don't need a million floating graveyards too."

Waira's eyes strayed past the smoke of the furnaces to the jungle. "Why would they try to leave?"

"Who?"

"You know who." Waira gestured to the remaining corpses on the conveyor belt.

"They were crazy, obviously. There's nothing out there. And even if they avoided getting caught – once we finish here, there won't be anything left. How can they live without tools, homes, cars, electricity – all those things?"

"I don't know. That's why I asked. At best those men probably would've found some hideous death in the jungle. And at worst, they get executed."

"Maybe they were tired of working."

Waira watched the last of the hanged men fall into the furnace. "Well, they're retired now."

Augusto sighed and shook his head, and tossed a femur on the conveyor belt.

Waira wrested the lower half of a skeleton from her cart onto the belt and then glanced over her shoulder. Not too far away in the center of a plaza, a demolition crew was dismantling a fountain. Hammers and crow-bars rose and fell in their hands. Sweat glistened on their faces. But every so often, Waira saw one of them stare off at the distant trees. Did they also wish to abandon their work and flee to the jungle?

She turned back to her work and helped Augusto put the last of the skeletons onto the conveyor belt. They watched it fall into the furnace. The flames grew high for a minute before dying off. Gray smoke trailed into the sky.

***

At the evening meeting, tension hung in the air like the humidity. No one wanted to provoke Tzinia after the execution earlier that day, but people couldn't keep from complaining about the day's stifling heat.

"A fifteen minute break isn't enough," said someone in the crowd.

"I can barely get my temperature down in that time," said another.

"Might have to shorten the days. Ten hours, maybe. Maybe eight."

Tzinia waved her hands dismissively. "It's just not possible. The medical staff has assured me fifteen minutes is more than enough time to rest."

"The doctors are wrong. You tell them to go out and move heavy equipment for half a day with only fifteen minute breaks and see what they say then."

Tzinia narrowed her eyes. "Are you telling me what to do?"

The man who had spoke grimaced. "No."

Tzinia stared down the man for a moment longer before scanning the rest of the crowd. "It's hot, yes, but we're all still here. We're all still working. The Project is going according to plan. Just today I received word that Mexico is finished. Mexico! The pacific coastline. The Yucatan. The Sierra Madres. Free, clean, unhindered by man's clutches. And here we are in Bolivia and we are not done. The rest are – Sucre, Santa Cruz, Cochabamba, La Paz! All finished. The beautiful Andes rise unburdened by mankind's filth. So tell me – what is a little heat and work when we are so close to completion?"

The grumbles in the room died down. Tzinia scanned the room, a satisfied expression on her face. She looked down at her notes and up, and then smiled.

"Have a good night."

As everyone filed out of the meeting hall, Waira could hear Augusto grumble under his breath. When they were far enough from anyone to overhear, she spoke up.

"What's wrong?"

Augusto turned toward her. "How can she call everything filth?"

Waira gestured to the decaying brick building on the corner. "Because a lot of it is filth."

"But not everything," said Augusto, storming away from the road and into the adjacent field.

Waira hurried after him. Augusto cut across the field at a fast pace and didn't stop until he reached the graveyard. He wove around the graves and then stopped.

"What are you doing?" Waira whispered.

Augusto ignored her and lowered himself into the grave. Waira watched the darkness swallow him up. It was like he had descended into the underworld. A minute passed before one of his hands grasped at the grave's edge. Waira reached down and grabbed his hand, and helped him up. In his free hand he held the skull-mask. The metal mask eerily reflected the moonlight.

Augusto held it up so they both could look at it. "It's not filth," he said in a soft voice.

"No. It's beautiful," said Waira.

"I won't let her destroy it. I don't care if they're destroying everything else. I won't let it happen to this."

"You don't have a choice, Augusto. Maybe if you contact the archeologists they will take it into orbit and put it in one of their museums."

"No. It belongs down here. Whoever this was – was clearly important. And whoever buried him honored him with this mask. They both belong here."

"Look, Augusto, I agree with you. But our opinions don't matter. The decisions have all been made. We're just gravediggers here."

Augusto suddenly smiled. "You're right," he said, and walked away from the graves.

Waira followed him. "What do you mean, I'm right? What are you doing? Where are you taking the skull?"

"You shouldn't come with me. It's dangerous."

Waira didn't know what he was talking about, but wasn't about to leave Augusto. He wasn't thinking clearly. He came to the end of the field and entered an alley. This was one of the last standing areas of the city. After so much time spent on soil, walking on hard ground felt odd. Augusto stopped at the end of the alley at a quiet road. He looked both ways before jogging across the asphalt to the other side where a small park grew.

Waira crossed after him. "Where are we?"

"The Plaza de Armes. They cleaned it last week. I saw it on the weekly progress report."

Augusto crossed the sidewalk to the border of the park, stepped over the yellow DO NOT CROSS tape, and slipped into the shadows.

Waira hesitated, knowing once a section of land was cleaned it was illegal to trespass, but followed Augusto anyway, worried about her partner. They wound through the light underbrush and around the towering palm trees whose fronds seemed to glitter in the moonlight.

They came to a clearing a few paces wide, and Augusto sank to his knees. He scooped up two handfuls of dark soil.

"You see – a gravedigger can't do much, but we can do this."

He scooped more soil away, forming a hole about a foot deep. He picked up the skull-mask. "Here, because this area is already cleaned and scanned, they will never find this. Here it can be buried like it was meant to be." He set the skull-mask in the hole. "Sleep well."

A sharp click cut the silence. Waira spun around to see the barrel of a gun pointed at her head. Waira looked up from the gun and saw Tzinia, holding the gun, smile. Behind her, lights whirled to life, flashing blue and red. Soldiers with machine guns fanned out in a semi-circle around Augusto and Waira.

Tzinia looked them over. "I never figured you two for vandals," she said.

"We're not," said Waira.

"Looks like it to me."

"I'm just burying something," said Augusto.

Tzinia's eyes narrowed. "Burying? Burying what?"

Augusto reached down and brought up the skull-mask. "I found it in the graveyard, but I couldn't destroy it. It belongs in the ground."

"That's not for you to decide. And further, you've illegally crossed the park's perimeter and desecrated the land. These are severe infractions."

Augusto stepped between Tzinia and Waira. "This was all my idea, ma'am. She had nothing to do with it. She kept trying to stop me."

Tzinia's hand played on her pistol grip. "You know the penalty for trespassing."

"I do, ma'am. And I take full responsibility. This was my fault."

Tzinia motioned to the nearest soldier. "Take this one back to the holding pen."

The soldier grabbed Augusto's arms roughly and yanked them behind his back, forcing Augusto to drop the mask. Tzinia picked up the mask and looked it over.

"I'll hold on to this for now. Before I have it melted down for scrap metal," said Tzinia before turning to another soldier. "Take the other one back to the barracks. One hanging in the morning will be enough." She looked at Waira as the soldier put a hand on Waira arm. "I don't know if you're lucky or unlucky to have such a stupid friend. But he saved your life."

As Waira was led away, she was able to glance back once and meet Augusto's eyes. She'd never seen a deeper sadness.

***

A knot had formed in Waira's stomach and had grown tighter with every hour that passed. It was several hours since she had been escorted back to the barracks and Augusto put under arrest. On the public notice board, the announcement had already been made: *Augusto Cabesa De Vaca will be executed at dawn.*

Waira lay on her bunk, pretending to read a magazine, but her mind burned with questions and fear. The wall clock's second hand seemed to blur by, stealing away the time Augusto had left. Waira switched from one side to the other, and back again. The lights dimmed at ten and she put away her magazine. Women in nearby bunks pulled up their sheets and closed their eyes. Waira copied them, but did not sleep. At eleven, the lights went out entirely. Waira's heart pounded so loud she feared it would wake someone.

What was Augusto feeling at that moment? Was he scared? Sad? Waira balled her fists. It wasn't fair, but she was angry at him. He knew the rules, but he had flaunted them. And now he was going to pay the price.

She would be assigned a new partner. But it wouldn't be the same. She already missed him. She rolled over and squinted at the wall. The clock, lit faintly with LEDs, read eleven forty-five. She took a deep breath and sat up, and slid on her pants and shoes. She grabbed her bag and exited the dorm.

Outside, the cold wind tossed her hair, making her shiver. She pulled her jacket closer and walked away from the building.

Twenty strides later, a whistle chirped and a uniformed man rushed toward her. Waira held up her hands.

"What are you doing out here so late?" he asked.

"I have to use the restroom."

He pointed a thick finger at her bag. "What's that for?"

"Things a woman needs that a man doesn't."

The guard's air of authority vanished, replaced by sheepishness. "Well, hurry along then. And don't get lost."

Waira turned and walked into the darkness. Adrenaline ran through her and her heart raced, but she managed to keep a steady pace. When she reached the restrooms she quickly bypassed them, and hurried across the field beyond. She'd walked the field everyday for months, but there, in the dark of night, it was as if walking there for the first time.

She reached the corner of the field and slowed. Black pools of night scattered across the ground. The empty graves were like hideous mouths.

She found where she had worked earlier that day and picked up the short shovel. Its weight in her hands gave her strength. She set off across the field, leaving the graveyard behind, avoiding the clusters of work tents, and angling toward a small building on the far end of the barracks.

It was commonly called the holding pen, but the small temporary wooden building was really a jail. Workers who had disobeyed rules, been cited for disorderly conduct, or any number of infractions, were held there for as long as their sentence lasted. And for those sentenced to death – the holding pen was their final stop before the gallows.

Waira hunched down next to a boulder and watched the jail for several minutes. There was only a single guard, just outside of the front door. The building itself wasn't large, a single-story construction, with small windows every few feet along the walls.

Waira padded forward. She started at the nearest wall, dangerously close to the front of the jail, and began peering in windows. When she reached the fourth window, she saw a pair of eyes looking back out through the window.

"Augusto?" she whispered.

She heard someone draw a quick breath. "Waira? Is that you?" It was Augusto's voice.

"Yes. It's me."

"What are you doing?"

"I came to get you out."

"What? No. You'll get caught."

"Not if you lower your voice. What kind of floor is in there?"

"Dirt."

"Can you dig?"

"No. My hands are tied behind my back."

"All right. Just stay put. I'll do the work."

Before Augusto could argue, Waira crouched down and slid her shovel into the hard, packed dirt. She had to go slowly so that she made as little noise as possible. Inch by inch, she formed a hole just next to the wall. She knew it had to be at least a couple feet deep to be deep enough for Augusto's wide frame.

By the time she'd dug a foot deep, her hands ached from the effort. Clumps of rock were wedged in the ground and she couldn't risk the noise of the metal shovel striking them, so she had to claw at them with her fingers. When the hole was deep enough, she began digging toward and under the edge of the building. She had to lower herself in the hole and lay on her back and claw away at the dirt. When her hand broke through the surface and into Augusto's cell, she knew she was nearly done.

"Go slow," Augusto whispered through the hole in the floor, "or they'll hear you."

Waira painstakingly pulled hunk after hunk of earth out of the floor until she guessed it was big enough, and then backed out and waited. She saw Augusto's head and shoulders appear in the hole, but he struggled to move. Realizing he was still bound, Waira grabbed him under the arms and slowly pulled him through. As he struggled to a sitting position, Waira found a small hand mirror in her bag, broke it, and used the edge to cut through Augusto's ties.

Augusto rubbed his wrists just as a light shone on them.

"Don't move," said the guard holding the flashlight.

Waira and Augusto were still as the guard approached them. In his other hand, he held a gun and waved it at them.

"It looks like there will be two hangings in the morning," said the guard, smiling. "Now come with me."

The guard motioned with the gun for Waira to move first. As he did, Augusto rose to his feet, swinging the shovel. The blade struck the guard in the temple, and he dropped in a heap.

Waira's eyes were like saucers. "What did you do?"

"Saved your life, and mine," said Augusto.

"We have to get away from here." Waira looked around. "And fast."

"I hope you have a plan."

"Sort of, but I don't know if it'll work."

"Then let's go. Help me with the body." Augusto began lifting the guard. Waira helped him. "He's alive, but what do we do with him?"

Augusto motioned for her to follow his lead. They carried the guard to the front of the jail and propped him up on the chair outside the door. They let him slump to the side as if he were asleep.

Augusto began to walk back toward the camp, when Waira caught his arm. "Where are you going? We can't escape that way."

"I know, but there's one thing I have to do before we go," said Augusto, pulling away.

Before Waira could stop him again, Augusto was hurrying toward the camp. Despite her reservations, Waira followed.

When they neared the camp, Augusto changed his route and circumvented the camp to the other side, far away from the general barracks. Here, the managers, directors, and project leaders were stationed. Augusto crept from one small bungalow to the next until he stopped.

The bungalow looked no different than the others nearby, except for the nameplate just below the dim porch light that read: Tzinia Mogoñon. Waira tugged on Augusto's sleeve. When he looked back, she shook her head emphatically NO. Augusto waved her back and knocked on the door. No answer came and he knocked again louder, and stepped to the side of the door. A muffled voice was followed by footsteps.

"This better be important!" growled Tzinia as she unbolted the door and swung it open. "Who's there?"

Augusto backhanded the shovel into Tzinia's face with a metallic thud. Tzinia dropped to the floor. Augusto looked around to make sure they went unnoticed, and stepped into the bungalow. Waira followed. Augusto grabbed Tzinia by the foot and pulled her out of the doorway, and Waira closed the door.

"I knew you were crazy, but this is beyond..." said Waira.

Augusto ignored her and strode to Tzinia's desk where atop a stack of reports sat the skull mask. In the amber light of the overhead lamp, the mask took on an earthy glow. Augusto picked it up and tucked it under his shirt.

"Really? You're worried about hiding it? Don't you think finding you would trump finding it?" asked Waira.

Augusto smirked. "You coming, or staying here?"

Seconds later, they were out of the bungalow and closing the door behind them. They moved quickly, but didn't run. They knew running would make them look suspicious, should anyone catch sight of them. So they moved with purpose, hoping they seemed like they were on an errand of importance.

When they left the light of the camp, Waira took the lead and stole across the dark fields. They passed the graveyard where the headstones shone under the moonlight like disembodied giant teeth. They wove around the headstones and out of the graveyard, and crossed a field of broken, rocky soil to the furnaces.

"Here we are," said Waira.

"Why?"

"Well – the perimeter is monitored with motion detectors, so if we try to cross, the alarm will sound, and the soldiers will be onto us within minutes."

"So we better run fast," said Augusto.

"No, we'd never outrun them – they have their scanners, guns, vehicles. But if we can cross the perimeter without giving warning, we would have enough time to escape."

"Sure, but what about the motion detectors?"

"Look," said Waira, pointing at the conveyor belt. "The belt leads to the furnace just beyond the perimeter, but the alarm never goes off when we send bodies through because the scanner knows everything on the conveyor belt is dead."

"Right – because anything on the belt falls into the furnace right after it's scanned."

"Exactly."

"So we'll burn to death."

"No, we just have to roll off right away," said Waira.

"That sounds dangerous."

"Look – I'll go first to make sure it works."

Augusto shook his head. "Not after breaking me out of prison. I'll go first."

He began climbing onto the conveyor belt, but Waira grabbed his hand. "I don't want anything to happen to you," she said.

Augusto shot her an irascible grin. "You can profess your love for me once we're both on the other side."

Waira rolled her eyes and pushed him onto the belt. "Try not to get singed."

Augusto lay down on the belt and was slowly taken toward the furnace. It crept along, painfully slow, until it stopped a few feet from the furnace, directly beneath the scanner. Augusto lay perfectly still with his eyes closed. The bulb glowed yellow-white for a long moment. Then the belt pushed forward. Augusto spun around and leapt from the belt, landing on the ground. He waved and motioned for her to join him.

"Remember," he whispered, "you can't bring anything unnatural with you. So toss the skull-mask over the scanner and I'll catch it."

"You'll toss nothing," said a different voice.

Waira turned. Cloaked in the shadows, Tzinia walked toward her. Her forehead and jaw were purple and red, and blood ran from her nose and at the corner of her lips.

"You thought you'd attack me and get away with it so easily?" asked Tzinia. "Attempted murder is punishable by death." Tzinia drew her pistol. "We'll start with him."

She aimed at Augusto, but Waira grabbed her hand. Tzinia hissed and backhanded Waira, but she kept her grip. Tzinia grappled with Waira, trying to point the gun at her, but Waira kept it away. Waira slugged Tzinia in the gut and smacked the gun out of her hand. Tzinia growled and lunged at Waira, slicing at her face with her long nails. Waira felt fire where blood was drawn.

Waira slung her arm around Tzinia's neck and pulled tight. Tzinia snarled and clawed at Waira's arm, but after months of digging and heavy lifting, Waira's arms were like iron.

Tzinia bit down hard on Waira's arm, and Waira lost her grip. The pair rolled on the ground, exchanging punches and trying to get their hands around each other's neck. They fought their way to their feet, but their legs tangled and they fell in a heap.

Tzinia batted Waira's hands out of the way and closed in on her neck. Waira gasped, clawing at Tzinia, but the maddened woman seemed to have abandoned pain. Tzinia forced Waira on her back. Waira couldn't breathe. She flailed around for a weapon, but couldn't find anything.

Then Waira's fingers closed around the item in her back pocket. She swung at Tzinia with all her strength; there was a sharp crack and Tzinia went slack, collapsing to the ground, her head lolling to one side. Her eyes were open in the shock of death.

Waira scrambled back, gasping. She stared horrified at the rib-bone embedded in the base of Tzinia's skull.

"Are you all right?" asked Augusto.

"I think so." Waira looked herself over. "Yes. I'm all right."

"Then you must hurry. Someone will come looking for Tzinia."

"What about the body?"

"Leave it."

"But someone will find it."

"Not until morning. By then, they'll know we're gone anyway."

Waira approached the scanner and stopped just before it to toss the skull-mask into Augusto's waiting hands. She then returned and kicked the gun into the darkness. She patted down Tzinia's body and heaved her onto the conveyor belt.

"What are you doing?" asked Augusto.

"She's wearing biodegradable clothes," said Waira. "She can burn with the rest of them."

The conveyor belt rolled along. Waira moved back far enough so that she could watch as the scanner read Tzinia's body and then pitched it into the furnace. Waira then climbed onto the belt and lay back, playing dead as the scanner passed over her. When the belt moved again, she rolled off and fell into Augusto's waiting arms.

Hand in hand, they ran into the jungle.

***

The quebracho trees rose up high as they neared. Mighty branches hung heavy with bright green leaves and wide snaking vines. The wet lush air was heavy with the scent of pollen and rich earth. Unseen birds sang and insects droned. The underbrush was thick, near impassable, except for their winding path.

Augusto and Waira stepped out of the brush and into a small clearing filled with mounds of dirt. They wove their way around the mounds until they reached the lone jatropha tree. In its shadow was a hole about three feet wide.

"Are you ready?" asked Augusto in a hushed tone. "No torches this time."

Waira scanned the foliage beyond the clearing. Though she could not see it, the camp was close by. She looked up. The setting sun had set fire to the sky and the moon had begun to rise. "I'm ready as ever."

Augusto went first, lowering himself into the hole, and into the tunnel. Waira followed quickly after him. They moved slowly, taking care not to bump the bamboo braces that supported the walls and ceiling. Augusto counted out loud, knowing the number of paces to the end of the tunnel. When he reached ninety-two, he reached out and felt the dirt wall.

"We're here," he said.

He felt along the ground until his hands came upon his makeshift shovel – a partially hollowed-out length of bamboo. Digging the tunnel had been hard work, but their muscles were used to it after so many months digging up bodies. Now, only a few feet remained. Augusto gripped the shovel tight and got to work.

Thirty minutes later, his shovel broke through the dirt wall to an empty space beyond. He paused and listened, and when he heard nothing, he whispered to Waira.

"We're here."

He carefully dug away the rest of the dirt until he could fit through to the other side. After the pitch dark tunnel, the moonlight seemed like a floodlight, and it was clear where he stood: in an excavated grave. When Waira joined him, she looked at the grave, and smiled. They cautiously peeked out of the grave, taking measure of the layout of the camp, specifically the sleeping quarters.

Together, they climbed up out of the grave like spirits reborn, seeking out others like them who would choose to live free.

Caleb Jordan Schulz has nomadic blood. He's trekked in the Andes, dove in the Yucatan, and camped in the Amazon jungle. Many of his adventures have made their way into his writing, which have appeared in *Innsmouth Free Press*, *Crossed Genres Year Two*, *Ray Gun Revival*, and *Scape*. When not traveling or writing, he works as a freelance editor and illustrator.

His web musings can be found at http://www.theright2write.blogspot.com.